THE ALPHA'S SECRET

THE RAVEN CHRONICLES: BOOK 2

MISSY DE GRAFF

STONE PHOENIX PRESS

Edited by Zero Alchemy
Cover design by Paradise Cover Design

ISBN 978-1-7370270-3-4
ASIN B0C2L1R5Z8

The moon shines brightest when going through the dark night of the soul...

CHAPTER 1

LUCINDA

A DARK SHADOW looms outside and circles the cabin. It stops underneath the window of the kitchen and paces back and forth as the sun rises. The silhouette of a wolf stretches along the leaf-scattered ground. I know who it is before he enters.

Caiden. Alpha of the Blood Moone Pack and my true Fated Mate.

His once-striking solid white wolf is turning a dingy gray as the cursed beast residing within him fights for control. *Damn that witch for cursing him all those years ago. Though, it wasn't until recently, when him and I met, that the beast began to change him.*

Caiden shifts from his wolf-beast to human form and steps into the main room of the cabin. "I thought I'd find you here."

"Yup, I'm here." My legs dangle over the edge of the couch, and I wiggle my bare feet to get warm by the heat of the fire.

The cabin is Caiden's special place, deep in the woods away from everyone and everything. He comes here when he needs to relax and unwind. I come here to get away from daily pack life.

Caiden crosses the room, and my heart flutters at his nakedness as he heads to the bedroom. The sound of drawers opening and closing comes from the room, then he walks back into view wearing red plaid flannel pants and an oatmeal thermal shirt.

My lips twitch, exposing a wry smile. *Damn, he looks sexy.*

"Is everything okay?" he asks.

"Yeah." But everything is far from okay. I'm freaking out. Caiden and I are at the center of everyone's attention. I have a twenty-page survey to complete for the planning of our mating ceremony, and that's just to decide what food to serve.

I close my eyes and turn my head away from Caiden.

As the daughter of an Alpha, I was raised to be a Luna—the wife of an Alpha—and a leader of a pack. I know what's expected of me as the mate of an Alpha.

But I've always done what I wanted, when I wanted. The list of rules and regulations the Blood Moone pack has—not to mention their unwritten traditions and unspoken expectations—is daunting.

When I was born, my father promised my hand in marriage to Dylan, my childhood best friend, until that damn witch cursed him, too. And now he's Caiden's Beta, second-in-command.

I smirk at the irony of our complicated history.

Dylan and I are still working to salvage our prior friendship. However, I'm realizing that my time alone as a rogue living outside of a pack, which Dylan forced, changed me in ways I don't think will ever be fixed.

"Then what's up?" Caiden asks.

"Nothing. I'm fine."

Lie.

Why am I lying to Caiden? He's my mate, and not just my mate by marriage, but my Fated Mate. Our souls are bound to each other by destiny. I should trust him with everything. Don't I expect the same from him? Would he—has he ever lied to me?

I watch him through the slits of my eyes.

No, I don't think he would ever lie to me.

My heart drops to my stomach, and queasiness stirs from lying to him.

He sits on the couch, lifts my legs, and drapes them across his lap.

With a calm yet serious tone, he says, "Lucinda, I can tell when something's bothering you."

"No—" I take a deep breath and let out a long sigh. My shoulders slump forward, and I dip my chin to my chest.

Do I look as pathetic as I feel?

A quick glance at Caiden's piercing stare answers my question.

"I know you want to slow things down," he says, "but our pack has certain traditions we can't ignore."

My pulse quickens at the thought of the mating ceremony and the Alpha's ritual. *Why am I nervous?*

"I told Mia to lay off the planning for a few weeks, but as the Alpha, the pack holds me to a certain standard." He tilts his head back and runs his hands through his hair. His jaw tightens and his nostrils flare. "By claiming you the way I did, we already broke several of the traditions. And keeping it a secret from the pack was careless."

Breaking tradition, as other pack members have made very clear, is taboo.

"I know." I reach up and brush his cheek with the backs of my fingers. As our skin touches, the little sparks soothe my nerves, and I smile.

Caiden rests his head against my fingers. "Mia thinks she

can drag out the planning possibly until late summer or early fall, but not more than that. Even that is pushing it."

Bless Mia Moone, my best friend and soon-to-be sister-in-law. She's excited about planning the ceremony, but she also secretly worries about her brother. I think she hopes that once he's officially mated, his wolf-beast will calm down.

"Will that give you enough time to settle whatever is bothering you, or are you having second thoughts about us?" Caiden asks.

"What? No, never." I crawl over and straddle him so I can stare into his never-ending blue eyes. "Caiden Lee Moone, I love you with every piece of my shattered heart. You found each part and glued it back into place with your kindness and affection. I will never doubt our love or regret our mating."

"Then what is it?" he asks.

I fidget on his lap, and he grabs my hips to hold me still. Leaning forward, I lay my head on his shoulder and whisper, "Your pack is overwhelming."

The jerk of his head and change in his heartbeat cause me to shift my weight. I draw back and study him. His eyebrows knit together, and a deep crease forms across his forehead.

I shrug.

Is this a surprise, or did I offend him?

I bite my lower lip. "I don't know. Maybe it's me."

"Talk to me. Tell me what's going on in that head of yours." He taps on my forehead. "Especially since you won't use the damn mindlink."

Yeah, because giving it to me before I am officially accepted into the pack is just another rule you broke.

I snuggle closer to him, and his arms tighten around me. The scent of bergamot wafting off his body calms my racing pulse and relaxes my inner wolf.

"I haven't really been part of a pack for a while—"

"Five years," Caiden says. "That's not too long."

True, but a lot happened in those five years. I'll never sleep the same again. Well, unless I'm wrapped in my security blanket of bergamot.

"It's actually been much longer. Ever since the bond first struck and Dylan stepped away from me... he was the to-be Alpha, so everyone took his lead. They left me alone, and I was treated as an outcast in my own pack."

"I had no idea—"

"It's not your fault. Dylan probably doesn't even realize it either," I say. "And your pack is at least five times the size of mine, so it's a lot to take in."

"Don't worry about it. You're my mate, and nothing else matters." He twirls a piece of my long chestnut hair between his fingers.

Yeah, I'm his mate. That's the problem. But I can't tell him that because he won't understand. What else am I, though? Where do I belong in the pack, other than as the Alpha's Mate?

"What is it—four more weeks, and you'll have met everyone in the pack?" Caiden asks. As if that's supposed to cheer me up.

Yeah, four more weeks of pure hell. If only he knew what those stupid parties were like—everyone judging me based on how I look and what I say. I hate that tradition with a passion.

"How are the meet and greet sessions going?" Caiden asks.

"You mean the weekly potential new member parties?"

He shoots me a disapproving look.

"Oh, they're swell." Sarcasm drips from my lips.

Under normal circumstances, one of the Blood Moone Pack's traditions is that a new person who wants to join the pack will socialize with the current members for a period of time and then the pack members vote—yay or nay.

However, with the large influx of people wanting to join after leaving Felix's band of rogues, the Elders have created parties. Groups of twenty potential new members meet with roughly fifty pack members in a casual setting to socialize, and the groups rotate each week.

It's been a long six weeks, and there are still four more to go.

But these people are more than happy to do what it takes to get away from Felix.

Most of them had been with him for so long, they didn't know another lifestyle existed.

Living in the wilderness, constantly on the run, moving and looking over your shoulder is no way to raise a family.

Living in misery and fearing your leader...

I shake my head, remembering what it was like to live among them when I was mesmerized by Felix, the rogue Alpha.

"Is there something you're not telling me?" Caiden asks.

I shake my head against his chest.

"Are you sure? Because your heartbeat is racing."

Just tell him already. The problem is us.

The members treat me differently because I'm the Alpha's mate. They're either extra warm and friendly or cool and distant. If I'm lucky, they'll be indifferent.

Though, I'm more interested in those that are borderline hostile. One woman accused me of special treatment. Which is when I decided I wanted to be accepted on my own merits, not because of who my mate is.

Tears well up in my eyes and threaten to fall. *Damn it.*

The pack rumor mill is torture.

I love Caiden so much, but sometimes I wish we waited to mark each other. I wish we took things slow and followed their stupid traditions. Then I could've been accepted, or not accepted, into the pack for who I am, not because Caiden's scent is all over me and threatening their judgment.

"Lucinda." Caiden's voice pulls me from my thoughts, and he wipes away a tear that escaped. "Talk to me."

I take a deep breath and say, "Sabrina's always there."

He nods, then kisses my cheeks, my forehead, and my lips in the gentlest kisses he's ever given me. I close my eyes and slow my breathing. *I don't deserve him.*

"I know," he says. "The Elders reprimanded her with community service, and part of that includes potential new member activity."

Sabrina deserves a harsher reprimand for what she did—instigating an overthrow of the Alpha. Community service is a slap on the hand. I emphasize rolling my eyes.

Sabrina is like a slimy worm, able to wiggle into and out of whatever she wants, and I don't understand why. I'm glad her and Dylan are no longer dating. That is something I couldn't condone as Luna of this pack.

I'm grateful that, in his spare time, Caiden is teaching me the inner workings of the pack politics, which include the different programs and organizations they have.

Caiden said he'll help me find a position after I'm accepted. But at the new member meetings, they tell us it's hard for new pack members to get a position.

Why is everything so complicated? And I still don't understand the role of the Elders.

"I thought Mia ran the community outreach programs?" I ask.

His lips move down my neck, and he breathes against my warming skin, sending little shockwaves traveling through my body.

"She does," he murmurs. "But since she was busy with Sammy and Grace's ceremony, she was too distracted to fight against the Elders decision."

A small smile plays at my lips. *Sammy and Grace.*

I'm so happy for them. Their mating ceremony was flawless, just like their uncomplicated love and pack life will be. They left for their ultimate honeymoon with no specified timeframe for their return.

Caiden's lips leave my neck, and he cocks an eyebrow. "So, it's just Sabrina that's bothering you?"

At the mention of her name, his ocean blue eyes flash red —the cursed beast within him is fighting for control.

Does he realize how often it happens? It happens more often than not these days.

Our small and intimate group of those directly involved decided not disclosing everything to the pack was best. So, we haven't told them about Caiden, Dylan, or even Felix's curse. Gavin said, *"In simple terms, it's on a need-to-know basis, and the general public doesn't need to know."*

I couldn't agree more.

Of course, pack members have noticed Caiden's escalating aggression and mood swings, though. It's just another thing they blame on me.

One lady called me "scandalous." But she didn't stop there, she continued to batter me verbally. First, I caused Caiden to break pack tradition, then also to break the pack rules.

What's next? Where will it end?

But the sad part is she's right.

The red flaming orbs have overtaken Caiden's eyes, and his movements become forced and jerky. He flips me onto my back so that I'm lying sprawled on the couch, and he supports himself above of me. His red eyes roam my body, and he licks his lips with a hungry gaze.

"No." I scoot out from under his body. Rolling off the couch, I land on the floor with a thump. Turning back to

Caiden and his penetrating stare, I muster all my control and say, "Not right now. I'm not in the mood."

I stand up and rush to the bedroom without sparing another look back. I want Caiden more than ever, but not like this, not when his beast has control.

After entering the room, I make the mistake of turning around to close the door. We lock in an intense stare down.

His Alpha calls to me, his wolf calling to his mate.

It takes all my strength to ignore him and not be submissive.

To ease the tension, as painful as it is, I flash a smile through the small opening, then latch and lock the door.

I flop onto the bed and curl up under the covers.

Now I wait out the tantrum of the beast in the other room.

CHAPTER 2

LUCINDA

I LIE in bed and wait for Caiden to come to me. I know better than to make the first move. I did that once, and I won't be doing it again anytime soon.

My thoughts drift to Cody—my fearless best friend, who always had my back, regardless of the circumstances.

When there is a light tap on the door about an hour later, I sit up.

"Lucinda." Caiden's voice cracks.

After one of his blackout sessions, he struggles to piece things together for a while. He once explained that the experience is similar to waking up from a coma after several years and not knowing what's reality versus a dream.

The corners of my mouth tug up as I crack the door and peek through the small opening. Caiden stands with his shoulders slumped and his head rolled forward.

I open the door wider and lean against the doorjamb, studying Caiden's forced movements. "Hey."

"I-I'm sorry," he says and blows out a chest of air. "Are you okay?"

"I'm fine."

"Did— What happened?" He runs his hands through his hair and curls his fingers, digging into his scalp.

"Nothing happened." I swing the door open and collapse into his chest.

My wolf has been deprived of her mate long enough.

"I love you," he whispers and kisses the top of my head. "If I ever hurt you—"

"You would never hurt me."

"You don't know that."

Pulling back, I stare into his eyes. "I do. And *if*—and that's a big if—anything were to ever happen, then it wouldn't be you in control. You know that, right? It would be the beast. He isn't you. You aren't him. You aren't a beast."

His head leans forward against mine, and my stomach flutters in anticipation of his touch.

I need him as much as he needs me for balance. I haven't figured out how he balances me yet, but I know he does. I'm not cursed with a raging beast like him, but I'm much calmer in his presence. And his touch is still my personal security blanket.

Lately, he hasn't been making it to bed at night, either working late on patrol or out in the forest to run off some extra dominance issues. He says it's the beast he struggles with, but sometimes, I wonder if it's me. Dylan jokes that I'm too dominant.

"When I first arrived to the cabin this morning, I should have started off by saying I was worried about you."

"Why's that?" I ask.

"You weren't in bed when I came home last night." His warm breath tickles my neck.

"I left you a note."

He pulls a few inches away from my face and smirks. "Yes, I saw that. What did you use to write on the mirror?"

"Dry erase marker."

His eyebrow raises and my lips pucker.

"Well, and I borrowed some of Mia's red lipstick for the kiss."

He leans in close and whispers against my lips, "Does she know?"

"Does it matter?" My lips brush over his, and my veins pulse.

I trace my fingers up his chest and wrap my arms around his neck. I need him.

With a flick of my tongue, I tease his throbbing lips.

His lips part, and I'm granted entrance. Strong hands grab my hips and slip under my shirt. When his fingers touch my bare skin, a fire ignites in my body, and I press my chest closer into his.

But he pulls away and turns his head.

This is all too familiar; the pack contacts him via the mindlink at the worst moments.

Sighing, I step out of his arms and go sit on the couch to wait. After a minute or two, he joins me.

"I'm sorry about that." He sits next to me.

"I know."

Doesn't the Alpha ever get time to himself without being criticized? My dad always made leading a pack look so easy, or maybe my pack wasn't as needy.

Caiden brushes the backs of his fingers across my cheek, then tilts my chin up for me to look at him.

"I need to leave town," he says.

My eyes widen. He never leaves. "Is everything okay?"

"Yes, everything's fine. I was actually going to talk to you about this last night but—"

"I wasn't home."

"Right." He plays with my hair.

"Where are you going?" I ask.

"Into the city for a meeting."

"When do you leave?"

"Tomorrow morning. Although, I need to head back now. Something just came up that I need to take care of before I leave." His shoulders slouch as he frowns.

"Oh okay." *There goes our alone time.*

"But tonight, I'm all yours." He flashes a devilish grin.

I return a mischievous smile. "Promise?"

"Pinky promise." He holds up his pinky finger.

Rolling my eyes, I shake my head and giggle, but then I lock fingers with him. "Pinky promise."

This is something he started right after we marked each other. Mia had everyone in our little circle pinky promise to keep our markings a secret. Caiden has since taken the pinky promise to be our thing.

"Good." His eyes sparkle.

He stands and heads for the kitchen. I drag my feet and follow behind him. My shoulders slump forward and I wipe my sweaty palms down my thighs. He turns and eyes me with a studious gaze.

He reaches up and tucks a few strands of loose hair behind my ear. "You don't have to come back yet, if you're not ready."

I peer at him with grin and then crush into his chest, wrapping my arms around him.

"Thank you," I whisper.

He gives me one last kiss, then shifts into his wolf and leaves.

I lounge on the couch and stare into the fire. The last few remaining flames crackle and hiss, while the embers simmer and glow orange. My mind wanders, thinking of nothing in particular.

And then, one big pop from the dying fire startles me, and I'm pull away from my daydream.

What am I doing? I want time alone with Caiden, and I

love running in the forest. *Dumbass*. I just missed the perfect opportunity. My gaze darts to the clock; he's only been gone ten minutes. I bet I can catch up to him.

With a renewed purpose, I dart outside, quickly undress and toss my clothes into my tote bag. Shifting into my wolf is second nature, my bones break down and reform within seconds. I snatch the tote bag up with my teeth and the thunder of my paws upon the earth disturb the silent forest as I race after Caiden.

The cool air ruffles my fur, and the singing birds calm my restlessness. My pace slows, and I relish this time alone in the forest.

Felix is still being held within the Blood Moone territory, and I know Caiden has regular visits with him.

For several weeks after Felix was captured, I wasn't allowed near him. And even though I know Caiden would now let me see Felix, I have no desire to. I'm done with him. I want the past to be left along, and just to forget about him.

Any thoughts of catching up to Caiden and spending time with him vanish. It's just my wolf running in the forest, free of all worries. My paws pound on the ground and the raw earth is freeing to my soul. I chase after a frolicking butterfly, drink from a mountain stream, and roll around in the meadow. The long grass scratches my back, and I lay in the warm sunshine with my belly exposed.

But all too soon, the sun fades marking late afternoon and begins its downward journey. I've played in nature long enough; it's time to face reality. My mate is waiting for me at home.

Recently, I've noticed Caiden's wolf showing signs of aggression when I'm naked and signs of overprotection during my shift, which is when my only weakness is exposed. Despite the action annoying me at first, I know he's under enough stress dealing with Felix, and I don't need to complicate things more.

To help ease Caiden's dominance issues, I've started to shift discreetly. When going on runs in the forest, which is the only time I've been shifting lately, I do it in the tree line behind the Pack House and then re-dress before entering the house again. Hopefully, this small act helps.

After shifting and dressing in the tree line, I make my way across the lawn to the Pack House, but Dylan steps out from the gazebo and intercepts me. I stop walking but continue to gaze at the Pack House.

The Alpha, Beta, their family members, and mates live in the Pack House. Since Caiden only has Mia left alive in his family and Dylan has no one, currently we only have five people living together. The Pack House also contains the Alpha's office. Things can get a little chaotic with random pack members always coming and going in my new home.

But, right now knowing Caiden is inside those walls stirs my wolf's need for the warmth and comfort of her mate.

"Hey, Lux, you got a minute?" Dylan asks, his voice pulling me from my inner thoughts.

"Sure." I shuffle over to him. Dylan is the only person in the world to call me Lux. And after all that we've been through, a part of me is glad he still does. He's the only person left in the world from my original pack, so he's the only one that knows my life as a child; he understands my sorrow and emptiness for the place we once called home.

He guides me back to the gazebo, sits down, and pats the spot next to him. "Come sit down."

I sit on the bench and turn to study him. "What's up?"

"I have something for you."

My cheeks burn with the intensity of his stare.

CHAPTER 3

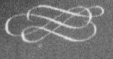

CAIDEN

SMALL GOOSE BUMPS ripple up my spine as I watch Lucinda sleep. My nostrils flare and my temples throb.

She's keeping secrets from me.

I grit my teeth and storm across the room. I pull out a canvas duffel bag from under the bed, grab a handful of clothes from the dresser, and shove them into the bag. While I continue to find things and toss them into the open bag, my thoughts stray to the events from last night.

I was going to surprise her with a romantic dinner under the stars so we could spend time together. And it was dusk when I rounded the corner of the backyard to find her.

Two shadows sat huddled together in the secrecy of the gazebo.

Dylan and Lucinda.

Dylan leaned in close and pulled something from his pocket. Her eyes widened as she took the gift and threw her arms around him in a long embrace. A necklace dangled from her hand.

Even thinking about it now makes my wolf growl. In a split second, I ditched the idea for the impromptu dinner and instead shifted and ran for the woods. Not returning home until well after dark when I was certain that Lucinda would be asleep.

I should be grateful that I didn't arrive home to another note written on the dresser mirror, but maybe that would've been better.

Sitting on the edge of the bed, I zip up the duffel bag and kick it as I steal a glance at Lucinda. I originally planned on a day trip, but after the exchange I observed, I need time to myself to think and cool off.

All the tightness in my chest relaxes when her eyes open and she flashes her dazzling smile.

"Hey." She sits up and wraps her hands around me from behind.

A warmth rushes through my body, and my wolf excites at the tender touch from our mate.

"Hey." I reach up to hold her hands tight to my chest, then dip my chin to kiss her knuckles. I can't stay upset with her. "I'm sorry, I didn't mean to wake you."

"It's okay. Where were you last night? Is everything okay?" she asks.

"Yes, it's fine."

But it's not. And I don't want to ask about last night. I want her to tell me about Dylan and the necklace.

"Are you sure you don't want me to ride along and keep you company?" She spins around to sit in my lap.

I wrap her in a tight embrace, and I lean my forehead against hers. "I'd love for you to go, but this meeting is best done alone. And it may take longer than just a day."

She tilts her head toward the duffel bag that sits at my feet. "How long will you be gone?"

"Just two, maybe three, days." I lift her chin up to meet my gaze and search her captivating hazel eyes for anything that will tell me what she's thinking and feeling.

But her gaze flits away, and she plays with the collar of my shirt. "Is there anything you need me to do while you're gone?"

"No. Dylan can handle any pack business."

Her shoulders slump.

I know this isn't what she wants to hear; she wants to help with pack business. But our pack has certain traditions, and members don't accept change well. Until our official mating ceremony, she won't be viewed as my mate or the Luna of this pack.

I brush my lips against hers and whisper, "I'll miss you like crazy."

"Oh yeah?" She smiles, wraps her arms around my neck and grinds into my lap.

"You are positively evil." I grit my teeth.

"Make sure you remember that, Mr. Alpha. Traveling alone to the big city that's full of temptations all meant to distract—"

"No one could ever distract me when I have you." I smash my lips into hers, and her moan sets my skin on fire. My wolf doesn't want to leave her embrace, but I must.

As I pull my lips away, she giggles like she knows what she's done to me.

"Believe me," I whisper, "I don't want to, but I need to get on the road if I hope to make it before dark."

She nods, and I reluctantly step from her embrace but keep her hand in mine. I steal one last kiss, then head out of the room. Our fingers interlocked, she follows me outside.

I toss my bag into the backseat of my black Hellcat, turn to face her, and steal another chaste kiss.

Her fingers fiddle with a black leather cord around her neck. I stare at the pendant hanging between her breasts—a teardrop made from dark green quartz. My jaw clenches.

Reaching up to touch it, my fingers graze the smooth stone. "What is this?"

"Oh, this? It's nothing." Rising to her tippy-toes, she leans in and links her hands behind my neck.

My hand is forced to let go of the pendant as she closes the space between us, and my thumbs graze her breasts as I wrap my arms around her and pull her tight.

Why is she lying to me? If it's nothing, she'd tell me that Dylan gave it to her.

I study her gaze and reach up to angle her face to mine. I release my frustration in our kiss. Hard and rough. My dominant wolf is marking his territory on her burning lips.

She moans against me, and I draw back. Lucinda's eyes flash open and then she lays her head against my chest. I hold her close.

Dylan's energy fills the room, then he clears his throat.

"Yes?" I ask, turning my attention to Dylan, who is now standing a few feet from us, without separating from Lucinda.

"The radio just reported a broken-down tractor trailer on the interstate," he says.

Great.

The drive is around seven hours, with no traffic. But driving on the interstate, you can never be sure when accidents will happen.

"Thanks for the update," I say to Dylan, then turn my attention back to Lucinda. "Well, I better hit the road. The drive is long enough without the added delay."

"Okay." She gives me a soft kiss before I release her from my embrace.

As I slide into the driver's seat of my black Hellcat, she says, "Oh, I programmed my new number into your cell phone."

"Did you now?" I smile and start the engine.

She closes the door, and I roll down my window. She leans in for one last kiss. "Call when you get there."

I nod, and she backs away to stand next to Dylan.

In the rearview mirror, Dylan and Lucinda walk into the Pack House, and I can't stop the feeling that things will be different when I return. But this trip is necessary. They deserve an explanation.

During the mindless drive, doubt creeps into my thoughts. *What am I doing?* The meeting will be over before it even begins, but it needs to be done. I need to be the one to tell Elizabeth's parents before they hear rumors from other pack members. The parents of my lost mate deserve to know the truth.

Am I being selfish? How will the truth about Lucinda and me be any comfort for the death of their daughter?

I want them to understand that I'm not taking just anyone as a new mate. I need to tell them that Lucinda is my Fated Mate, and a witch cast a curse to mask her years ago.

Who am I kidding? They won't believe me. It sounds crazy as hell.

The accident only delayed my trip by an hour, so I pull up to their house around three o'clock in the afternoon. I pass their house, turn around in the cul-de-sac, and park along the curb a few houses down. I lean my head on the steering wheel, gripping it tight, and take a deep breath.

Well, here I am.

This house stirs memories I haven't thought of in years. Elizabeth lived here when we first met. I picked her up on that doorstep for our first date. Our first kiss was standing outside the black front door, though it used to be painted cranberry red.

I've only seen her parents once since the attack that ended with the death of their daughter, and I never told them specifics about how Elizabeth died.

They don't need to know every detail of the gruesome horrors. No parent needs to visualize that. But they never forgave me for returning alive when their daughter didn't. And I can't blame them for that.

My phone vibrates in the cup holder, and I see a new text message.

Lucinda: *Miss you.*

Me: *Miss you too.*

Lucinda: *Are you close?*

Me: *Just got here.*

Lucinda: *K. Call when you're done. I have something to tell you.*

Me: *K.*

Shit. Did she wait for me to leave town to tell me about her and Dylan? No. She wouldn't do that. But what else could she possibly have to tell me? What happened since I left this morning?

Pushing those thoughts aside, I step from the car and cross the street to the house. I came to do this. I'm here. Now I need to focus and do it as calmly and politely as possible. They are the only wolves on this street, so I don't want to cause a scene.

I knock on the large double doors and take a deep breath as I straighten my posture.

Elizabeth's father opens the door, and his piercing glare stabs through my heart.

"Alpha." His formal tone slices through my soul. I've never felt such disdain from a pack member.

CHAPTER 4

LUCINDA

As Caiden drives away, a mixture of anxiety and nervousness swirl together in the pit of my stomach. I rub my tummy to soothe the queasiness.

Am I that attached, or do I sense things will be different when he returns?

After the last flash of the taillights disappears in the distance, I turn and head into the house. Dylan follows behind me in silence, mumbles something about a shower, and darts upstairs.

Needing something to fill the void of Caiden's absence, I venture into the kitchen. Typically, this room is full of various pack members, but this morning it is empty. I open several cabinet doors in search of a bowl. Upon finding a white porcelain cereal bowl, I grab the box of frosted shredded wheat with fruit in the middle that's sitting on the counter and then climb to sit on the bar stool.

My stomach growls in anticipation of food.

Sabrina's voice cuts through the silence. "Hi Lucinda."

I look over my shoulder and nod in Sabrina's general

direction. She takes this gesture as a welcome to sit on the empty bar stool next to me.

The vile stench of rancid eggs mixed with sickly sweet perfume carries through the air, lingering around Sabrina, causes me to lose my appetite. I slide my bowl a few inches in front of me on the counter.

"I know we didn't get off to a good start," she says. "But I'd like to start over with a clean slate."

My jaw would have hit the floor if it were open. Our eyes meet, and I search her gaze for an explanation or hidden agenda.

"Can we be friends?" She extends her hand.

I drum my fingers along the edge of the counter, ignoring her. I never liked Sabrina, for several reasons. But the Elders conducted their investigation on the charges of a conspiracy to overthrow the Alpha, and they cleared her name.

For the annoyance caused to Caiden, her punishment is six months of mandatory community service—part of which is to help out around the Pack House as needed.

She wipes her hand down her thigh.

I wish the Elders had consulted Caiden before assigning her to the Pack House. Well, I assume they didn't, though I never asked Caiden his thoughts about their decision. But I can't imagine he approves of Sabrina being around all the time.

Mia and Gavin also don't like Sabrina in the Pack House because she involves herself in things that she has no business being a part of—like planning the Alpha's mating ceremony.

Yesterday, when Mia and I were discussing the season, she offered her opinion based on when flowers are readily available. It actually made perfect sense, but still, she's annoying.

Sabrina shimmies off her stool and heads toward the fridge. She grabs a bottle of water and leans on the counter across from me. "After talking to you and Mia about your ceremony yesterday, I thought more on the topic, and I know the perfect date and place."

"Really?" My voice remains dry and void of excitement.

"Yes." Her eyes sparkle.

I pull my bowl of cereal back in front of me. "Please share."

"June 21st."

I roll my eyes. "That's a very specific date."

"It's the summer solstice, and this year, it'll be on the full moon."

"That's an interesting idea." I hide a grin and stare into my bowl.

"Picture this." She glides around the counter to stand behind me. Wrapping her left arm around my shoulder, she uses her right arm to paint the picture in front of me. "Your ceremony takes place in the middle of the forest at the pavilion Caiden built with his dad. It begins at midnight, and no other light is needed other than the bright light of the full moon."

"As long as it isn't cloudy." I can't let her see my excitement, but her idea does sound intimate and romantic.

"True. But I have a feeling everything will be perfect this year." She sits next to me again.

"Unless it rains."

She places her hands on her hips. "Are you always this pessimistic?"

"I'm not pessimistic, I just live in the real world."

"And what's that supposed to mean? Are you not allowed to dream?"

I shrug and play with the spoon in my bowl.

"I'll take care of everything. You won't have to worry about a thing," she says.

"What about Mia?"

"Oh, Mia will have plenty to do with the rest of the planning."

"The rest?" Apparently, I'm so far out of touch with ceremony planning.

"Food, flowers, music, attire, invitations," Sabrina says. "And all the other stuff like that."

Right. Everything else on Mia's daunting questionnaire. My head spins. I never knew there were so many details needed. I've only ever attended one ceremony when I was eight years old, and it wasn't for an Alpha.

I turn to look at her. "So what will you do?"

"I'll take care of the venue," she says. "And don't worry, I'll coordinate with Mia for decorations and catering."

I stir my cereal and stare into the bowl, and then finally look at Sabrina. "Fine. It does sound perfect. But..." I hold up my finger. "We'll need to have a backup plan in case it's cloudy."

"I'll string white lights and lanterns in the trees."

"And in case it rains?"

"I'll secure a secondary location."

"Deal."

Sabrina leans in for a hug with a squeal.

What the hell did I just do? Did I just set a date without first talking to Caiden? And did I just hug Sabrina? Hell must be freezing over.

Gavin walks into the kitchen. "What're all the squeals about?"

I eye Sabrina and she smiles, but her lips remain closed.

"Where's Mia?" I ask.

Gavin motions upstairs, I assume her bedroom.

Time to face the music.

I turn to Sabrina. "I'm going to go talk to Mia."

She nods and squeezes my hand. A strange sensation builds in my chest as I look at our hands. I assume her action is meant as a sign of comfort, but I can't help feeling that it means something else to her. Weird.

I shake off the eerie feeling and go find Mia.

I peek my head into Mia's room. She stands in front of her dresser mirror, brushing her hair.

"You got a minute?" I ask.

Mia rolls her eyes. "What did Sabrina want today?"

She despises Sabrina more than ever before. Mia claims the Elders gave her special treatment for some unknown reason. A conspiracy of sorts.

"How'd you know?"

"Her rancid stench is all over you."

I cross the room and stand behind Mia, looking into the mirror over her shoulder.

"She had more advice for the ceremony." I bite my lower lip and wait for Mia's blowup.

"Oh yeah? And what does she have to say now?"

I narrow my eyes, and I tilt my head in question.

She shrugs. "What? Can't a girl be curious?"

"She had a suggestion for the date and location," I say.

"Really?"

I nod.

"So, when and where?" Mia asks.

"June 21st."

"I thought you wanted more time, so I was going to try and stretch it out for a fall date."

"I know, and I appreciate that. But I can't be too selfish. I need to compromise. Will you have enough time to plan for June?"

"Of course. I can do anything." Mia's nose scrunches and her lips pucker. "But—"

"I know that face. But what?"

"The questionnaire you filled out isn't helping. Your answers are all over the place. How am I supposed to plan your dream ceremony if you can't tell me what your dream is?"

So far, so good. Let's go for more.

I let out a long sigh. "Sabrina suggested having it in the forest at the pavilion."

Mia's eyes roll up as she ponders this new information. "Yes, that could work. It would fit in with the outdoorsy mood you wanted based on some of your responses."

"And at night—"

"Nope, no way. Can't do it." Mia crosses her arms over her chest.

"Are you sure?"

"It'll be too dark, even with candles. And the amount we would need to provide enough light could burn down the forest."

"June 21st is a full moon. Close your eyes and picture the light of the full moon shining down and illuminating the ceremony."

"OH MY GOD! That is classic and romantic." Mia squeals with excitement. She claps her hands repetitively in front of her body, and her eyes dance with renewed joy.

"I thought so too."

"I better get started."

Here goes nothing. "So, since you have a lot of other stuff to take care of, Sabrina offered to help with the venue."

Mia's eyes narrow and turn black. "What do you mean *help*?"

"Only that she could get the venue set up and ready. It

would free you up to deal with the more important stuff like food, entertainment, attire, invitations—"

"In other words, she doesn't want to help me, she wants to plan the venue."

"Right."

"Fine. But I want her to run all final decisions through me." Mia stabs her thumb into her chest.

My heart swells and threatens to burst. I dare not show her my excitement, so I give her a brief hug and say, "Deal."

Mia and I talk about several more aspects of the ceremony, and a few hours later, she leaves with Gavin to go shopping.

I'm exhausted, but I pop my head into the kitchen on my way upstairs to get ready for bed. Sabrina is sitting at the table organizing the pack's mail. I give her a thumbs-up, and she smiles the most genuine smile I've ever seen from her.

I hope I didn't just make a deal with the devil.

After going through my nighttime routine, I crawl into bed.

The new black cell phone that Mia gave me rests next to me in contrast against the red satin sheets, filling the empty space Caiden's left in our bed.

My hands drift over the silky sheets, and every few minutes, I check for a new message. I really want to talk to Caiden tonight. I want to tell him about the day I had with Mia... and Sabrina. But maybe I won't mention Sabrina.

Caiden knows I love him, and he understands things are moving too fast for me. After all, I lost my family and everyone I ever knew. I need time to process it all.

With a loud sigh, I exhale. Opening up and talking to Caiden about everything I feel, is the right thing to do. But, I don't want to upset him, or have him get the wrong idea.

Who am I kidding?

He probably already has the wrong idea. I thought I was doing a good job of hiding my hesitation over the mating ceremony, but Mia called me out on it today. She said my enthusiasm was lacking, especially considering the fact that Caiden had already claimed me and that I even had the gall to mark him.

I really wish we waited.

But when I think about the perfect picture that Sabrina painted—the secluded and romantic ceremony—a wave of calmness rushes over me, settling my jittery nerves.

I know he was upset by my reaction when we last talked about our ceremony, but between conversations with Mia and Sabrina, I can picture the perfect dreamy ceremony for us, and I want to share it with him.

A smile creeps across my face as I think of Caiden's excitement when I tell him I've picked a date, and butterflies swirl in my stomach.

I play with the stone around my neck. I should tell Caiden about the necklace too.

When he asked about it earlier, why didn't I tell him? *Dylan gave me this.* It's easy enough to say.

Why do I feel weird saying it then?

The necklace was actually my mother's. Dylan's mom was keeping it for me until I was older, and she gave it to Dylan the night he was named the next future Alpha of the Dark Raven pack.

The smoothness of the stone is centering. The quartz has a zen about it, or maybe it's my imagination. Either way, when I touch the surface, a calmness soothes my mind and soul, leaving me grounded and fully rejuvenated.

Glancing at the clock again, I yawn. My eyes involuntarily flutter, and I struggle to keep them open.

Caiden, where are you? I fumble with the phone between my sleepy fingers and send him a short text.

Me: *I guess the meeting ran late. Hope all is well. Going to bed. Love you.*

Immediately, the status turns from *Delivered* to *Read.*

The three bubbles appear in the text thread, and my heart pounds in anticipation of his message. A burning desire stirs deep in my stomach. I ache to talk to him.

And then, the bubbles disappear.

No response.

CHAPTER 5

CAIDEN

From the other room, Elizabeth's mother, Amber, hollers, "Who is it, dear?"

Elizabeth's father, Wilson, grunts and turns his back to me. He leaves the front door open and retreats down the foyer.

I step inside.

Amber walks into the hallway just as I close the door behind me.

She pulls me into a warm hug. "Caiden, so nice to see you. What do we owe this honor?"

I awkwardly hug her in return. "I wanted to talk to you about something."

Wilson yells from the other room, "If it's about that rogue you took as your new mate, you can just turn and walk out the door now."

My gaze drops to the floor. *That's exactly why I'm here.*

"Come in and sit down." Amber motions me to the kitchen. "How about a cup of coffee?"

"That would be great, thank you."

Amber calls down the hall, "Wilson, come in here."

"He's got nothing to say that I want to hear," Wilson yells back.

"He came all this way, the least you can do is—"

"Is what?" Wilson storms down the hall and bursts into the kitchen. "Our daughter is dead because of him. And now, he gets to take a new mate and live happily ever after. Horse crap. That's what that is."

I cradle the mug of hot coffee Amber gives me and watch the dark liquid ripple from my shaking.

"What are you really doing here?" Wilson asks. "Do you need our approval so you'll sleep better at night?"

In a stern voice, Amber says, "Wilson, that is enough! Remember who you're talking to. This is our Alpha."

Wilson mumbles under his breath and glares at me from across the room.

My wolf doesn't like Wilson's tone, but I hold back. He means no harm to the Alpha. *He has a right to be a father.*

"It's true," I say. "Elizabeth is dead because of me. I wasn't strong enough to save her, and I have to live with that. While I get to live on and take a new mate, she doesn't. And yes, that is why I'm here."

Wilson pulls out a wooden chair from under the kitchen table. "Then speak, boy, and be done with it."

After a deep breath, I tell them about the witch, my curse, and Elizabeth's cruel death. I explain to them about Dylan's curse, Felix and his inexcusable wrongdoings, and then I let them know about Lucinda. About how Lucinda and Mia met, why she came to our pack, and how I fell in love with her.

And then I admit that the bond between me and Elizabeth was superficial and not real, though I loved her all the same. I loved her for who she was, not because of any bond.

Tears stain Amber's cheeks. She sniffles, but her smile warms my heart. She walks over to me and embraces me as I imagine an approving mother would her son.

Relief washes over me. Not because she approves, but because I am finally able to talk to them about Elizabeth.

I am finally free of the dark secrets I kept from them. Maybe I will finally be free of the guilt I carry and can forgive myself for failing her.

But I know that is a long time in coming—nothing happens overnight.

Wilson stands up, his shoulders droop, and his head falls forward. Amber releases me and glides over to Wilson. A small sniffle is muffled upon their embrace. He reaches out his arm to me, and I cross the floor to take his extended arm in a forearm embrace. *It's done.*

"Would you like to stay for dinner?" Wilson asks. "Amber is cooking her famous braised chicken with white wine sauce."

My mouth waters just thinking about it.

"I'd love to."

Wilson and I head into the family room to watch TV while Amber finishes cooking.

I check my phone—no messages.

My fingers glide across the smooth face of the phone while I zone out. I want to send Lucinda a message, but what do I say?

It'll be better if I wait and just call her after I leave.

Slipping the phone back into my pocket, I lean into the soft leather chair and try to relax.

Wilson toys with the remote, sliding the battery cover on and off as he flips through channels on the tv.

Suddenly, the front door bursts open.

My wolf startles, and I jump to my feet at the commotion.

Wilson rolls his eyes while Amber rushes through the family room to greet the new visitor.

A sweet aroma—a mix of apple, rose, and vanilla—fills the room and tickles my senses.

I study the visitor as Amber talks in a hushed tone. The young woman has tattoos on her wrists and shoulders.

"Caiden?" she squeals as she crosses into the family room, dodging Amber.

"Leah?" I ask, needing to confirm she is Elizabeth's younger sister. "Look at you, all grown up! Has it really been so long?"

She rushes toward me and jumps into my arms.

Wilson's voice booms through the still air. "He is your Alpha! Stop this nonsense and show him respect."

Leah takes a step back and winks. "He was my brother-in-law before he was my Alpha."

"Well, he isn't anymore. Your sister is dead, and he's taken another mate. Now he's just your Alpha." Wilson adjusts his weight in his chair.

Large round eyes stare at me, and she wrinkles her forehead. "So, the rumors are true?"

I nod.

Amber steps next to Leah and grabs her hand. "We weren't expecting you tonight. Is everything okay?"

Leah turns to her mom and smiles. "Yeah, everything's fine."

"Then why are you here?"

"Can't a girl stop by and see her parents without an ulterior motive?"

The oven timer rings, and Amber rushes into the kitchen, mentioning something about checking on dinner.

Wilson closes the distance between him and Leah and reaches for her. With his thumb, he turns her face from side to side. "What have you done to yourself this time?"

He mutters under his breath and walks out of the room.

For the first time since she arrived, I take a good look at Leah. A small diamond stud sparkles in her nose, and her ears are covered in piercings, which peek out from behind her wispy hair.

"So..." Leah swings her arms as she talks.

Realizing I've been staring, I clear my throat and force an awkward smile. "I haven't seen you in what, five years?"

"Something like that. I didn't see you at the funeral."

"Right. I—"

"It's okay. You don't have to explain yourself to me."

I motion to the couch. "What have you been up to?"

"Well, I graduated from college last year."

"What did you study?"

"Event planning." Leah sits on the couch next to me and pulls her legs up to her chest. "It's a competitive field, and I've been having trouble finding full-time employment. For the last few months, I've been working as an independent consultant for PR relations and social media outreach. But I'm in between gigs right now."

"Why don't you come down to the Pack House next week? We can talk to Mia and find you some work—only if you're interested, of course."

"Really?" Her lips curl into a grin. "I mean, yes, I'm interested."

Amber steps into the doorway, wiping her hands on her apron. "Interested in what?"

"I asked Leah to come down to the Pack House next week. My sister Mia may have a job for her."

Amber inhales and her eyes widen. "Alpha—"

"Please, call me Caiden."

"Caiden." Amber bows her head. "That is too generous of you. Thank you."

"No thanks needed."

Why is it generous of me? I'm not giving her special treatment, am I? With the influx of new members from Felix's band of followers, Mia must be overwhelmed. And I didn't promise a job. I said we would talk to Mia and maybe find her a job. I'd do this for any pack member, wouldn't I?

I give my head a slight shake and smile.

Leah asks her mom, "How long until dinner is ready?"

"Oh! It's ready now. Dished up and on the table getting cold." Amber motions toward the kitchen.

"Wilson!" she shouts up the stairs. "Dinner!"

Wilson insists I sit at the head of the table, and Leah sits to my right, with Amber on my left. Wilson sits next to Amber and as far from Leah as possible.

Elizabeth mentioned her sister and father didn't get along, but I always assumed it was because Leah was the rebellious type of teenager.

"Leah, honey," Amber says as she sips her wine. "Your hair is different."

Leah's grave expression curves into a smile. "I bleached it blonde with the tips fading into a rose gold. Do you like it?"

"It's different." Amber tucks into her food.

———

After dinner, Wilson excuses himself and retires to bed. Amber begins to clear the table of the dirty dishes, and I stand to help.

"Don't worry, Mom, we can do this and then I'll see Caiden out," Leah says.

"Thanks, dear." Amber gives me another long embrace and then follows Wilson upstairs.

I continue collecting the dirty dishes and move them to the sink. "It was really good seeing you, Leah."

She brings over the last few glasses. "Do you have a few minutes to chat?"

"Sure."

She leads me back into the family room, and we sit on the couch.

"It's really none of my business, but I'm curious about your new mate."

"Lucinda?" My voice raises as I say her name.

Leah nods.

"Okay. What do you want to know?"

"About your bond."

Straight to the point.

A smile plays at my lips and a tightness twists in my stomach. Just thinking of Lucinda, my wolf yearns for his mate.

I tell Leah everything I told Amber and Wilson. Strangely, it isn't as awkward this time around.

Leah hugs a pillow in her lap. "Why do you think the witch cursed you?"

"Of everything I just told you, that is your question?"

She raises her eyebrows and nods.

I run my fingers through my hair and sigh. "I have no idea why she picked Felix, Dylan, and me to curse—"

"That's not what I meant. I mean, why do you think you are cursed? The beast you call him? You say he is a curse. Why?"

"He is aggressive and I can't control him—"

"Has there ever been a moment you could control him?"

My nostrils flare and I close my eyes. The image of Lucinda lying on the ground, covered in blood as I hover over her, ready to strike the final blow, fills my mind.

"Once," I whisper.

"Tell me about it."

I'd prefer not to. However, the words tumble from my mouth. "I was the uncontrollable raging beast. Lucinda was trying to stop me, and I almost killed her."

"But you didn't."

"I saw her lying there, and it's hard to describe. Something inside me snapped. Almost like the two pieces of my soul, me—well, my wolf—and the beast, collided and fought internally with each other." A low laugh erupts from my dry throat. "I know that sounds insane."

Her lips curve into a playful purse. "A little, but I've heard worse. So, what happened next?"

"I won the battle inside me and shifted back to my human form."

"Is the beast still within you?"

"Yes."

"But you can control him now?"

"Yes. But it's not easy. It's not like controlling my wolf."

Leah's lips curve into a wide smile, and her eyes sparkle. "Maybe Lucinda is your beast's mate."

My heart pounds, and my hands grow clammy.

My beast's mate. What does that even mean?

My phone buzzes, and I glance down to see a message from Lucinda. I quickly type a response, but then delete it. *I'll call her later.*

I turn back to Leah. "What do you mean my beast's mate?"

Pulling her legs onto the couch, she spins to face me. "I dunno. It just seems that she can control—or at least help you control—the beast. And Elizabeth didn't. So, something is different."

"It could just be the real fated bond versus the fake bond—"

"True. Or it could be something else. Tell me more about Lucinda."

I shift my weight to get comfortable and tell her all about Lucinda. Everything from my first impression of her, our run through the woods, our time in the cabin, and everything she shared with me about her past.

"She's an alpha female?"

I smirk with pride. "Yes."

"Interesting. I think I'd like to meet her."

"You will. Next week. Now, it's getting late. I really should be heading out."

"Where are you staying?"

"The old motel on the corner."

"Seriously? No. I will not allow that. You should stay here in the guest room."

"I—"

"I'm not taking no for an answer. My mom always keeps the room ready for guests. She won't mind. And I'm sure she would've offered earlier if she knew where you planned to stay." Leah punches me on the shoulder. "Come on."

I reluctantly nod. "I'll grab my overnight bag from the car."

Leah stands on the porch watching me. The light from the moon casts a shadow over her face, and her silhouette dances against the house. I rub my eyes with the back of my hand. *I must be more tired than I thought. Shadows don't dance.*

As we reenter the house, I say, "I plan to leave before sunrise to head home."

"Okay. But please don't wake me before you leave. I'll say bye tonight." She laughs and leads me to the guest room.

After closing the door behind me, I collapse on the bed. My feet hang off the small double bed, and I twist and turn all night. Vague memories of Elizabeth swirl through my dreams. Some are happy, but most are dark and sad thoughts.

I grow restless as shadows lurk on the edges of my vision, only to disappear when I turn to see them.

Shadows don't dance or stalk. If they aren't shadows, what are they?

CHAPTER 6

LUCINDA

MY PHONE BUZZES on the empty pillow next to me. I open my sleepy eyes and blink several times to fully wake up from a dream. I'm glad to be awake, but I can't remember why.

What was the dream about? I remember Caiden. Something happened to him—or he did something—and my pulse raced as I screamed. Damn it! Why can't I remember?

My phone buzzes again, and I raise my shaky hand to grab it.

"Hello?" My scratchy morning voice hurts my ears.

"Hey, Lux," Dylan says. "Do you want to go on patrol with me today?"

I hold the phone in front of me to look at the screen. I heard right. It's Dylan. What a rude awakening. I was hoping to hear Caiden's voice on the other end.

"Where are you?" I ask.

"Outside your door."

"Why did you call, dumbass?" I snort and pull the covers over my head.

I want to go back to bed and remember that dream. Something inside me tells me it is important.

"Because you didn't answer when I knocked on the door," he says. "Hurry up. I want to leave in ten minutes."

I glance down at my phone—zero missed calls and no new messages—and take a deep breath.

Caiden must've been up late and is still sleeping. He probably won't be home until this evening. I shoot him a quick text before I get up to let him know I'll be gone for the day but will see him tonight.

He hasn't responded by the time I'm ready, so I leave my phone on the dresser and head downstairs to meet Dylan.

"So where are we going?" I ask.

"The northern border," he says. "I know you're not used to the mindlink yet, but it's vital we communicate today, okay?"

I roll my eyes. "Fine, okay. Mindlink open."

"Great, let's go."

I slip off my robe before shifting into my wolf and then follow Dylan into the forest.

I've always wanted to go on a patrol, but Caiden hasn't let me yet. I know it's not because I'm female—he has female patrol wolves. It's because I'm his mate. He doesn't want me near danger.

I do not want to be near Caiden when he finds out that Dylan took me on one of his watches. A small roll of goose bumps races up my spine, and my wolf whines in protest. She is torn. She's like me; we're excited about going out on patrol, but she doesn't like going against her mate's wishes.

Caiden once asked me how I could forgive Dylan so easily. I told him that Dylan is all I had left of my prior life. While he isn't a blood relative, he is the only surviving Dark Raven pack member. Therefore, he is my only living family. Caiden accepted this explanation and understands. *I hope.*

Dylan and I have drifted closer these past few weeks, and

the fire of our old friendship has rekindled. But there are no romantic feelings on either side. *I think.*

Dylan moves at a decent speed while racing through the forest. He maneuvers over the fallen trees and around the underbrush with an amazing grace that's a joy to watch. I follow, staying a length behind him and to his right.

All too soon, we're racing. It's an old game we played as children, seeing who could be the most daring and pull off the best stunts while running through the forest at top speed.

I soar past him, leap over a dead tree, and come skidding to a halt. My hackles bristle and my ears lie flat as I crouch low. Dylan leaps over the tree and lands behind me.

"Lux, what is it?" he sends through the mindlink.

"Something's not right." I sniff the air and snarl. "Don't you smell that?"

Raising his nose to the air, he sniffs. "What is that?"

"Not good whatever it is. I don't like it."

Dylan's eyes narrow as his lip curls, exposing his sharp incisors. "Let's get out of here."

"Shouldn't we find out what it is?" I take a cautious step forward with my nose to the air, trying to pick up the scent.

"No."

I turn and pounce, knocking him to the ground.

"What do you mean, no?" *If it's because I'm the Alpha's mate, damn him!*

"Lux, we have protocols for stuff like this."

"What's the protocol?" I roll off him and stand with my back to the strange scent.

"A team of trained guards and trackers will go investigate."

Lies. I snarl. "Why? Are you scared?"

"It's how we do things. If you ever want to be a patrol wolf, then you'll need to abide by our rules."

"When will they go?"

"I've already alerted them, and they're on their way here. They'll pick up the scent and track it back to the origin. They'll report what they find."

"Fine."

"I want to show you something anyway," Dylan says. "This way."

He turns to his left and motions for me to follow. I take another look over my shoulder and a shimmer, like that of the sun gleaming off metal, glints in the distance. My lips pull back as I snarl.

"Lux, let's go," Dylan says in a deep voice.

Ignoring him, I raise my head and howl into the sky. Soon, there's an echo of howls in response. *Good. Dylan was telling the truth.*

"Satisfied?" Dylan asks.

After sniffing the air once more to take a memory of the strange scent, I turn back to him and follow his lead.

This time, our pace is much slower. We are less playful and more cautious. But I can't resist admiring the forest and all its beauty. It is stunning this time of year. Winter is ending, and the forest is beginning to become alive again.

Dylan leads me to a series of untouched caverns that jut out from the side of the mountain. "This place is good to know in case you get stuck out here in bad weather."

"These caves would be fun to explore."

He glares at me. "Many people have gotten lost within this system and never seen or heard from again."

"Then why are you showing them to me?"

Dylan stares at me for a beat without blinking. "This place makes a great shelter if you stay on the exterior, but do not explore deeper into the cave system."

I glance back at the cave entrance.

"Lux, do you understand me?"

"Yes, fine. I'll stay away."

Dylan turns around and I follow his lead. *Of course, I'll be back one day.*

He shows me other things to watch out for while conducting a patrol of the border—unnatural disturbances of the forest floor, fallen trees, broken tree limbs, dead animals, and all the while paying attention to different scents drifting in the air.

Apart from his instruction, the conversation between us is quiet. There is no discussion of the prior event, but I can't stop thinking about the way that scent made my stomach queasy.

My nose wrinkles remembering that retched smell.

Dylan tosses a rabbit at my feet for lunch. It's not much, but it'll do until we get home. It's been a while since my wolf has feasted. She dances with delight at the sight of fresh blood and raw meat.

My stomach churns.

Suddenly, Dylan stands. His ears stand erect and then flatten as a low growl rumbles in his chest.

I glance to the sky and black wings soar just above the treetops. A growl erupts from my throat. *That damn bat!*

Dylan's nose twitches as he watches me, but we both turn toward the sound of twigs breaking. To the human ear, this person would be considered stealthy, but not to our heightened senses.

I head toward the sound in the forest, but Dylan nudges me in the opposite direction, and I comply. He leads me into a thick briar patch, and as soon as we're fully hidden, he shifts into human form and I follow.

"What is it?" I ask.

"I don't know, but something isn't right," he says.

"Do you think it's the same thing from earlier?"

"No."

"How do you know? Where's your team?"

"I don't know. But the forest is too quiet." He crouches and peers through a little hole in the briars.

"Except for that damn bat," I mutter under my breath.

"You mean raven."

"No. I mean ba—" I look up to find a raven perched on a branch directly above us. "Whatever. He's annoying too."

Can't I ever go anywhere without either a bat or raven following me?

"You know him, do you?" Dylan smirks.

Just then, the raven swoops down and lands a foot from Dylan's knee. I narrow my eyes at the damn bird. *What is he up to? He's never come this close before—usually, he just watches from afar.*

"He seems nice enough to me." Dylan reaches out his hand for the raven to climb onto his finger. "There's something different about him. His eyes—"

A soft twig breaks not too far from where we hide in the briars.

Suddenly, the raven takes flight and bursts through the briars. A swish echoes through the silent forest—the sound of an arrow flying through the air. The hair on my forearms prickles, and I fight the urge to shift. My wolf would never fit in this small hiding space.

The pungent smell from earlier drifts on the light breeze, and the repeated short shrill of the raven, followed by whispered mutterings, grow silent as the intruder retreats back into the forest.

"I think that was the same thing from earlier," I say to Dylan through the mindlink. He nods.

"Where is your team?"

"They're not responding."

"Should we follow it?"

Dylan glares at me and his nostrils flare. "No, we should head back."

"But—"

"Lux, please don't argue. It'll be dusk by the time we get back anyway. I'll show you the southern border next time."

"What about the eastern and western borders?"

"On the east, we're protected by the ocean, so we don't have a regular patrol schedule. And on the west, well, we're protected by the mountains, which is a natural barrier."

"And isn't that where Felix was camped?"

"Yes."

I raise my eyebrows.

"The truth is, I don't think anyone wants to go west," he says. "Too many memories from the massacre that happened there several years ago."

"The one where Caiden's parents were killed?"

"Yes."

"Do they know who attacked?"

"No. After meeting Felix, I assumed it was him."

"It wasn't."

His eyes narrow. "How do you know?"

"He told me—"

"And you believe him?"

"I do. He has no reason to lie about it."

Dylan stares at the ground, yet he nods in agreement.

"Besides, he said he heard about it and then watched them torture Caiden's mate, Elizabeth. Felix actually thought it repulsive."

"Really?"

I nod. "So, any other leads?"

Dylan's face twists, and he bites his lower lip.

"What is it? Tell me!"

"I've been going through the old pack records."

"You found something?" I ask.

"Not exactly. I've been looking for anything that might be about witches, curses, or anything like that. There isn't much, and pages are torn out of several of the journals. But I found something—"

"Have you told Caiden?"

"No, I want to wait until I have more of a theory before going to Caiden. Right now, it's just a bunch of questions and a few letters and journal entries that talk nonsense. But I think they are talking in code. If I can just break the code..." He stares at the ground, lost deep in thought. He looks up to me and says, "Let's keep this between us... for now."

"Agreed. Are we telling Caiden about what happened out here today?"

"We can tell him what he needs to know."

"Which is?"

"There was a strange scent. But I want a report from the men first when they return."

"If they return," I whisper.

Dylan's jaw clenches and he closes his eyes. "Come on, let's head back."

Our run back is all business, and Caiden contacts Dylan through the mindlink to say he's home.

Why didn't he try to contact me? Or did he? Was I blocking him?

When we arrive back at the Pack House, I slip into my robe, which is exactly where I left it in the Mudroom.

After dressing, I turn to Dylan and say, "Hey, thanks for today. It was fun."

His smile widens, exaggerating his dimples.

"And I was wondering," I say as I step closer to him. "Since both my father and Caiden's father are dead, would you give me away at our ceremony?"

"I would be honored," he says.

I fling my arms around his neck, and his arms wrap around my waist.

"Thank you," I whisper and kiss him on the cheek before pulling him closer for a long hug.

And then my nose twitches as a spicy bergamot scent drifts down the hall. *Caiden!*

I pull away from Dylan, and he smiles.

"Go on," he says, motioning with his head toward the hall.

Butterflies swirl in my stomach. *Why am I nervous to see Caiden?*

CHAPTER 7

CAIDEN

MY FAVORITE SCENT of mint and honey drifts through the air in the Pack House. *She's home.* I step out of my office and turn down the hall toward her scent. But I immediately stop. In the floor-length mirror that hangs on the wall, I see their reflection.

Lucinda in Dylan's arms is not a welcoming sight for a mate.

I force my fist into a tight ball to channel my frustration.

"Caiden," drums through the mindlink.

Unable to focus, I snap. "What?"

After what I just witnessed, I need a cooldown run. I dig my nails into my weathered and calloused skin and storm back into my office.

One of my guards sends through the mindlink, "I found someone in town."

"And?"

"He was hiding in the shadows and acting suspicious, so I approached him—"

"Hurry up and get to the point."

"Somehow, he's masking his scent, but he's a wolf," he says. "His name is Cody, and he asked to speak with you."

"Cody?" I sit down. After all this time, could it be the same Cody that ran with Felix? "Okay, bring him here. And keep it quiet. Stay to the back roads."

There is no need for anyone to know he's here, if it is the same Cody.

"Caiden." Lucinda's voice rings down the empty hallway. "I know you're home, where are you?"

I turn to look out the window at the calm forest—my sanctuary. "In the office."

"There you are," she says walking into the room. She stands behind me and rubs my back, leaning her head on my shoulder. "Everything okay?"

"Fine." I inhale the irresistible scent of mint and honey that radiates off her.

I turn and engulf her in my arms, holding her tight. My nose twitches as I catch the scent of cumin and fresh cut grass drifting through the air. The beast that resides within me stirs and whines. He doesn't like other male scents being on our mate.

A fire ignites in my chest, and I need to extinguish any doubt that Lucinda is our mate. Resting my forehead against hers, I lift her delicate fingers to my lips and place gentle kisses on them. A spark of mischief glimmers in her hazel eyes as her lips curve at the corner.

If only she knew the power she has over me.

My lips find hers in a frenzy like no other. If the large mark on her neck at the sweet spot below the ear isn't warning enough for others to stay away, then I need to claim her in other ways. My scent needs to overwhelm the delicious mint and honey.

Nibbling on her lip, a low moan escapes her and drives my wild desire. I grab her thighs, picking her up and carrying her to my desk. Our lips never part. She runs her fingers through my hair, and tingles travel all the way down to my feet. I need her like I've never needed anyone before.

Once at the desk, I knock off everything that is in the way with one swift movement of my right arm. A loud crashing fills the room as the items hit the floor.

Oh well. I'll pick it up later.

I set her down on the desk, her legs spread wide, and I lean between them. Hands roaming down her body, I find her hips and pull her closer to the edge. *God, I need her.*

"Lucinda—" I moan, but my voice is muffled as her lips crash into mine.

Her nails graze my back, and she fumbles with the hem of my shirt.

I pull away from her, quickly tear my white T-shirt off over my head, and drop it to the floor. As I grab for her shirt, my thumbs brush her nipples, and she shudders under my touch.

We work together to unbutton her shirt, but my idle fingers are impatient. I reach in to fondle her breasts while she continues to work on the buttons. Her nipples form stiff peaks as I roll them between my fingers, and her heavy breathing tells me she's enjoying my touch.

"Caiden, I love you," she whispers against my neck. Her sweet breath warming my skin.

That is exactly what I need to hear and my wolf needs to know. She loves us. We are hers, and she is ours.

Finally, her shirt hits the floor and our eyes meet, mixed with lust and love.

A heavy burden is lifted and my heart surges. My hands and lips move over her with a new agenda, and her hips begin to rock in a rhythm that calls to me. Her fingers find the button and zipper to my jeans. She traces my waistline, teasing me, and it's my undoing.

In a frenzy, I rip down my pants and they pool at my feet.

A giggle plays on her swollen lips and I reach for her, my fingers intertwining in her hair on the back of her head.

A small knock taps at the door, followed by a throat clearing. "Caiden?"

I stand upright.

Dylan calls again from the other side of the door, "Caiden."

"What?" A growl slips out.

My mate is half-naked in front of me, dripping with moistness, needing me to put an end to her misery.

"Cody's here."

"Cody's here?" Lucinda slips out of my grasp and reaches for her shirt on the ground. She quickly dresses and rushes for the door, then turns back to me. "Did you know?"

I nod as I reach for my pants and shirt.

Turning on her heels, she strides toward me with her eyebrows furrowed. "How long have you known he was here?"

"Not long," I say.

"Were you going to tell me?"

"Yes." I pull my shirt over my head.

She places her hands upon her hips. "When?"

"Later."

And just like that our sweet and sensual moment together is ruined.

Flipping her cascading chestnut hair over her shoulder, a rush of mint and honey is sent floating through the air.

My manhood throbs with anticipation, and my wolf tears at me from within to throw Lucinda down and have our way with her. But no, I won't do that to her. I will never allow my wolf to escape during our moments together.

Lucinda rips the door open, putting an end to my thoughts.

Dylan smirks on the other side. Lucinda rolls her eyes and looks down the hall.

We spot Cody at the same time, though our reactions are much different. She takes off running and flings herself into his arms.

"Just a tip," Dylan says to me through the mindlink. "Try to remove that scowl on your face before Lux sees it."

"What?" I ask.

"She won't approve."

Dylan motions for Cody and Lucinda to follow us into the office.

"Cody, what are you doing here?" Lucinda asks.

Dylan closes the door and the deadbolt latches.

Cody's gaze darts around the room. "I'm tracking a witch."

"A witch?" Dylan walks across the room to stand next to me.

Cody nods.

My nostrils flare as I hold back a growl. "I would know if there's a witch in my territory."

"I mean no disrespect," Cody says, "but would you really?"

Our eyes lock. He makes a valid point. *Damn it.*

I fold my arms across my chest. "I'm listening."

"After everything that went down in Felix's camp..." Cody glances toward Lucinda. "I was holed up recovering for a few days. That's when I first came across the witch. So, I followed her."

Lucinda leans forward. "You followed her here?"

Cody nods.

Dylan paces back and forth. "What does she want?"

"I think she lives here," Cody says.

I mutter through a clenched jaw, "We have a witch living right under our noses?"

"It would appear that way."

I lift my arms behind my head and lace my fingers tightly together. Lucinda stands beside me and rubs my arm. Her gentle touch helps to calm my rising temper.

"If she lives here, then obviously, she doesn't mean us any harm." Lucinda's voice is steady and comforting.

Cody clears his throat. "I'm not so sure about that."

I lower my arms and jerk my head to him faster than a rubber band flying through the air. "What do you mean?"

"I've been watching her for several weeks, and she's had a few interesting meetings."

Dylan snarls in Cody's direction. "Care to elaborate?"

"They've hired an assassin," Cody says, his voice lowering as he says the last word.

"They?" I ask. I didn't miss the part about the assassin, but the mention of more than one witch caught my immediate attention.

"A male witch came to meet with her, then they hired the assassin."

My pulse races, my blood rushing through my veins. *Two witches in my territory. This can't be good.*

"Who is the target?" Dylan asks.

I follow Cody's gaze as it drifts and settles on Lucinda. He says nothing, but the look in his eyes says it all.

"Me?" Lucinda's voice shakes, and I wrap my arms around her midsection to keep her upright.

"That makes no sense." Dylan's barely restrained voice breaks the silence. Like mine, his wolf is near the edge of pushing through his barrier of control.

I grit my teeth and take a deep breath before speaking. "Why do the witches conspire against Lucinda?"

"Because they fear her," Cody says.

"They fear her? Why?"

"You're still holding Felix, right?" Cody asks.

"What does that matter?" I snap.

"We need to talk to Felix. I need to tell him—"

I storm across the room to stand face to face with Cody. My power vibrates in my wake, and Cody's eyes widen in shock.

"What do Felix and the witches hiring an assassin to kill Lucinda have in common?" I ask.

"Everything," Cody whispers. "But Felix can explain it better than I can."

Dylan touches my shoulder and moves me away from Cody. He steps between us and says, "Try me."

Cody takes a deep breath and lets out a long sigh. "Okay, short version. The witches have been trying to kill Lucinda her entire life. They just didn't want it traced back to them."

Dylan turns to look at me, and we both glance at Lucinda. She shrugs and shakes her head.

Cody clears his throat. "Why do you think the payment for Dylan's curse was her death? They wanted Dylan to kill her. Fortunately for us, they underestimated Dylan's strength and ability to control himself."

Dylan's gaze bores into Lucinda, and she turns away with a blush rising to her cheeks. I recall their long embrace earlier, and a low growl vibrates in my chest. Lucinda steps next to me, wraps her arms around my waist, and squeezes.

"That still doesn't answer why they want her dead," I say.

"Felix will have to answer that. It has something to do with her parents," Cody says with a sincere but sad face.

I nod and look to the forest where the sun is setting. "It's getting late."

"Caiden." Lucinda steps in front of me. "We should go talk to him now."

"I need a run to calm myself before talking to Felix," I tell her through the mindlink.

Lucinda doesn't have the mindlink closed right now, but I still have to force the message through to her. When she gets my message, her eyes widen and she takes a step back. Her eyes roam my body, as if just noticing my tense posture, bulging veins, and shaky hands.

"Okay," she says out loud. She adds through the mindlink, "But I'm coming too."

The heat and passion from earlier return, and my body aches for her touch. I give a slight nod of approval.

Turning to Dylan, I say, "I need to run. When we return, I'll arrange for us to meet with Felix. Until then, will you see that Cody has everything he needs?"

Dylan nods.

Cody grins at Lucinda. His eyes gleam of approval; he must have noticed our bond. She runs to him and gives him a quick hug.

My teeth strip at the sight of Lucinda in Cody's arms.

CHAPTER 8

LUCINDA

CAIDEN and I waste no time darting through the house, leaving our clothes thrown in piles on the floor behind us. I'm careful to shift into my wolf within seconds of removing my clothes, no need to torment the raging beast within Caiden more than he's already agitated.

Through the mindlink, I ask Caiden, "How did your meeting go?"

"Fine." He quickens his pace.

"Is everything okay?"

He turns, and his red glowing eyes drill into me.

My hackles bristle. I fight the urge to stop running and let him calm himself, but I can't do that. "I know it was a stupid question with everything Cody just said, but you don't have to be like that."

I glance back toward the Pack House.

"Leave," he says.

"What?"

"Go back. I'll be fine."

"No." I push forward to stay alongside him. "Caiden, you

aren't alone, not anymore. You have me. And we'll get through this—together."

He nods and picks up his pace even more, dodging trees and leaping over fallen logs. I love a good run, but this is borderline self-destructive.

"Is something bothering you?"

"No." He surges forward.

Lie. He is agitated and unfocused. He has been since he returned from his trip.

I leap over a fallen tree, though when I land there is another and another. My paws press against one of the dead logs to get more momentum, but I slip on the luscious green moss that's covering the side of the log.

A small whimper escapes as I tumble to the ground. "Caiden—"

He slows and stops to look at me about five hundred yards ahead of where I lie.

I press to stand and limp to him, watching each move my paw makes on the pine needles that cover the forest floor.

"Are you hurt?" he asks through the mindlink. Although, his tone is more of an Alpha checking on a pack member than Caiden checking on his mate.

"I'll be fine. Maybe a sprain."

He holds his position but turns his back to me.

As I approach him, I ask, "What's wrong?"

"Nothing." He circles me as he would prey.

I hold my position, but there is a distant and cold look in his eye that causes the fur on my back to bristle. His eyes glaze over and turn solid onyx as he continues to circle.

Caiden's massive white wolf pauses directly behind me. Ears erect, a low growl erupts from him.

I flip around, strip my teeth, and let loose a snarl. My ears lie flat, and I lower my head near my front legs. *If he wants to fight, I will fight.*

"Caiden..." I call to him through the mindlink, but he has it blocked.

He crouches back and pounces. His sharp claws dig into my back, and I yelp. But I quickly respond by flipping him off and pouncing on him.

I wrap my teeth around his shoulder. I don't want to hurt him. It's not him that has control right now; it's the beast within him. But I won't let him hurt me without a fight.

I sink my teeth into his flesh. Warm blood drips down my muzzle and fills my mouth. He yelps, but the sound quickly turns into a growl. He throws me from his back with such force, I land ten feet away. I smash into a tall pine tree and lie under its umbrella of dark green branches.

Caiden stalks over to me. His fur bristles as he closes the distance between us, and his lips curl, exposing his sharp incisors.

"Caiden." I try again through the mindlink.

Still nothing. The past few weeks he's struggled to control the beast, but this is the first time I haven't been able to bring him back.

He'll never forgive himself for this.

When I manage to stand, my legs are wobbly underneath my weight. But there's no time to gain full strength, as Caiden charges toward me. On pure instinct, I raise my head and let loose a howl into the sky.

Caiden skids to a halt and falls onto his side in order to avoid ramming into me. He's shifted into man form.

Luckily, my solid black wolf hides blood very well. He doesn't need to know what happened. I shift and run to him as he stands.

"Lucinda," he whispers into my ear.

"Where were you?" I ask.

"Did I—" He wipes the blood from my back.

"It's not mine." It's not a complete lie.

He reaches to my bite mark on the back of his shoulder. It's already started to heal, but he can feel the wound.

"I'm sorry about that." I look up at him from under my lashes. Tears threaten to roll down my cheeks.

His eyebrows raise, and he eyes me suspiciously. "As long as I didn't hurt you."

"No, I'm fine," I say. *I will never tell him what he did.*

His hand brushes across my cheek, and I lean toward his warm skin.

"Can we sit and talk a while?" I ask.

The pained look on his face tries for an unconvincing smile, and he guides me a few feet away to sit under a tree. I crawl into his lap and lay my head against his chest. His grip tightens around me, and he holds me so close I can hear his heart beating at a rapid pace.

"I don't know what happened," he says. "It's been harder—"

"I know."

"Is it that obvious?" he whispers.

I nod against his chest.

"What's happening to me?" His warm breath tingles on my skin. My mate's mark throbs and my pulse quickens.

His loud sigh causes me to jump, and Caiden pushes me off his lap. He abruptly stands, turns away from me, and heads deeper into the forest.

Sitting like a damn fool, I squint in his direction. After a few seconds, I stand, race after him, and call out, "We'll figure it out."

When I catch up to him, he's stopped at the edge of a small stream. I stalk toward him, careful not to disturb his peace. Once I'm confident he won't leave again, I rub his back and say,

"We'll figure it out together," I say. I walk around to the front of him and look up into his eyes. "Guess what?"

I hope a change of topic will distract him enough to lighten his mood.

His forehead raises and our eyes meet.

My heart pounds in my chest. "I picked a date."

He cocks an eyebrow. "A date?"

"For our ceremonial mating ritual."

His eyes widen, then a large grin creeps onto his face. This is a genuine smile, not a failed attempt. My heart soars with relief. He closes the distance between us.

"Is that right?" he asks. "And what day would that be?"

"June 21st," I whisper as his lips nip at mine.

"The summer solstice." He outlines my lips with the tip of his tongue.

"Yes," I moan. "Is that okay?"

"It's perfect." His mouth moves down to my jawline, and he trails kisses along my neck, ending at his mark. The kisses burn on the sweet spot.

My hands roam his body, and my nails glide across his bare back. His wounds from earlier have healed.

"How did you come up with that date?" Caiden asks as he continues his trail of kisses down my collarbone.

"It doesn't matter," I say. *I don't want to ruin this moment by mentioning Sabrina.*

He lifts his head so fast, I flinch at the movement. The intense look in his eyes causes my nerves to falter.

"Why doesn't it matter?" His tone changes from light and playful to dark and crude. "Was it someone else's idea?"

My shoulders slouch as I step away from him. *The moment is ruined. As all of our moments have been recently.*

"Yes—"

"Who?" Again, the deepness in his voice startles me.

I bite my lower lip. "Sabrina."

His face distorts and relief washes over his features. *Apparently, that wasn't the person he was expecting.*

"Caiden." I reach my hand out for his. "What's bothering you?"

He steps closer to me and takes my outstretched hand.

"Nothing." He presses his lips into my knuckles. A smile spreads across his face and warms my soul.

But the expression is fleeting. His eyes widen and he pushes me to the ground. He crouches over me in a protective stance, his arms tense and his muscles bulging.

"Caiden—"

He shushes me. A growl erupts, but this time it's not directed at me.

His head scans the area, searching for something. Then I smell it. The same pungent scent I smelled earlier with Dylan.

An arrow zips through the air and lands in the dirt inches from my head.

Shit! Is this the assassin?

My heart thumps in my chest at a rapid pace.

"Stay down," Caiden whispers in my ear, "and open the damn mindlink."

I nod.

"Patrols are on their way," he says through the mindlink. "When Gavin gets here, I want you to shift into your wolf and run like hell."

"What about you?"

"I'm going after this bastard."

I look over my shoulder, and his eyes meet mine.

His once beautiful blue irises show nothing of the man I love. Instead, they are two glowing red embers.

I'm not sure which is more terrifying, the red or black beast... At least he still has control of the red-eyed beast, I think.

CHAPTER 9

CAIDEN

CROUCHING to meet Lucinda's distant stare, I brace myself for her to protest being left behind. To my surprise, she nods in agreement.

Good. I'll be able to focus and hunt better knowing she's safe.

Her eyes widen, and the distinct hiss of another arrow flies through the air. I twist around and push her down into the soft earth. As I shield her body with mine, the sharp tip of the arrow grazes across the exposed flesh of my bicep.

Lucinda looks at my bleeding arm and then to me. Her voice is small and timid as it comes through the mindlink. "Please don't leave me."

"Gavin's here. I'll see you soon." I press my lips against her forehead.

I nod to Gavin as he approaches from behind Lucinda, and shifts from his wolf into human form.

"Take care of her," I say as I turn to leave.

"You know I will."

I give them one last glance over my shoulder. Lucinda stands and steps so she is positioned slightly behind Gavin. She reaches out and grabs a hold of his arm.

Flashing a smile, I turn toward the direction the arrow came. In one swift motion, I shift in midair.

Game on. It's time to hunt.

My senses are much stronger and clearer in my wolf form, so I inhale deeply to pick up the intruder, and my nose twitches with disgust. The scent is repulsive. It reminds me of snake musk, a mixture of rotten eggs and dead fish baking in the hot sun.

What kind of monstrous creature did the witches hire as an assassin? Because if this is the scent of a witch, I would know one was living in my territory.

I find the tree and overgrown underbrush the intruder used for cover while watching us with ease. The scent is everywhere. I shift and kneel to feel the earth—the leaves and dirt are disturbed.

We have an impatient assassin. Interesting.

The guttural croak of a raven startles me, and I shift back into my wolf just in time for another arrow to land an inch from my paw.

Keep it together, I tell myself. *Stay in control. We need him alive.*

But the beast within me is fighting for control, and it appears this assassin is either a bad shot or toying with us. The fur on my neck bristles and my lips curl. Saliva drips off my incisors and pools in the dirt.

I snarl and crouch down at the ready.

There's a glimpse of movement about twenty yards away. I take off running at full speed and pounce on the assassin's back as he turns to flee.

My claws pierce his brown cloak and dig into the soft flesh of his back. A high-pitched scream echoes through the empty forest, and I flip the person over. After I claw through the hood covering his head, I step away and rear back on my haunches.

A woman lies in front of me. Her purple eyes widen as I stand over of her, growling. She reaches for her belt, but I'm quicker. I sink my teeth into the flesh between her thumb and fingers, and I shake my head to give it a good tear.

The raven swoops down and croaks, but it's too late. The assassin raises her left foot and kicks me in the ribs. A blade sticking out of the tip of her boot slices into me.

As she pulls the knife out of my skin, the wound burns with a fierce intensity. My nostrils flare, and I blow out a large breath, which stirs up a pile of dead leaves.

The satisfaction and curiosity that crosses her face causes alarm and makes me wary. *She's no longer afraid. But I'll give her something to fear.*

I can't fight the beast any longer. Gritting my teeth, I send a silent message to Lucinda. *Please forgive me.*

A raven's croak rings in my ears, and I look up. Sooty black wings dive from above and perform an acrobatic roll before gliding gracefully to the ground.

The bird walks with a swagger and stops at my bloody paws. Its beady eyes stare at me, then it opens its knife-shaped beak, and a deep gurgling call echoes, causing my hackles to bristle. The raven croaks one last time and takes flight, soaring far into the distance.

I raise my paw to look at the blood. It doesn't appear to be mine.

Time to survey the damage.

My eyes scan the forest floor, and it is stained red. But the assassin is nowhere to be found.

The beast never lets his prey escape. What happened?

I press my nose to the ground and search for the scent. *Nothing.*

Something isn't right. My eyes dart around, looking for a blood trail. There should be a trail—if not visible, at least by scent—but still, nothing.

I stomp my front paw into the ground and growl, flaring severe pain. The knife wound to my ribs and the slice on my arm from the first arrow have yet to heal. And I have an arrow lodged in my right shoulder.

Lucinda's voice pushes through the mindlink. "Caiden, where are you?"

I survey the area one last time. There is no new scent of blood, the wretched stench of the assassin, or any other clue as to where she went.

I hang my head low and respond to Lucinda, "I'm headed home."

With every step, my shoulder burns with pain. The arrow is still lodged deep in my flesh, and I can feel its weight pressing into me.

However, the intensity of the pain is from deep within the wound. An internal flame ignites my blood and sends the sensation of cut glass coursing through my veins. I fear this isn't an ordinary arrow, so I pick up my pace, which only causes my blood to pump harder and faster through my body.

When I arrive home, I burst through the back door and grab the pair of flannel pants I left sitting on top of the dryer.

Lucinda rushes in and drapes her arms around my midsection, and I tense at her touch. My skin has become overly sensitive—every movement and every touch feel like a jagged stab wound.

"Caiden, what is it?" Lucinda pulls away from me and takes a step back. Her eyes roam my body and she raises her hands to cover her mouth with a gasp. She reaches out a hand to touch the arrow protruding from my shoulder.

"Please don't touch it," I say.

Her eyebrows raise. "Are you okay?"

"I'll be fine. But I do need it removed, and the wound on my arm and chest should be cleaned and stitched so I can heal quicker."

Lucinda nods. "I guess you found him?"

My legs wobble under my weight and my vision blurs. I give a slight shake to my head to clear the fogginess. "Who?"

"The assassin or whoever was shooting the arrows."

"She..." I sway back and forth, rocking from heel to toe. I start to stumble forward, and Lucinda catches me.

The room spins and beads of sweat drip down my face.

Lucinda's voice is muffled and distant, but her mouth is still moving. She turns over her shoulder, and others rush into the room. The faces are familiar—Dylan, Mia, and Gavin—but they're all blurry. I can't focus.

"Stay with us," someone yells.

What's happening?

Whispers drift in my ear. The voices are low and muffled, but I sense the uneasiness of their wolves. My wolf is anxious as well. I strain to open my eyes.

Shit! Why won't they open?

My heart pounds in my chest, but then mint and honey drift through the air. Lucinda's power surges over me, calming my racing pulse. She's close, and she's beyond angry.

Where is she?

In the midst of my frustration, my wolf fights for control and forces my eyes open.

I'm in my room. Lying in my bed.

Through a groggy haze, Gavin and Cody come into focus in the dark hallway just outside my room. They are leaning close together, lurking in the shadows..

What are they talking about?

Lucinda shouts, "Caiden."

In the corner of my eye, her fingers touch my arm, but I don't feel the softness of her fingertips against my skin. I try to turn my head in her direction, but I can't.

DAMN IT! A growl escapes from deep inside my chest.

"Shh," Lucinda says. "Everything will be okay, now."

Her arm crosses in front of my face, and she tilts my head toward her. When she comes into view, the dark circles and swelling around her eyes send my wolf into a frenzy. A breath catches in my throat, but my lips won't move.

I send through the mindlink, "Why can't I move?"

Lucinda's eyes gloss over, and she blinks back tears that threaten to fall. Her nose scrunches. A tear escapes and rolls down her cheek. "Oh, Caiden. You're paralyzed."

"Paralyzed?" I'm glad my voice isn't working right now, or else my quivering tone would betray my emotions.

What good am I to Lucinda and the pack if I'm paralyzed?

Lucinda rests her head on my chest. Her close proximity calms the frantic beats of my heart, thought I can't feel the doodling with her fingertips upon my bare skin. "Calm down. The doctor says it's only temporary."

I release the breath I was holding. *Temporary.* "What happened?"

"You were poisoned," she says.

"How?"

"We think it was the broadhead on the arrow, or it could have been the knife that stabbed you, or both. Whatever it was, a weapon was laced with a unique poison and..."

My chest rumbles. "And what?"

Lucinda sits up and leans in close. I should be able to feel her warm breath on my lips, but I can't. "Caiden, this assassin means business."

"No, this assassin is a coward."

"A coward?" Her eyebrows raise and she furrows her forehead.

"Anyone that uses a poison-tipped arrow to kill their prey either isn't a good shot or can't stomach the kill. She's hiding behind the poison to finish the job as opposed to finishing it herself. She is a coward—"

"She almost killed you!"

"Almost. But didn't."

"You're right. YOU got lucky." Lucinda's eyes narrow. "You've only been unconscious for two days."

"Two days?"

She bites her lower lip and nods.

"Tell me everything."

"The pack doctor said the poison is deadly. Fortunately for you, it wasn't a strong enough dose to kill you in your wolf form, at least not immediately. With the racing adrenaline of your beast, the effects subsided until you shifted back into your weaker human state."

"And?"

Lucinda looks over her shoulder at the door. Cody and Gavin are gone.

"What aren't you telling me?"

"Caiden, you need to rest now. We'll talk more in the morning."

"Tell me now."

Lucinda's head snaps around so fast that her hair brushes across my lips. Her eyes widen as she gazes upon me. Her lips purse into a tight pucker. "No. Sleep."

A growl slips up my throat.

Lucinda stands and turns her back to me. "Rest. You need to regain your strength."

She walks out the door.

Damn it!

"Lucinda!" I yell through the mindlink, but she doesn't

return.

The pictures on the wall vibrate, and the oil lamp almost dances off the nightstand.

Dylan, Mia, and Gavin burst through the bedroom door.

Mia runs to my side. Her eyes fully dilated. "Caiden, you need to calm down."

Dylan and Gavin stand at the door, surveying the room.

What's going on? Did I do that?

Mia strokes my head. I imagine the gentleness of her touch. She looked at me with those same big blue eyes after Elizabeth died.

The sharp tip of a syringe glints in the sunlight before it disappears from view.

Mia's eyes soften around the edges, and her pupils constrict to their normal size as she leans down and kisses my forehead.

Through the mindlink, I say, "Mia, don't—"

"Rest my dear brother, just rest."

A heaviness pushes through the barrier of my rattling mind and my eyelids droop.

CHAPTER 10

CAIDEN

THE SOUND of chirping pulls me from my nightmare. Another sleepless night full of lies, death, and destruction. And those damn birds won't stop their irritating racket!

My wolf pushes through the invisible barrier that holds my eyes closed. I raise my arms to shield myself from the rays of morning sun that pour through the open blinds. My arms are weak and shaky, but they move with my command.

A smile plays on my lips, and I let out a deep sigh.

They were right. It was only temporary.

"Lucinda?" I call through the mindlink.

No answer.

"Luc—" I croak. My throat is dry, and my voice weak.

The vividness of my dream flashes in my mind, and my pulse races. There was a pool of blood at Lucinda's feet. She was chained in silver.

I killed her.

"LUCINDA!" I holler through the mindlink.

I wipe my clammy palms on the sheets and lift myself up, then swing my legs over the edge of the bed.

It couldn't have been real. It was only a dream.

When my bare feet hit the cold wood floor, I cringe. My feet are mostly numb, but the coolness creeps into my skin, and small pinpricks pinch just below the surface of my calloused feet.

Mia races into the room and catches me as I slip off the bed. "Hey! What are you doing?"

I force a swallow to wet my dry throat. "Where is she? Where's Lucinda?"

Mia's eye twitches, and she glances over her shoulder toward the empty hall.

My ears burn and my stomach twists. "Mia—"

"Calm down. She's fine." Mia helps me back onto the bed, but I refuse to lie down.

While I massage my legs to jumpstart the circulation, I ask, "Where is she?"

Mia bites the inside of her cheek and stares out the window. I follow her gaze and notice the birds are gone. A raven perches on the branch in their place. I squint to focus. *Is that the same raven—*

"Caiden, just rest, okay? You need to calm down and relax. The doctor said rest is the only way you'll get back your strength."

The raven flaps its wings twice and holds my gaze. Then it struts down the branch.

I rub my eyes and blink. *Am I seeing things?*

Turning my attention away from the window and back to Mia, I ask, "What did you inject me with?"

"It was a concoction the doctor mixed up."

"What was in it?"

"Does it matter?"

I steal a look toward the window, and the raven croaks directly at me. My lips twist. I close my eyes and shake my head. "Not really, but I still want to know."

I open my eyes as Mia lets out a deep sigh. She presses her hands together and folds them into her lap. "I'm not exactly sure. A little of this and a little of that. Some herbal stuff to flush out the toxin, calm your wolf, and help you sleep."

"Yeah, it knocked me out."

Mia bumps me with her shoulder and giggles. "It was supposed to."

My heart skips a beat as mint and honey swirl through the air. And then Lucinda walks into the room. "How are you feeling?"

"You're beautiful," I say and reach for her.

Her smile lifts my heart and eases my soul. Mia excuses herself, and Lucinda sits on the bed next to me.

"I've missed you."

"I've missed you too," she says. Her hand reaches up to fluff my hair that's stuck to my forehead. "I see you've sweated out the rest of the toxins in your system."

I shrug and brush my thumb along her bare shoulder. Her long sleeve shirt is simple, but the shoulders are cut out, and I love it.

"Caiden, we need to talk."

"About what?" My fingers trace the mark of her mate— my mark—on her neck.

She removes my hand and places it in my lap. "The witch and the assassin."

Releasing a sigh, I say, "Let's go talk to Felix."

"We already did."

"What? When?"

"Yesterday—"

"Without me?" The blood rushes to my head, and I hold back a growl.

"You were unconscious. We had to."

My eyes narrow, and I peer at her through tiny slits.

"Caiden Lee Moone, don't you dare look at me like that!" Lucinda's voice is deep and controlling. Her wolf projects her dominating power, which hits me with the force of a hurricane.

A growl rumbles in my chest and slips through my teeth.

"And I'm leaving," she says.

I knew it was only a matter of time. My lips curve into a snarl, and I squeeze my hands into tight balls.

"Don't." Lucinda stands and steps away from me.

My wolf threatens to take control. But it's not just my wolf, it's the beast. *Concentrate.* I hang my head low and close my eyes. *Stay in control.* I take a deep breath. *In, out.*

My nails grow long and pierce through the skin on my palm. My teeth extend and puncture my lips. *Shit.*

Lucinda's eyes widen, and her forehead wrinkles. She reels in the power she was forcing earlier, and in a low tone she says, "Caiden, you need to calm down."

"Too late," I send through the mindlink.

I push off the bed and race for the door.

The next morning, footsteps echo on the hardwood floor leading down the hall to my office. The scent of mint and honey drifts through the air and tickle my nose before the door knob jiggles, alerting me to the fact she entered.

I remain standing with my back to the door and continue to gaze out the window into my sanctuary. At one time, her delightful scent gave me peace, but now only the forest calms the raging beast within me.

"You didn't come to bed last night," Lucinda says in a soft voice from close behind me.

I watch the sun rise over the evergreens and then the

black tips of a raven soaring above the trees catch my attention. *What is it with that damn bird?*

Dropping my head to my chest, I let out a sigh. My father always told me that if you love someone, you can't force them to do your bidding. That would be controlling them, and there is no room for control in love.

I roll my shoulders back and lift my head as my posture straightens. Taking a deep breath, I say, "If you want to leave, I won't stop you."

Her fingers tuck inside my hands, and she squeezes. "I don't want to leave, but I have to."

I paced all night trying to understand her perspective. Protecting the innocent is her nature. And protecting this pack by leaving is honorable. Except she's my mate—the Luna of this pack—and running away isn't an option.

Mia had come to check on me last night after my return from the woods and explained their plan. Lucinda, Dylan, and Gavin have decided to leave. They are escorting Cody and Felix to meet the witch and to find out why she is trying to kill Lucinda. I should be going with my mate, but I can't. I am weak from the poison and need to rest. The shift and my run almost drained my energy.

But above all, I am the Alpha, and I can't leave my pack. Not with an assassin on the loose in my territory.

Now it's dawn, the group is getting ready to set out on their journey. The never-ending argument with myself must end. *She's going whether I agree or not.*

I take a deep breath and squeeze her hand. "I know. We're left with no other choice. It's a solid plan."

She has made up her mind, and there is no changing it. I love her too much to control her and force her to do something she doesn't want to do, which is staying here—with me.

Guilt washes over me as I realize my hardheadedness

wasted our last night together. Turning around, I wrap my arms around Lucinda and pull her close to my chest.

"Just promise me you'll be safe," I say.

"I pinky promise."

I back away, just enough to gaze into her beautiful hazel eyes. Most days they are the striking combination of moss green with rays of gold cutting through. But right now, they are a deep shade of hazelnut.

"And promise me you will come home," I say.

Her lips turn up in the corners as she leans closer. "Caiden, I love you too much to stay away. I will return, and when I do, we'll have our official mating ceremony."

"I thought that would be put on hold—"

"Mia and Sabrina are working together and will keep in touch with me for decisions via text." Her warm breath tingles as it sweeps across my lips.

"Sabrina and my sister, working together?" I cock an eyebrow.

She nods. "I know, crazy, right?"

"I can think of one thing crazier."

"Oh yeah, and what's that?"

I growl and pull her closer to me.

She blinks, and her eyes flutter open wide. Her surprised look turns mischievous.

Dark black pupils flash, but they quickly melt back to hazel, and she smashes her lips into mine. I kiss her with a wild passion, my wolf responding to the call of his mate. I tangle my fingers in her long hair and her hands roam with greed under my shirt.

Between breaths, she whispers, "I love you."

"What time are you leaving?" I glance at the clock on the wall.

"Seven."

I grab her hand and pull her out of the room. "Come on."

"Where are we going?"

"Upstairs." I turn around and put her back against the wall. Leaning in, I kiss her neck and say, "We have thirty minutes before you leave, I thought we could..."

She pushes me off, and I slam into the wall on the other side of the hallway. Clutching my hand, she pulls me down the hall and giggles as we run up the stairs.

"Whoa! Easy tiger," Gavin says as he steps out of his room and is almost plowed down by our eagerness.

Lucinda and I race into our room, and she closes the door behind us. I slam her back against the door, and my mouth devours her lips. I play with the hem of her shirt, and then I rip it off.

She whines. "That was my fav—"

"I'll buy you a new one," I say between breaths.

Her hand roams my chest and stops on my pounding heart. Her hazel eyes raise, and she looks up at me through her dark eyelashes.

"Are you okay?" she asks.

"Yes. Just a little winded."

"Promise me you'll rest while I'm gone."

I lean in and leave a trail of kisses on her neck.

"I'm serious. Take it easy until I get back, okay?"

"Mmm," I mumble against her dewy skin.

"Caiden!" She pushes my head away, and the darkness of her stare stabs deep into my soul. "Rest and regain your strength. If I hear otherwise—"

"You'll what?" Stepping forward, I close the distance between us. My nostrils flare as I tower over her.

She smirks and raises up on her tippy-toes. "Are you trying to intimidate me?"

"Is it working?"

"No." She traces her finger across my jawline.

Her touch sends little shocks rippling through my body, and I tremble.

A grin crosses my face.

Placing one finger under my chin, she leads me across the room toward the bed. "Come on, we're down to ten minutes."

If Lucinda ever finds out exactly how much control she has over me, she'll be the death of me. Or does she already know?

CHAPTER 11

LUCINDA

I DON'T WANT to leave Caiden, but at the same time, I'm looking forward to the freedom of being away. Not away from him necessarily, but away from the pack and everything else that makes life complicated.

When it's time for me to leave, I slip out from under Caiden's warm embrace and shimmy into my clothes in silence. With one more glance at Caiden, I kiss him on the forehead and slip out the bedroom door.

A ball of excitement and anxiety stir deep within me, and my stomach twists in knots. Standing at the top of the staircase, I clench my fists and take a deep breath. One more look to Caiden's room, then I glide down the stairs.

Sabrina's satin voice floats across the hall. She holds out a bag of cookies. "Here you go. I made these special for your trip."

"Thanks." I flash a smile and reach out and take the bag.

Mia pushes a cooler across the floor. "And I packed other stuff."

My eyebrows raise "What is all that?"

"Uh... Gavin gets a little grumpy when he's hungry," Mia whispers.

Gavin stomps down the stairs. "Are you talking about me?"

"Nope." Mia winks and muffles a laugh.

Gavin reaches for Mia. "I'm gonna miss you, babe."

Mia leans into him. "You'll call and text, right?"

Sabrina rolls her eyes and struts into the kitchen.

As I smile at them, Caiden's voice enters my head through the mindlink. "This will be their first time apart since they met."

He stands in the foyer near the front door, his hands tucked into the front pockets on his jeans.

Heat rushes to my cheeks. I stroll to him and wrap my arms around his sturdy frame. His strong arms wrap around me, and I relish this moment.

"I didn't want to wake you earlier," I whisper.

He pulls me away from the security of his chest and stares deeply into my eyes. "There is no way I would let you leave without saying goodbye."

My lips smash into his, and a small moan escapes.

Gavin clears his throat. "I'll get Cody, and we'll start loading the car."

Caiden kisses my nose once before turning to acknowledge Gavin. "Then it's time Dylan and I go retrieve Felix."

While the men get busy with their tasks, I help Mia carry out the overnight bags and the cooler of food supplies she packed.

Dylan and Caiden return with Felix, just as the back of the car closes.

I can't help but glare at Felix. The time spent in holding hasn't treated him well. His unkempt hair and overgrown beard ages him. My mouth goes dry and I force a swallow. So many mixed emotions swirl through my body. *I don't trust him.*

But, at the same time, I can't shake a feeling from deep within my soul urging me to trust him, if only on the topic of the witches.

Caiden and I discussed this briefly, he doesn't trust Felix either. But, since he, Dylan, and Felix were all cursed, we need to try and work together to figure this out. Goosebumps prickle my skin and I rub my arms.

Caiden grabs my hand and pulls me toward the front porch, away from everyone else standing around the car.

"I love you," I blurt.

He leans his forehead against mine. "Pinky promise?"

I giggle and hold out my pinky.

"I love you too," he says.

When his warm breath sweeps across my face, my cheeks flush and my mate's mark throbs.

"NO!" Dylan growls.

I whip around; he's standing toe to toe with Felix.

"Have fun with those two," Caiden says, motioning toward Dylan and Felix. "The entire walk from Felix's holding cell, those two acted like little boys and wouldn't stop exchanging an onslaught of heated words."

"About what?"

"I gave the car keys to Dylan, and Felix demands to drive."

"Seriously?" I slowly turn toward Caiden.

He nods.

"Can't you put a stop to this?"

"I could. But I find it more entertaining to watch them. Besides, you'll be in charge during your journey."

My muscles tighten. "What about Dylan?"

"What about him?" Caiden's straight face makes me smile.

He has faith in my leadership ability, but am I really capable?

I give Caiden a small peck on the lips and then head toward the car.

Caiden's hand brushes against my lower back, and he steps next to me, holding me in place. "Be careful, Lucinda."

"Always," I send to Caiden through the mindlink.

With one last kiss, I step away from him and head to where Dylan and Felix are still arguing.

With a gentle flick of my wrist, I say, "If he wants to drive, let him drive."

Dylan's black eyes pierce through me, and I return it with a growl.

I send Dylan a message through the mindlink. "You may be Beta, but on this trip, you follow my lead."

Dylan grunts and grudgingly slides into the backseat of the car.

The soft purr of the engine is a welcoming sound. We wave our last goodbyes as we speed down the driveway.

Felix breaks the silence before I'm able to turn on the radio. "Don't believe anything the witch says."

I adjust in the passenger seat to turn toward him. "If we can't believe anything she says, why are we even wasting our time meeting with her?"

When his knuckles turn white from gripping the steering wheel, I smirk. *He doesn't like being questioned.*

After a loud sigh, Felix clears his throat. "I'll rephrase. She will twist our words to make us question ourselves and everyone around us. Understood? Good. And let me do all the talking."

I cross my arms over my chest, slouch in my seat, and lean toward the window.

In every situation, Felix always needs to be in control. First, he had to be the driver; now he wants to be the main contact with the witch? *Whatever.*

"Is that understood, kitten?"

I flinch at the pet name Felix chose for me and my nose flares. "How many times do I have to tell you to stop calling me that?"

"Oh, I suppose it wouldn't hurt for you to tell me again." Felix's lips curl into a smile. "Though it won't do any good—"

A growl slips out.

Gavin rests a hand on my shoulder. "Easy now, Cinda. We still need him alive."

Dylan mutters, "For now."

Gavin blocks Felix from my immediate view by leaning across the center console to fiddle with the radio. "Okay. Enough talking. Let's get some music on."

I twist in my seat and gaze out the front window. *This will be a trip from hell.*

Several hours later, we arrive in the town Cody tracked the witch to.

The witch hunt begins.

We go directly to the house she was last seen at. No one is home. We spread out and search around the house, which turns up nothing.

I step away from the guys and pull out my phone.

Caiden picks up on the third ring. "Hello?"

"Hey, it's me."

"It's good to hear your voice," Caiden says.

"Are you busy? Did I interrupt—"

"No. I was just resting, that's all."

"Good. Glad you're taking my advice." I giggle.

"Are you there yet?"

"Yes. So far, no sign of her or anything unusual."

"How was the trip?"

"Just as you suspected. Horrible. I don't know who to kill first, Felix or Dylan."

Caiden's muffled chuckle comes through the phone, and my heart flutters.

"So, what's the plan now?" he asks.

"Cody's on a stakeout at the witch's house while the rest of us grab dinner and scout out the town." I nibble on my lip, hoping he doesn't ask more questions.

"It's getting late, do you have a place to sleep?"

Damn it.

"Yes. We found a room—"

"What do you mean *we*?"

I startle at the deepness in Caiden's voice, force a swallow, then take a deep breath. I prepared for this conversation, so here goes nothing.

"We are all staying in one room. It's a suite that has a separate bedroom, which will be mine. Cody has the car at the witch's house since he can identify her, so Felix, Gavin, and Dylan will fight over the floor, the pullout couch, and the cot."

Heavy breathing and a low growl rattle through the speaker.

"Caiden, I didn't want this arrangement either, but it makes sense."

"How?"

"Without knowing where the assassin is, I shouldn't be alone." This is the best answer I can give. I don't really mind being alone with an assassin hot on my trail, I just think our group should stay together and not split up.

After a long pause, a grunt comes through the phone, vibrating in my eardrums.

I grab the phone with both hands and whisper, "Caiden?"

"Fine."

"Hey, Lux, ready to eat?" Dylan yells from several feet away.

I nod.

Turning my attention back to Caiden, I say, "Okay, we're going to go get dinner. I'll call later. I love you."

With an audible sigh, Caiden says, "Be safe. I love you too."

———

The past couple of days is a blur. Gavin and I mostly stayed in our room, watching movies to pass the time. Felix's first task was to cut his hair and trim his mountain man beard to his usual sleek goatee.

Next, Felix and Dylan have been checking out this small town, and they finally agree on something. Our surveillance efforts have proven to be thorough.

The coast is clear, and we weren't followed. *No assassin on our trail.*

Caiden can rest easy knowing that I am not in danger.

Cody remained on the stakeout and the witch finally came home. He followed her to a small pub in town. Gavin and I meet up with Felix and Dylan.

We stand on the corner of a vacant sidewalk under a dimly lit street lamp. I watch the door to the small pub across the street from us. A few people have entered since we've been here loitering. And each time the door opens, smoke billows out, followed by loud cheers and blaring music.

Cody appears across the street and motions to us.

With long strides, we cross the street and open the old wooden door to reveal a lively Irish Pub. Stepping through the door, Felix surveys the patrons and finds his prey. I've always been amazed how graceful and elegant he moves while also displaying power and confidence with every step. It's not a common combination.

Cody nudges my shoulder, bringing me back to reality. A blush heats my cheeks when I realize I have stopped walking to stare at Felix.

"Come on." Cody tugs at my arm, and we follow Felix across the room.

Felix sits in the back corner between the fireplace and a big bay window. It's dark, the only light coming from a single votive candle that burns on the table. I slide into the booth across from him and then realize Felix isn't alone.

Stupid, Lucinda. What's wrong with you? Pay attention!

Cody slides into the booth next to me, and Dylan next to him, which leaves Gavin to sit next to Felix. I study the person sitting across from me. An older woman with tan, leathery skin. Purple eyes, I remember her. She's the woman I met the last time Felix held me against my will. She was the old cooky woman—the other captive.

Oh shit! She's the witch.

Felix and the witch whisper back and forth, but it's too loud in here even for my heightened hearing to know what they're saying. I tap my fingers on the table in time to the Irish ballad that's being sung in the background.

"Do you mind?" Felix asks, motioning with his head to my fingers.

"No, not at all." I continue tapping my nails on the table. I know I've been on edge the past couple days—my wolf misses her mate—but Felix would get on my every last nerve regardless of my mood.

He reaches across the table and slaps my hand flat. My skin burns under his touch, and I clench my jaw.

"So," I say. "Care to introduce us?"

"Of course, where are my manners?" Felix removes his

hand and smirks. "Ms. Talin, this is Lucinda Raven. And you know, Cody. Then we have Dylan Sparrow."

The witch's eyes glaze over with cataracts. It happens so fast, if I wasn't watching her so intently, I would've missed it.

At the sound of Dylan's name, her eyes widen, and a flame sparks behind her frosty eyes. She licks her lips in a frantic display, and my stomach turns in repulsion.

"And this is Gavin," Felix says, motioning to him.

The witch squints and focuses on Gavin for longer than I'm comfortable.

I interrupt her scrutinizing gaze. "And who exactly are you?"

"Lucinda, dear, don't be rude," Felix scolds.

"You're one to talk about being rude, and please don't call me dear."

"You may call me Nyla," the witch says. She adjusts her hood to cover her eyes, and it casts a shadow over her face.

I glance to Cody, and he shrugs. Dylan and Gavin look just as confused, if not annoyed at the theatrics.

"Okay, let's get on with it," I say to Felix.

"All in good time." He motions me to calm down.

A waitress shows up at the edge of the table. Her red hair clashes with the white shirt she wears.

"Hi, and welcome to The Salty Dog. Is this your first time here?" she asks and winks at Dylan.

He does a double take, then flashes his lady-killing grin. I curl my fingers, and my nails dig into my thighs.

"Yes. We're just passing through," Gavin says. "What's the house favorite?"

She flips open her notepad. "Well, since it's Irish Night, the special is the corned beef sandwich, but—" She glances over her shoulder and swallows. "I recommend the crab cakes or fish tacos."

"I'll take the crab cakes with water," I say and hand her my menu.

Cody, Dylan, Felix, and Nyla relay their orders next, leaving everyone to turn their attention to Gavin.

"Oh, I can't decide," Gavin says. "I'll try the corned beef sandwich, fish tacos, and the crab cakes. And can I also have a side salad?"

I turn my head in slow motion, and my eyes widen.

"Great. It shouldn't take too long for your order to be ready." The waitress turns and heads toward the kitchen.

"Really?" I send Gavin through the mindlink.

"What? I'm hungry," he sends back.

I shake my head and remember what Mia said about keeping him happy.

Felix shifts his body to face Nyla. In a calm tone, he says, "We've heard through the grapevine that a contract has been issued on Lucinda's life."

The witch remains still as a statue.

"Can you confirm?" The inflection in Felix's voice turns sharp and stern.

A shiver runs up my spine. When Felix uses this tone, it would be considered threatening to anyone.

"Aye," she says. "I have heard that too."

"Did you put out the contract?" Felix asks.

Nyla's gaze snaps to meet Felix's glare, and her eyes swirl multiple shades of purple.

"Do you know who took the contract?" Felix asks.

"You should've killed her when you had the chance," she says.

"Why do I need to be killed at all?" I blurt. Then I take a deep breath to find my composure and repeat myself. "Why am I a target?"

Nyla's eyes widen. "You haven't told her?"

Felix's stone-cold demeanor gives nothing away.

"Told me what?" I ask.

Nyla continues talking to Felix. "How much does she know?"

Again, Felix remains still and silent.

"Know about what?" I pound my fist on the table.

Cody's voice answers Nyla. "Nothing. She knows nothing."

My jaw drops as I turn my head to gawk at Cody. My heart falls to the pit of my stomach. *My rock. The one person I could always count on has been keeping secrets from me. But not just secrets, apparently life-and-death secrets—about me.*

"Please don't look at me like that," Cody says. He casts his eyes down under my burning stare. "It was for your own protection."

"My own protection?" I say, my words laced with sarcasm. "I'm tired of everyone else keeping secrets from me and claiming it's for my own protection, damn it!"

I glance between Cody and Dylan. They each turn their attention away from me and fiddle with their drink.

Turning back to Felix and Nyla, I say, "What do I need to know?"

They are once again talking with each other and ignoring the rest of us. I can only hear a few words here and there, but after my name is said several times, I can't take it anymore.

"Felix, hey, I'm right here. Don't you know it's rude to talk about someone—"

His growl takes me by surprise, and I snarl in response.

"Just calm down and be patient," Cody whispers. "There's a lot we need to talk about, but here probably isn't the safest place."

Dylan, Gavin, and I look around. Many of the prior patrons have already left, or are standing around the bar in the rear.

"There's actually not that many people left," Gavin says.

"And that is exactly why it's not safe." Cody takes a quick look over his shoulder. "It's the ones you can't see that we need to worry about."

"None of that makes any sense." I roll my eyes. *I just want to hurry up and get this over with so we can go home.*

"Yes, it does. Think about it for a minute," Cody says.

"Whatever. The next thing you're going to tell me is that Felix isn't some ruthless, unpredictable, psychotic killer—"

Cody's eyes widen and his forehead creases.

"Seriously?" I ask. "How are you going to get me to believe that Felix isn't all of those things?"

"With the truth, kitten," Felix interjects with his velvety smooth voice. "Do you think you can handle the truth?"

My gaze pierces through Felix, and my nostrils flare, but I remain calm and nod.

Two luminescent orbs pulse under the shadows cast by Nyla's hood, and her eyes glow purple. "I don't."

A warning growl slips up my throat. Glancing back to Felix, I say, "Try me."

CHAPTER 12

CAIDEN

MY OFFICE IS a place of business, not pleasure. I need to focus on pack business today, yet the daydreams of Lucinda won't leave me alone.

Before Lucinda waltzed into my life, I would escape to my cabin in the woods in order to be alone. Too often, I was criticized for the seclusion and much-needed peace and quiet. But today, the quietness of the Pack House is unnerving.

Until now, I hadn't realized how accustomed I'd become to the steady noise of a full Pack House. The constant commotion provided a distraction from my inner thoughts and doubts.

Only Mia and I remain at the house, but Sabrina still spends most of her time here during daylight hours.

It's been almost two full days since Lucinda and the group left on their journey to meet the witch. And the emptiness they left behind is weighing heavy on both Mia and me.

After their departure, Mia insisted that I rest, and I ended up sleeping all day. Then yesterday, she suggested I take another day to relax and regain my strength, so we both vegged out on the couch and watched movies.

But today, I need to be the Alpha and work on the pack business. There is a stack of grievances from pack members that need action. Ever since the influx of new members, the stack of letters is never-ending.

I let out a loud sigh and drop my pen. Stretching my arms above my head, I stare out the window, and my wolf whines.

A run would do us good.

There's a small knock on the front door, but in the silence of the house, the sound ricochets off the walls and echoes down the hall. My heart drops to the pit of my stomach; the run will have to wait.

When I turn into the hall, the sweet scent of apple, rose, and vanilla fills the air, and my pulse quickens. *Leah.*

Mia says from the foyer, "Hey, Caiden, look who's here! What a most welcome surprise."

Leah asks as I near, "You didn't tell anyone I was coming?"

"Hi, Leah. Welcome. I'm sorry, a lot has happened since I returned, and it must've slipped my mind."

"OMG! Let me tell you." Mia comes to life again with excitement in her eyes. "So, there's a crazy assassin trying to kill Lucinda, and she almost killed Caiden instead—"

I clear my throat. "Mia, that's enough."

Leah startles at my stern tone.

"Leah, it's not that I don't trust you—"

"But it's a need-to-know basis." Sabrina strolls into the hall from the kitchen. "And you don't need to know."

My nostrils flare and I grit my teeth. Sabrina has been very helpful the past couple of days, but she can be a real bitch sometimes too.

Leah's sky blue eyes linger on mine and then she looks

away and blushes. "Oh. It's clearly a bad time. I'm sorry to intrude. I'll leave and come back another time."

I give Sabrina a sharp look, warning her to shut her mouth. "Don't be silly, Leah. You're already here, and we've plenty of room."

"This will be great!" Mia says and gives Leah a hug. "It's been too quiet since everyone left."

Mia sends me a question through the mindlink. "Guest room?"

I nod.

Mia takes the tote bag from Leah's hands. "Come on up, I'll show you the guest room."

I step out of the way to let Mia and Leah pass. "Once you're all settled in, Leah, we'll talk. Until then, you're in good hands with Mia. And, about the assassin—"

"I won't tell anyone."

"I trust you. I've asked everyone involved to keep this incident quiet until we find out more information."

She flashes me a grin that lights up her eyes and accentuates her cheekbones. And then she and Mia race upstairs.

Sabrina puckers her lips and crosses her arms. I ignore her disapproval and head back down the hall to my office.

Soon after I sit at my desk chair, the click-clack of high heels on the hardwood floor echoes in the hall. Sabrina storms into my office, slamming the door shut with the heel of her boot.

My eyes drift away from the letter in my hand as she crosses the room with a great stride.

"Don't you think it's a little odd for your ex-mate's little sister to be here?" she asks.

"Elizabeth isn't my ex-mate, she is a former mate."

"What's the difference?"

"She didn't leave me. She died."

Sabrina picks at her nails. "Still playing the wounded boy—"

I slam my hands on the top of my desk. "If there's nothing you need, then get out."

"Oh, I was just wondering how Lucinda feels about Leah being here. I mean, it must be a little awkward for her."

"Enough!" I stand and thrust my finger toward the door. "OUT."

Sabrina crosses the room to the door. *Why do I let her get under my skin?*

She flashes me one last smile before stepping into the hall, then leans on the doorframe. "Caiden, you have a gentle soul. It's not your fault—you always have, even when we were kids. But it makes me wonder if you're the right person to be our Alpha. Will you be able to make the hard choices that are coming?"

A rhetorical question or not, I turn my back on her and focus on the forest. I won't give her the satisfaction of a response. She wants me to strike out in anger or to lash out at her with my dominating beast. But I'm not that type of Alpha. I won't lead with fear and aggression. *No. I won't do that.*

The latch on the door clicks closed, and Sabrina's vile stench of days old salty decay no longer floats in the room.

Finally, she's gone.

———

A warm hand rubs my shoulder.

I turn around, and Mia stands behind me with wide eyes. "Caiden."

"What's wrong?"

Mia wraps her arms around my midsection, and she collapses into my chest. I cradle her head in my arms.

"Mia, what happened?"

"It's okay, you know," she says.

"What is?"

"You're allowed to miss her."

"Who?"

Mia pulls away from my chest and looks up at me. The corners of her mouth droop as she fails at a grin. "Elizabeth."

Damn. Am I that easy to read?

"No," I say. "It's wrong in so many ways."

"Why?" The wrinkles on her forehead knit together and form a deep v. "Because of Cinda?"

I stare into Mia's all-knowing and all-seeing eyes. *When did my little sister become so knowledgeable on such matters of the heart?*

"You know, it's okay to still love Elizabeth. What you two had was real. And now you have Cinda. And what you two have is not only real, but it's powerful and inspiring."

I cock an eyebrow. "Powerful?"

"Yup." She grins. "I think what you and Cinda have will stand the test of time. A love they'll write about in a novel."

"Okay, I've heard enough. That's my cue to leave." I squeeze her hands and step away from her.

"Wait." Mia tugs at my arm. "Before you go, can we chat?"

"I thought we were, but yes, go ahead. What's on your mind?"

"You went to see Elizabeth's parents, didn't you?"

I take a deep breath and let it out. "Yes."

"Why didn't you tell me where you were going?"

"It's something I needed to do alone."

"I wouldn't have gone with you. But it would've been nice to know where your head has been. It's easier to gauge your mood." She shrugs and looks over her shoulder toward the sound of Leah's laugh echoing from the kitchen.

"I know it was rash inviting Leah here, but I hope we can make it work," I say.

"Me too. She's all set in the guest room, and with everyone gone, I could use some extra help around here. And maybe I can learn something from all that fancy schooling she had too." Mia flashes a smile and winks at me as she turns to leave the room.

What would I do without my little sister?

I follow her out of my office and down the hall. It's time to properly greet Leah and welcome her here.

"SABRINA!" Mia's voice rises as she turns into the kitchen.

Mixed emotions vibrate through the empty Pack House—anxiety, amusement, disgust. I hurry down the hall and swing into the kitchen just in time to see Sabrina lowering a kitchen knife. Her eyes are onyx, and she's face to face with Leah.

"What's going on here?" My power ripples in the air as I cross the room, and they both bow their heads in submission.

"Sabrina had that butcher knife in Leah's face! That's what's happening here," Mia says from behind me.

Sabrina raises her head just enough to glare at Mia.

I step between Sabrina and Leah. Looking down at Sabrina, I ask, "Do you have anything to say?"

She lowers her gaze to the floor and shakes her head.

"It was nothing," Leah says. "We were just having a little get-to-know-you chat."

I continue to stare at Sabrina, but I ask Leah through the mindlink, "Are you sure? Sabrina is a known troublemaker."

"It's nothing, really. Just a little misunderstanding," Leah says.

"If she bothers you anymore, please let me know," I send through the mindlink. My arms tense and my nostrils flare as

I let out a deep sigh, then I say out loud, "Let's go, Leah, I'll show you around."

Leah brushes her hands down the front of her thighs. "Okay."

With one last deep growl, I turn and walk toward the back door. Through the mindlink, I say to Mia, "Going for a run. We'll be back later."

"Stay calm and be safe," Mia sends back.

Leah follows me out the back door. Once our feet hit the grass, Leah asks, "Where are we going?"

I stop and wait for her to catch up. The afternoon sun catches on her cheekbones and highlights small freckles under her eyes. "Sorry about that. Sabrina gets on my every last nerve sometimes."

As Leah smiles, the fine lines around her lips deepen, giving off an otherwordly vibe.

"Sabrina amuses you?" I ask.

"Very much so."

"Do you care to share what that was about?"

"Are you asking as a friend or as my Alpha?" Leah's smile fades, and her eyes lock on mine.

My pulse quickens, and I blink several times before swallowing. "What color are your eyes?"

Leah chuckles. "Changing the topic, are we? Smart tactic."

"No. It's not that, it's just..."

"What?"

"Earlier, I could've sworn your eyes were just blue, and now they're—"

Leah shifts her weight and tugs on her earlobe. "Oh! Right. Caught me, color-changing contacts. They're like a mood ring for your eyes. Pretty cool, huh?"

"They're stunning. Like a deep violet or amethyst. They remind me of someone—"

"Really? I don't know anyone with purple eyes," Leah says, but her stifled laugh doesn't reach her eyes.

I glance over Leah's shoulder; Sabrina is watching us from an upstairs window. *Is she in the guest room?*

"Mia, check on Sabrina, please," I send through the mindlink.

Turning my attention back to Leah, I ask, "So, what would you like to see first? The forest or the town?"

Leah's lips purse. "The forest."

I fight the urge and restrain my wolf from shifting. Being so close to the open wild of the forest, he wants to hunt. "Shall we run?"

Her eyes lift to meet mine. "Can we walk?"

Leah twists her foot in the ground, and she shifts her weight under my questioning gaze.

"I don't really do the whole wolf thing often," she whispers.

My jaw clenches and my arms tense. I've heard of people rejecting their wolf—denying the other half of their soul—but I've never met anyone.

When my nostrils flare, she takes a step away from me. "It's not that I don't like my wolf or anything like that. It's just—"

"What would cause you to keep your wolf locked up?"

"I'm a city girl." Her high cheekbones turn a dusty pink, and she shrugs.

I've often wondered how our kind who live in the city, and even the suburbs, deal with their wolf.

"So, you suppress her?"

"Who?"

"The other half of your soul—your inner wolf?" I narrow my eyes.

"No! Never. It's not like that."

I let out a sigh and rub the back of my neck. "Then please explain."

"My whole life, I've only ever shifted twice a month."

I tilt my head. *Limiting my wolf... I can't fathom that.*

But I nod. "It's been a while since I've actually walked in the woods. A change will be nice."

Her lips purse and then widen into a grin, and she follows me into the forest.

"So." I clear my throat and swallow. "What did you do with your wolf growing up?"

Leah swats at a spiderweb that she walked into. "Every other weekend, Mom would take me out to the state park."

"So you went camping?"

Her chin drops to her chest, and she watches her feet as we step through ferns that cover the forest floor.

"If you don't want to talk about it—"

"No, it's fine." She kicks at a rock. "Mom said I was special and didn't need the extra help or more time spent with my wolf. So, we only stayed a few hours."

I stop walking. Standing face to face, I peer down at her. "Well, if you ever want to stretch your legs and run, these woods are great for it."

"I like this forest, it's full of life." She kneels next to a patch of thorny vines.

My nose twitches as something approaches.

From under the vines, out steps a gray fox. Her coat is sleek and peppery black with glossy reddish undertones. She flips her bushy tail and brushes it across Leah's face, causing her to giggle.

"A friend of yours?" I ask.

She turns to look over her shoulder. "Maybe."

My shoulders tighten and I clench my fists. *My wolf wants to play.*

"Do you have any friends in the forest?" Leah asks as she strokes the back of the fox and rubs her pointy ears.

I lift my chin and glance through the tree branches overhead. "Maybe."

Leah's smile calms my wolf, and as she stands, the fox runs off. "What is it?"

"What is what?" I ask as my gaze follows the path of the fox.

She reaches up and lowers my face to hers. "Your forest friend. What type of animal is it?"

"A raven."

Leah's eyes swirl with shades of purple, light and dark all mixed in one. The beauty of them mesmerizes me, and the varying shades are hypnotizing until the rough croak from above startles me.

The black wings of a raven flap on a nearby branch.

Mia calls through the mindlink, "Caiden, you'd better hurry home."

I say to Leah, "You can stay out here if you want, but I need to head back."

"Okay, I'll leave with you. I think it best to take slow steps to acquaint myself with the forest."

The raven takes flight from its perch, leaving a melody of croaks in its wake.

Is the raven warning me of something or disapproving?

CHAPTER 13

LUCINDA

I DRUM my fingers on the table at the pub and scowl at Nyla. *Who the hell does she think she is?*

My patience is almost gone, and they've still not revealed the truth. "I'm waiting."

Nyla's thin hand extends from under her cloak to wave in the air. "Very well, proceed."

My gaze drifts to Gavin, and his eyebrows raise with his shrug. In my peripheral vision, Cody and Felix exchange a look, and I know they're talking through the mindlink. When Cody opens his mouth, I put my finger up to his lips.

I point to the waitress heading our way with a tray full of food. "Hang on."

As soon as we have our food and the waitress leaves, Cody clears his throat. "Well, you see—"

"I am not the monster you'd like to believe," Felix blurts out.

I glare across the table at him. "Prove it."

He opens his hands, palms facing up. "Ask me anything, I'm an open book."

"Fine. Why did you kill my father?" I ask.

"Oh, kitten—"

"I told you to stop calling me that," I whisper.

"Lucinda," Felix says with a grin, "your father is alive and well."

My fork drops from my hand and clanks on the plate of food. "What do you mean my father isn't dead? I saw you kill him."

"No. You saw me kill the Alpha of the Dark Raven pack."

"Right. My father."

"He was not your father," Felix says. His left eye twitches, and he watches me with such intensity that a shiver runs up my body.

I grip the napkin in my lap. "Your words are like poison. You like to speak and let the words slowly twist around, sucking the life out of people and doing damage—"

Nyla's hand flies out from under her cape, and she slaps me across the cheek. "Watch your tongue. You would be wise to listen to him and heed his words."

I jump. Shocked more by her words than her actions, I grind my teeth and crack my knuckles as I glare across the table at her.

Gavin snarls at Nyla, and Dylan raises his steak knife.

I reach up and remove the knife from Dylan's hand. "Settle down, I'm fine."

My ego is bruised, and as I rub my cheek, I know full well that I'll have a mark to show for it later.

Cody leans toward me, bumping my shoulder. "It's true, Cinda, just hear him out."

I nod and fix my attention across the table at Felix. His grin makes my wolf tense.

Felix taps his fingertips on the table in an irritating, erratic manner. "Any more questions?"

"We'll come back to the question of my father in a moment," I say. "Why did you kill the Dark Raven Alpha?"

Felix strokes his goatee. "Ah, yes. That is a good question."

After a moment of silence passes, I ask, "Well?"

Felix sips his drink and wipes his mouth with his napkin. "You see, all is not what it seems. I went to question him—"

"About what?" Dylan mumbles with a full mouth of food.

"If he, Alpha of the Dark Raven Pack, made a blood pact with the Vampire Nation," Felix says. "And it turns out, he did."

Gavin belches and then asks, "A blood pact with the Vampire Nation?"

Dylan and I exchange a confused glance. In unison, we ask, "What and what?"

Nyla shakes her head with disapproval. "Such babies, and these are the saviors?"

She continues rambling in another language that I've never heard.

Turning my attention back to Felix, I cross my arms. "Start talking."

"As it turns out, a few years before you were born, the Dark Raven Pack entered into a blood pact with the Vampire Nation. They agreed to turn over their firstborn son to the damn bloodsuckers."

"Why would they do that?" I ask.

Felix shrugs. "That I don't know. I've never been able to understand their reasoning."

Dylan plays with the food on his plate, pushing it around with his fork. "But if that was more than twenty years ago, why is it important now?"

Felix lets out a deep sigh. "The Dark Raven pack isn't the only pack to do such a thing. Several others did as well. And now, all of the firstborn sons are coming of age—"

I slam my fist on the table. "Wait. Back up. So you didn't follow me to the Dark Raven pack?"

"No, kitten." Felix winks. "It was a nice bonus finding you there, but alas, it was a mere coincidence."

I slump in my seat to lean against the hard wooden back of the booth and peer out the window. The guilt over the slaughter of my pack that's weighed down my heart just lifted a little.

"And the other packs you slaughtered?" I ask.

"All the same," Felix says.

Gavin's eyes are as dark as coal and fixed on Felix. "Dude, you really don't like vampires, do you?"

Cody throws up his thumb, pointing toward Felix. "They killed his father."

"I thought Felix killed his own father," Dylan says.

A dark and sinister laugh erupts from Felix. "Where did you ever hear such a story?"

"I read it in the pack records."

"Of course, you did, of course, you did," Felix says.

"That is the rumor that's been going around," Cody says. "No one wants to acknowledge that vampires exist, but believe me, vampires are real, and they pose a serious threat."

"Okay, slow down," I say. "If you slaughtered the Dark Raven pack—"

Felix holds up a hand. "Lucinda, if you can't keep up..."

I roll my eyes. "Why did you drink their blood and cut out the Alpha's heart?"

A grin spreads across Felix's face. "Ah yes. I was wondering when that was coming."

Cody smashes his hand into his face. "I knew you went too far that night."

"Theatrics," Felix says to Cody. "I needed to keep up appearances. And, Lucinda, I cut out the heart to ensure he was dead and would stay dead."

"Stay dead?" Dylan asks.

"Yes. Stay dead and not rise as a bloodsucker."

"And drinking the blood?" I ask.

"I tasted their blood to see if it was pure or had been tainted."

"Tainted with what?" Dylan asks.

"Vampire blood," Cody whispers.

"That'll work?" Gavin asks. "I thought—"

Nyla taps her long fingernails on the tabletop. "They've been experimenting."

"Experimenting how?" Dylan asks.

Felix's gaze bores into mine, and heat radiates through my veins.

I whisper, "Me."

"What? How?" Dylan and Gavin ask in unison.

"The Alpha of the Dark Ravens." Nyla spits on the table. "He made a blood pact to give up his firstborn son. And he did. But it didn't work out as planned. They made another blood oath. This time, he gave them rights to his mate for one night."

"What?" My eyes sting, but I refuse to shed tears.

Cody watches me with worried eyes as he whispers, "Lucinda is a half-breed. Her father is a vampire, and her mother is a wolf."

My pulse rises and beads of sweat run down my spine.

Leaning around Cody, Dylan catches my attention. His onyx pupils give me the strength to stay in control.

Gavin snorts as he chews quickly to clear his mouth. "So what does that mean? She's a half-breed, so what, who cares?"

Felix motions to Nyla and says, "The witches don't know much about half-breeds, and it scares them. That's why they want her dead."

"We're not scared of her." Nyla speaks between her teeth.

Felix's dark laugh brings my attention back from the

foggy haze I was drifting into. I glare at Nyla. "Did you kill my brother?"

Dylan questions, "Your brother?"

I've never talked about my brother, so I don't know why it surprises me that Dylan doesn't know about him.

Gavin's eyes are wide with excitement. "Get out, you have a brother?"

Nodding, I say, "I was told he was my twin."

"Yes, child," Nyla says. "Your mother gave birth to twins. You were born first. She struggled with your brother and died before he was born."

"Oh," I say.

I guess that's why Dad, or the Alpha, always said my brother killed his mate. It's all making sense now.

Wait! Something isn't adding up.

I focus on Felix and blurt, "Why did you attack the Blood Moone pack and try to kill Caiden?"

"Ah, I was wondering how long it would take you to remember your dearest lovesick mate," Felix says. "The Blood Moone pack never entered into a blood pact with the damn vampires, and that's why Caiden was cursed."

Dylan chimes in. "How do the curses fit into the puzzle?"

I begin to protest, but Felix holds up a finger to shush me and turns to Dylan. "The witches visited the three strongest packs that did not take an oath with the vampires, and they bestowed a gift to each future Alpha of the pack to ensure the new generation would not side with the vampires."

I turn to Nyla and ask, "Why were the gifts a curse?"

"It's all in the eye of the beholder, child. You see a curse, when I see a gift," she says.

Doubt spreads within me, and I turn back to the guys.

"I've been thinking about this," Cody says. "Felix was given the gift of power, which has enabled him to be a strong leader. Caiden was gifted with strength, which will protect his people. The two of them together, leadership and strength, would yield a force to be reckoned with. If they joined together to form a single pack—"

"I'm going to stop you right there," I say. "Back to attacking Caiden."

"Just because Caiden's father stood against the vampires, didn't mean Caiden would. I needed to make sure he hadn't sided with them," Felix says.

"So, you tried to kill him?" Dylan asks.

"Oh, that? No, no. Nothing like that."

I growl. "Please enlighten us."

"I heard so much about it from the witches over the years that I just wanted to see his beast."

The smile on Felix's face sends blood rushing through my veins. *No one plays with my mate's life like that.*

Cody places his hand on my leg and squeezes. Once again, I'm able to fight back my wolf and remain in control.

"So why were you so intent on claiming Lux as your mate?" Dylan asks.

With a small shrug, Felix says, "The witches wanted her dead. If she were my mate, I would be better situated to protect her."

"You have an excuse for everything, don't you?" I say.

"They aren't excuses. They are facts and truths."

I roll my eyes. "It was a rhetorical question."

"Whoa, so let me get this straight," Gavin says. "You didn't kill Lucinda's dad, so he's alive, and he's a vampire. But you did kill the Dark Raven Alpha and the entire pack because they supported the vampires. You didn't kill your own father, the vampires did. And you and Caiden were given special gifts to help you lead an army to fight against the vampires."

Felix grins. "You are cleverer than you let on."

Nyla asks, "What is your name again, boy?"

"Gavin," he says.

"Yes, yes, but Gavin what? Where are you from, boy?"

My ears perk up. As long as I've known Gavin, I've never asked much about his past, where he came from, or why he was rogue. I figured we all have a past, and if he wanted to share, he would.

"Gavin Wisteria."

"Yes, yes you are. Wisteria of the O'leander pack," she says. "So, Gavin is what she named you."

Gavin's eyes narrow as he stares at the witch. His forearms tense and the muscle in his jaw pulses.

I clear my throat. "Didn't you say the witch visited the top three strongest packs?"

Nyla snorts, but no one answers.

I reach behind Cody, nudge Dylan's shoulder, then motion in Gavin's direction.

Dylan nods and attempts to change the subject to divert the attention off Gavin. "So Lux is a half-breed and has a twin brother that died at birth."

Bless him.

Nyla twists her fingers around her glass. "Rumored. But not confirmed."

"What?" I ask. "If you haven't confirmed I'm a half-breed, why are you trying to kill me?"

"It hasn't been confirmed that your twin brother is dead," she says.

I rest my elbows on the table and grab my spinning and throbbing head. Everything I've always known isn't true.

At least I know one thing in my life is real and true —Caiden.

He is my mate and my rock to keep me anchored when life gets crazy. I wish he were here to wrap his strong arms around me and chase away the shadows of doubt.

"He might still be alive?" Dylan asks.

"We haven't been able to confirm either way," Felix says, shooting dagger eyes at Nyla.

When I find my voice, I ask, "Why do you think he didn't die like the records say?"

"There is a rumor that he was born a half-breed, but not like you," Nyla says. "Your Alpha turned him over to the vampires."

How am I ever going to explain this to Caiden? What will he think? Will he still love me? Oh god! Can I have pups, or will they be little bloodsuckers?

I sway in my seat, and Cody wraps his arm around my shoulders to steady me.

"I think that's enough for tonight," Cody says.

"You mean there's more?"

Felix nods, and says, "But nothing that can't wait until the morning. We covered all of the major points."

"One last question," Dylan says. "Why are the witches involving the wolves in a war against the vampires?"

"Short answer," Felix says. "Because they can."

Knowing that my entire life is based on a lie sends chills racing down my spine.

I can't wait to get home to Caiden. But... How can I go back, knowing the assassin is still out there and hellbent on killing me? And will Caiden even accept a half-breed mate?

CHAPTER 14

CAIDEN

MY NOSE TWITCHES as we near the Pack House. Unfamiliar scents drift through the air, and my wolf is wary of the strange odors. Upon entering through the back door, a loud commotion and then a continuous low hum breaks out. I run through the kitchen, and Leah is right behind me.

I stand in the foyer, peering into the family room. "What's going on here?"

Mia waves her hands through the air in an erratic motion. "They just stormed in and started all this."

Leah mumbles something under her breath.

Four burly men, all of whom are dressed in brown robes, hum a chant—twisted words in a foreign tongue. The early afternoon sunlight streams through the windows, and light reflects off their bald heads. If they weren't in my house it might have been beautiful and relaxing to listen to.

A rumble vibrates in my chest. "STOP IT NOW!"

The men turn in my direction, but their chanting doesn't stop. They stand unfazed by my shouting, and they appear to be annoyed by the intrusion. One of them scowls in my direction, and others flare their nostrils, careful to avoid eye contact with me.

Elder Charles crosses the floor to stand a few feet in front of me. "Calm down, we mean no harm."

Through the mindlink, I say to him, "Don't make me repeat myself."

He turns and motions for the odd men to stop what they're doing.

Sabrina glides across the room to meet me in the foyer. "Caiden, they're here to help."

"Help with what?"

Elder Charles locks eyes with me but doesn't answer my question.

My nails pierce through the calloused skin on my palms, and my canines protrude over my lips. My chest rumbles as I narrow my eyes. "You don't come into my house, without my permission, with unwelcome strangers, and—"

"How dare you," Elder Charles says in a low hum.

I take a step closer and glare down at his frail form. "I am your ALPHA."

"You, sir, may have the title, but how do you expect to keep our respect when you break pack rituals and keep secrets? You're lucky—"

"Are you threatening him?" Mia's eyes widen as the words tumble from her mouth. Her right hand rests on her chest, which rises and falls as she takes deep calming breaths.

Elder Charles shrugs. "I've warned him before."

My fists curl into tight balls and I punch through the air, pointing at the door. "GET OUT!"

Elder Charles's face turns a ghostly white. My eyes must be onyx because I'm on the verge of losing control.

He glances over his shoulder and nods to the four strange men. They pull cowl hoods over their bald heads and shuffle their bare feet across the floor.

"This is not over, we'll be back," Elder Charles mumbles under his breath.

I snarl, which causes him to jump, then he steps around me to leave as the other men follow behind him.

Sabrina steps forward. "They were only trying to help."

"Help with what?"

"The Elders heard about the assassin the witches hired."

"How do they know about that?"

"Does it matter?"

"Yes," I hiss through my clenched jaw.

"I told them."

Mia growls. "That wasn't your place."

My arm muscles tighten as I ball my fists. "You disobeyed a direct order. I requested everyone that knew of that incident keep it quiet."

"I only meant to help," Sabrina says. "I thought they may know how to track and kill the assassin."

"And did your disobedience pay off?"

"All they knew was how to protect us."

"How?"

"They called upon old friends—those men that were here."

"Dark blood magic is nothing to use foolishly." Leah's eyes transform into sleek purple orbs.

Sabrina scowls. "They are only activating protection wards."

"I've heard enough," I growl. "Sabrina, leave."

"But I haven't finished my work yet." Sabrina bats her eyes and tilts her chin to look as innocent as possible. "The Elders are expecting—"

"I don't give a damn about the Elders!"

"Caiden, be careful." Mia's voice blares through the mindlink. I glance at her, and she lifts her eyebrows, fixing me with a pointed stare.

I take a deep breath and then release all the air from my lungs. "Fine. Sabrina, finish your work for the Elders. And then leave."

A wide grin spreads on Sabrina's face and she nods. I brush past her to storm down the hall toward my office.

A couple hours later, I'm still sitting at my desk to review more pack paperwork, but my mind is drifting to simpler times of my youth and then to nights with Lucinda in our cabin. I stare at the overflowing box and several tote bags full of journals, notebooks, letters, and other loose records that have been waiting for decades to be filed.

Sabrina walks into my office, her vile stench causing my stomach to churn.

"I can do that," she says.

"No, I'll do it."

"Do what?" Mia pops her head inside the door. Sabrina and I both turn to look at her. "What? I was just walking down the hall and heard voices."

"I'm straightening up the pack records," I say. "Organizing and taking inventory of everything."

Mia crosses the room and stands next to me, looking at the pile of stuff that sits at my feet. "Why in the world are you doing that?"

"To make room for the records of the new members." I shrug.

"It's busy work. Let me do it." Sabrina's tone is cold and calculating. "I'm sure the Alpha has more pressing matters to deal with."

I still don't trust her, especially not with the pack records.

"I said, I've got this."

Both Mia and Sabrina startle, and I realize my tone is sterner than intended.

"Here, I'll help." Mia bends to pick up a stack of loose papers. Through the mindlink, she says, "It'll be a nice distraction. I miss Gavin already."

I nod and hand her a spiral notebook and pen for inventorying the letters.

"Sabrina, if you've finished your work for the Elders, you're done for the day," I say and turn my back to her.

After a moment of silence, her soft footsteps shuffle down the hall and the front door opens and closes.

Finally, she's gone.

"What do you know about those men that were here?" I ask Mia.

"Nothing." Her eyes droop in the corners. I study her pale face and the dark circles that line her puffy eyes.

I wonder why being away from Gavin is taking such a dramatic toll on her.

Leah's voice drifts through the mindlink. "They are from The Brotherhood."

I jerk my head up and look around.

I cross the room and stick my head out the door, peering down the hall in both directions. Sniffing the air, I follow the riveting scent of apple, rose, and vanilla to find Leah lounging in one of the arm chairs in the family room. Her right leg is perched up on the arm while her other sits on the floor, and she's twisted in the seat so her head rests on the other arm of the chair.

When I enter the room, she turns and looks at me from upside down.

"What did you say to me?" I ask.

"Those men that were here. They are from an ancient fraternal order called The Brotherhood." Leah twists in the chair to sit upright.

"How do you know that?" Mia asks from behind me.

My eyes narrow at Leah. "Were you eavesdropping on us?"

"I wasn't trying to. But it's so quiet in here that your voices carried down the hall," she says.

I nod. *That could be true.*

I rub the back of my neck to release tension. "Tell me about this order."

"I'd have to research them again to get all the details, but what I remember is that more than a thousand years ago, the Lord and Lady of the Witches came into a disagreement, which divided the witches into two groups. A fanatic group of men that followed the lord separated even further and thus became known as The Brotherhood."

Mia asks, "How do you know all this?"

"My mom has some old books that I read when I was younger." Leah shrugs.

"What type of books?" I ask.

"History books," Leah says. "The history of us."

"How does she have those?" I ask. *I've heard of such books but never known anyone to have them. Especially a non-Alpha family to have them in their personal library collection.*

Leah bites her lip. "I think they were passed down from generation to generation. You know, like a family heirloom."

I cross the room to stand in front of Leah. "I'd like to see those. Will you go get them and bring them to me?"

She swallows. "I'm not sure Mom will like that much. But as long as it's kept between just the three of us." She glances to Mia. "No one else can know about these books."

"We'll keep it a secret," Mia says.

"That includes keeping it from your mates," Leah says.

I glance over my shoulder and make eye contact with Mia. We both nod.

"Agreed," I say. "And one more favor—take Mia with you."

Leah's eyebrows raise.

Through the mindlink, I add, "I hope a change of scenery will help distract her until Gavin returns."

Leah's lips turn upward. "Of course! I'd love the company."

Mia starts to protest, "Caiden, I really should stay—"

"You'll only be gone two days at most. It will be good for you." I walk over to Mia and wrap my arms around her. "Hopefully, by the time you return, Gavin will also be home."

She wraps her arms around me and whispers, "Okay. I'll go pack an overnight bag, and we'll go ahead and leave."

"Wouldn't you rather wait until the morning?"

"No. I'd rather get on the road." Mia glances out the window. "Then we'll be home tomorrow, as opposed to the day after."

"It'll be easier to get the books if Mom's asleep anyway," Leah says.

"You're not going to ask her for them?" I ask.

"Technically, they're mine and she's just keeping them safe for me."

I rub the back of my neck. "Leah, I hope that's the truth."

———

While Mia and Leah pack their overnight bags, I busy myself with scraping together some snacks for the road. *Trail mix, peanut butter crackers, chocolate bars, and apples—that should work.* I grab several bottles of water and throw everything in a bag. By the time I'm done, so are they.

Walking them out, I say, "Drive safe."

"Always." Leah tips two fingers to her forehead in a salute.

Through the mindlink to Leah, I add, "Take care of her."

"I'll treat her as if she were my own sister."

I give Mia a hug and whisper, "Be careful."

"You too," she says back.

The vile stench of Sabrina causes me to roll my eyes. *She's returned.*

"What do you want?" I snarl at Sabrina as she climbs the porch steps.

"I have important business to discuss with you."

"How important? Can it wait?"

"It can wait until they're gone. Where are they going?"

I stiffen. "It doesn't concern you."

"Your new little stray is going too, though. How does it concern her?"

My lips pull tight into a silent snarl.

Sabrina's bottom lip puckers into a pout. "Your little rogue mate better hurry home to her big bad wolf. You get grumpier by the hour."

I scowl, and after waving to Mia and Leah, I turn and enter the house, leaving Sabrina on the porch.

"Have you heard from her?" Sabrina's voice echoes down the silent hall.

"Who?" I ask.

"Lucinda. Has she called you recently?"

I stop in front of my office door. My fists clench into tightly formed balls, and I take a deep breath.

"I see." Her silky voice drifts on the air.

Closing my eyes, I take another deep breath to calm my wolf.

Sabrina's fingertips brush across the top of my back, shoulder to shoulder, and then down my arm. "Are you sure she'll come back?"

I grit my teeth. "Of course, she'll come back."

"Have you heard from any of them?" Sabrina steps around me to stand face to face. "Who knows what they really had planned."

"I'd watch what you say. You're awfully close to—"

"Close to what?" She flips her dark hair over her shoulders. "To telling you the obvious truth?"

A deep rumble erupts from my chest. "You don't know the meaning of the word truth. The only things you speak are lies."

Sabrina looks up at me with her pale blue eyes. "Is that what you think of me?"

Her eyes begin to swirl—the blue mixing with lavender. *They remind me of Leah.*

"If you'll excuse me, I have a lot of work to do."

I stiffen as Sabrina grabs my elbow. "Right. But before you go, there is that little matter of business I need to discuss with you."

Jerking my arm away from her grip, I open the door to my office. "Come, sit."

"Those men that were here found signs of a witch nearby." Sabrina's cool tone matches her once more icy blue eyes.

"What type of signs, and where?"

"They picked up a trail of magic that had been cast in the forest."

My head drops back, and I release a deep feral growl.

"They would like to come back and finish activating the protective runes."

"I thought they were protective wards?"

Sabrina's eyes flutter, and a rosy blush creeps into her cheeks. "Oh right. Aren't they the same thing?"

"You tell me."

Sabrina steps backward and stumbles over the small bronze spittoon that decorates the floor of my office. A childhood obsession that my mother indulged in.

I raise my eyebrows. "Nervous?"

"No." Sabrina stops moving and stands tall. She lifts her chin and rolls her shoulders back. "So, can they come finish?"

After a beat, I say, "When Mia and Leah return, I'll think about it."

"Cai—"

"You're dismissed." I motion to the door with my head.

CHAPTER 15

LUCINDA

WHEN WE STEP out of the tavern into the dimly lit street, the cool night sends ripples through my body. A shiver runs up my spine, and I cross my arms over my chest.

I wish I had a jacket or Caiden's warm arms to wrap around me.

Felix and Gavin rush ahead to get the car. Cody walks next to Nyla, and Dylan leads me down the sidewalk, the whole time my mind races with everything the witch just said.

My twin brother might still be alive, and I had an older brother too. She never said what happened to him.

I force a swallow to coat my dry throat.

And my father is a vampire. I'm a half-breed with mixed blood.

I stare at the back of Dylan as I follow his lead.

How will I ever explain this to Caiden? Will he still love me the same?

My pocket vibrates, and I stop to pull out my phone.

"Hi, Caiden—"

"Lucinda, it's so good to hear your voice," Caiden says.

"What's wrong?" *I miss him, I really do.* I motion for Dylan to continue walking.

"Nothing," he says. "Can't I call you for no reason?"

"Caiden, you forget how well I know you. What's up?"

"Nothing you need to worry about now. I'll fill you in when you get home."

I reach the curb, and my head stays on a constant swivel as I cross the vacant street. Glancing to the sky, wispy clouds cover the stars. *Won't this godforsaken night ever end?*

"Speaking of, do you know when you'll be home yet?" Caiden asks.

I stop in the middle of the street and sniff the air. The light breeze carries a strange yet familiar scent.

My nose twitches as the scent swirls in my nostrils, and I sneeze. I spin around to study the area behind me, my wolf on high alert. *I remember this scent. I smelled it when Dylan and I were out on patrol a few days ago.*

"Caiden..."

"Lucinda, what is it?"

"I have to go."

"Don't you dare hang up." A growl slips through the phone.

"Fine. Calm down," I whisper. Through the mindlink, I send, "Dylan, something isn't right."

He stops walking and turns to look at me; his nose twitches. He smells it too.

"Lux! Watch out!"

I duck and kneel just as a bat grazes my head.

"They're here!" Nyla's scream echoes through the silent night.

Caiden's voice bellows through the phone. "Lucinda, what's going on?"

"Lux, get out of there!" Dylan runs toward me.

I look over my shoulder. A swarm of dark objects emerge through the thin layer of clouds.

"LUCINDA?" Caiden roars again.

"Bats, a swarm of bats," I say, my breath short and soft.

Dylan and Cody reach me at the same time. They both close in around me in a protective manner.

"Let's go," Dylan says.

I steal another glance to the night sky as human shapes materialize behind us. *Shit.*

"This can't be good," I say.

"Damn bloodsuckers." Cody pushes me and Dylan forward and turns to face them.

"CODY!" My fingers fumble, and I drop the phone. My lips pull tight into a lethal snarl as the vampires near Cody.

Dylan wraps his arms around me and squeezes tight, which stops me from shifting.

I let loose several waves of power from my inner wolf, and the vampires flash wicked grins as they grab Cody and take to the sky.

Apparently, some of them can fly even when not in bat form. *Something Nyla didn't mention.*

Caiden's deep voice bellows through the phone. "LUCINDA!"

Dylan picks up the phone and examines it. Surprisingly, it isn't shattered.

"Hey, Caiden," he says.

"Where is Lucinda? What is going on?" Caiden's growl pierces my ears in the now silent air.

"Lux is fine. She's right here."

"Let me speak to her."

Dylan holds out the phone to me. I close my eyes and take the phone.

"What the hell do you two think you're doing? Get in the

damn car!" Felix says from inside the car beside the curb with a snarl.

In all the excitement, I didn't realize he'd pulled it up next to us.

As I continue to watch the dark shadows fly off into the distance, Dylan pushes me into the backseat, and I slide in next to Gavin.

"Lucinda?" Caiden asks.

"They took Cody," I say.

"Who took Cody?"

"The vampires," I whisper.

"I want you home, NOW!"

"Caiden, I... I can't."

"Lucinda, come home." Caiden's voice is low.

"I can't put the entire pack in danger. The assassin is still out there—"

"We're taking care of that."

"No offense, but I don't think you can."

"Lucinda, please, come home. I'll keep you safe," he says.

"Caiden, I can't." My stomach churns. All I want is to curl up in his arms.

A howl echoes through the speaker, followed by a distinct crash, then the line goes dead.

Shit!

Dylan raises his eyebrows and says, "Not good."

Gavin flips his phone shut. "I can't reach Mia."

Nyla turns around from the front seat and asks, "What's happening?"

"I assume the beast has taken control," Felix says. "Am I right?"

I bite my lower lip and scroll to find the Pack House land-line. *Someone, please be home.*

On the second ring, a female voice picks up. "Hello?"

I pull the phone from my ear to check the number.

"Hi, who is this?" I ask.

"Leah," she says.

My eyebrows pull together as I rack my memory. I don't recall meeting or hearing about a Leah in the pack.

A series of snarls and growls echo in the background and then another howl. Leah gasps. "I'm sorry, I have to go."

She hangs up.

The phone drops from my ear and slides into my lap. I stare at the screen until the backlight dims. *What just happened?*

"What's going on?" Dylan asks.

"Who is Leah?" I ask.

"Haven't a clue," Dylan says.

I look to Gavin. He tugs on his right earlobe and shrugs.

"Lux, come on, we need to get you home," Dylan says.

I turn to face him and growl. "Home? I can't go home, not now."

"Lux, it's the safest place for you," Dylan says.

Nyla speaks up. "He's right. If both the witch's assassin and the vampires are after you—"

"And that is exactly why I can't go back! Why doesn't anyone understand?" I take several deep breaths to clear my mind. "Gavin, what do you think?"

"Cinda, you're in the middle of a storm, and it's only going to get worse. You need to lay low, and we need to keep you safe."

"I can't go back to the Blood Moone territory. Caiden knows even less about what's going on than I do," I say. "If I go back to him, with the vampires and the witches both trailing me—"

"Witch," Nyla says.

"What?" I ask.

"Witch. Singular. Only one witch is tracking you."

"Oh, that makes a world of difference," Gavin says. "Thank you for clarifying."

I turn to look at him, expecting to see a smile, but his face is stern and serious. When he notices me watching him, he smirks and shrugs.

"Am I driving us back?" Felix asks.

"No! If I return, it will be like wrapping up a package with a nice little bow, delivering it to Caiden, and waiting for it to explode." I cringe at the thought. "I won't put anyone else in danger. Cody risked his life and was taken because of me. I'm going after Cody."

"Then I'm going too," Dylan says.

"Neither of you will get very far without my help," Felix says. "And Cody is like a brother to me, so of course I'm going. And, you do realize I never had any intention of returning to be held captive."

I roll my eyes. I'll cross that bridge when the time comes.

"All of you are fools," Nyla says in her gravelly voice.

I turn to Gavin. He's chewing on his thumbnail and staring out the window.

"Gavin, will you take Nyla back to Caiden and explain things to him?" I ask.

He looks to me with solid black eyes. My pulse quickens, but he quickly calms down, and his pupils restrict back to normal.

"Yes," he says.

"And then will you start preparing the Blood Moone Pack—"

"Preparing for what?"

"War," Felix says.

Through the mindlink I add, "But don't tell Caiden everything we learned. I should be the one to tell him about my father, my brothers, and my mixed blood."

Gavin's eyes soften and he nods.

Felix pulls into the parking lot of our motel and tosses the keys to Gavin. "Here."

"Won't you need a car?" Gavin asks.

"I can get another one easy enough," Felix says. "And it'll be faster."

I roll my eyes.

Giving Gavin a hug, I whisper, "Be careful."

We climb out of the car, and Gavin climbs into the driver's seat, then we watch as the red of the taillights vanish in the distance.

I turn to face Dylan and Felix. "Anyone have a plan?"

"Find Cody," Dylan says with a wide grin. *Smartass.*

Felix smacks him upside the head. Felix has a natural air of authority about him and all of the refined social graces of high society, if only he wasn't such a power-hungry ass.

Once we enter our motel room, I ask, "How are we going to find Cody?"

Felix tugs on his well-groomed goatee. "I know a guy."

"You know a guy." Dylan's tone drips with sarcasm.

Felix nods and dismisses him with a wave of his hand.

"So where do we find this guy?" I ask.

"He can always be found at the Chateau de Paris," he says and stares out the window.

"Okay, so where's that?"

"Not far from here, maybe a couple days' drive northwest."

"Near Chicago?" I ask. My insides quiver at the thought of being near Chicago. I spent almost a year there after I left Felix—the first time.

"Yes, near there." Felix stands as still as a statue. It's eerie.

"Is something wrong?" Dylan asks. *He must've picked up on it too.*

"Chateau de Paris is not a nightclub that you can just arrive at without an invitation," Felix says.

"How do we get an invitation?" Dylan asks.

"You don't just get an invitation." The inflection in Felix's voice rises with anger, and he grips the metal radiator in front of him.

"Do you know someone that could get us in?"

Felix growls, and I jump. Dylan turns to me, and we share a puzzled expression. *I guess Felix doesn't run in those circles anymore.*

"I might have a connection," I say.

Both heads snap in my direction, their eyes wide and foreheads raised, creating wrinkles.

"Do you now?" Felix says.

I bite my lower lip as my cheeks flush with warmth. "Yeah."

Dylan watches me and narrows his eyes. I never told him about my time in Chicago.

"Kitten, are you waiting for an invitation?"

My gaze snaps to Felix and I glower. *I wish he'd stop calling me that..*

Felix snaps his fingers. "Come on now, make the call."

"The call?" I ask.

"To your contact." Felix raises his voice and emits just enough power to get my heart pounding.

"Yeah, okay." I reach into my pocket and fish out my phone. Katie's number isn't saved, but I'll always remember it. I hope she hasn't changed it.

"Hello?" She answers on the second ring.

"Hi, Katie."

"Cinda! No way. Girl, I was wondering if I'd ever hear from you again," Katie says. "Hang on a sec... okay...done."

"What's done?"

Katie snickers. "I saved your contact info."

"I'm sorry for leaving the way I did." I turn my back on the guys and twirl my hair.

"It's cool, I get it. No worries here. Are you in town?"

Felix steps in front of me and motions for me to hurry up.

"Actually—"

"Awesome! Girl, we gotta hang out. Where you staying?" she asks.

I sprawl across the bed. "It's a spur of the moment trip, and I haven't thought that far ahead."

Katie laughs. "You haven't changed, still the same Cinda I remember."

"I'm just passing through and I heard about this nightclub."

"Which one?"

"It's called Chateau de Paris."

"That place is the bomb, seriously. It's off the hook! You wanna go?"

"I'd love to!"

"When you get in town, come on over to my place," she says. "Gotta go. Love you girl. Bye!"

"By—" She hangs up the phone.

Same old Katie. It'll be fun to hang out with her again. She was my first female best friend, and she'll always be dear to me. She's also the first human friend I ever had.

"What did your contact say?" Felix asks, and Dylan watches me from across the room with a scowl.

Like they couldn't hear her high-pitched squeals through the speaker.

I study them for a moment. The light banter reminds me of the old days, with Dylan and Felix at different times in my life. Before they both brutally crushed my soul. *Have I forgiven them so easily, or am I escaping to a familiar past in order to run from my future?* No time to think about that now.

I set my phone on the nightstand and smile. "We're in."

"Just like that?" Felix asks.

I nod.

"Do I even want to know?" Felix drums his fingers on the small round table.

"Nope." I smirk.

Felix doesn't need to know everything.

CHAPTER 16

CAIDEN

ONE OF MY patrol members contacts me through the mindlink, and the urgency wakes me from a night terror. I squint at the bright sun that floods the room.

"What do you want?" I ask through the mindlink.

Having slid out of bed, I stumble to the window and close the curtains before collapsing onto the bed again.

The patrol member's voice quivers. "There is a man here that requests your audience."

Unusual, but also something I cannot ignore.

I sit on the edge of the bed and rest my elbows on my bent knees.

"Does he say anything else?"

After a moment the guard responds, "He says he is Garcia, an emissary from the O'leander pack."

"Audience is granted. Bring him to my office," I say.

Last night was a restless night. After the phone call from Lucinda, I almost lost total control of my beast.

Thankfully, Leah was able to calm me down.

I'm grateful she forgot her house key and came back to get it. She arrived with Mia just in time to stop my beast from doing something I would regret. After, Mia wanted to stay home with me, but I insisted that she continue with her trip and go with Leah.

I have a feeling the book they're retrieving will play a crucial part in our future.

Mia reluctantly agreed, and Leah brewed me a large mug of herbal tea. She said it would help me to relax, keep calm, and sleep.

I tossed and turned all night, my dreams dark and grim. But my strength is slowly returning after the poison damage because I remained in control, and that is what matters most.

After showering and dressing for the day, I examine my cell phone and grunt. It's out of commission, so I call Lucinda from the house phone, but she doesn't answer.

My claws extend, and my muscles flex as I leave her a voice message. "Call me."

I stare at the phone for a moment before hanging up, perhaps my tone was too harsh. *I need more of that calming tea from Leah.*

As I walk downstairs, the vile stench of Sabrina infiltrates my senses. I clench my fists. The beast inside me is fighting for control.

I walk into the kitchen and check the counter for more of Leah's tea. *Damn, all gone.* I move to the cabinet and start pulling out boxes of tea bags in the hope I can find something calming.

Sabrina's silky voice floats across the room. "Can I help you find something?"

"No." I read the ingredients on one of the boxes.

Sabrina crosses the room to stand next to me. "It looks like you're looking for something."

I growl and continue scanning the different tea boxes.

"I never knew you drank tea," she says.

"Sabrina, take the day off and please go home."

"Nope, can't. I have a few things to do. And who would look after you if I left?"

I glare at her. I can't find anything that sounds calming, so I toss a box of tea across the counter and it hits the backsplash.

Sabrina picks up the box of tea and rotates it in her palm. "Are you looking for a specific tea or herb?"

I run my hand through my hair and let out a loud sigh. Turning to her, I say, "Yes. I'm looking for something that is calming and relaxing."

A smile brightens her face. "I have the perfect blend. Give me a few minutes to run home and get it."

"No, it's okay."

"I insist." Sabrina pops her hip. I nod.

She turns to leave. But when she gets to the front door, I call out to her.

"Sabrina, since you insist on being here, will you at least make yourself useful to me?"

She turns around. Her face is twisted into an expression of anger and excitement.

"I'm expecting a visitor later," I say. "So we'll need a meal prepared. Please stop by the store on your way back to get things."

"Who's the visitor?" Her pale blue eyes dim to a light lavender in the morning sun.

"Does it matter?"

"Yes."

My brows pull tight.

"If I know who is coming, it will help me decide what dish to prepare," Sabrina says.

That makes sense.

"An emissary from another pack," I say through a tight jaw.

"Who, which one?" Her eyes widen, and she takes a step

forward as she leans on her tiptoes.

I growl and walk toward the mudroom. Even if Sabrina's tea blend is as calming as Leah's, I still need a good run before meeting with this emissary.

After my run, I jump in a quick shower, and the cold water pours over my tired muscles.

The free time in the forest did more harm than I was expecting.

I let out a sigh and turn up the temperature until hot water scalds my sore body.

"Alpha, we approach," the guard sends through the mindlink.

I reach for the knob, but my fingers linger before shutting off the water. *Am I ready for this?*

Once dressed, I head down to my office, but Sabrina meets me at the bottom of the steps.

"Did you have a nice run?" Sabrina asks.

"Calming," I say as I pass her.

She walks down the hall and follows me into the office. She sets a mug on my desk. "I made you tea. It's been steeping for an hour, so it should be nice and strong."

My head tilts toward her. "What is it?"

"My special blend. It's chocked full of tranquil herbs," she says. "Oh, and I dropped in a dash of honey too."

I waft my hand above the mug, and the aroma stirs my wolf. *Mint and honey.* My heart aches for Lucinda. The mug is still warm in my palm as I grab it. The dark liquid is sweet on my tongue as it goes down. *This is much more delicious than Leah's blend.* I eagerly take another sip.

"I'm glad you like it," Sabrina says.

"It is very good. Thank you."

"Oh, and about your visitor. When will they arrive? I'm cooking a chicken, and it should be ready in an hour."

"Chicken sounds perfect. And he should arrive any minute now. We'll talk business before we eat." I lift the mug to my lips to drain the remaining liquid.

"Are you ready to tell me who it is yet?" Sabrina asks. Her eyebrows raise.

I place the empty mug on my desk and then lean back in my chair. My head falls back and rests against the soft, worn leather. "Garcia, the first warrior of the O'leander pack."

The stillness of the room causes restlessness in my wolf. I search the room, and my attention lands on Sabrina's lavender eyes that pierce through her narrow gaze.

"Do you remember him?" I ask.

Her relentless gaze sends chills deep into my soul, and my wolf responds with a wave of power rippling through the room. Sabrina shakes her head, as if she's forcing herself out of a trance.

"What?" she says. "No, no, I'm sorry, I don't remember him."

"Maybe when you see him. I've only met him once, and I will never forget—"

"Alpha Caiden?" A female voice rings through the house.

"He's here," I whisper to Sabrina.

She nods and turns to leave, but stops in the doorway. "I'll lead him in and then set the table for dinner."

I nod and remain seated. Even though he is a first warrior, he is not my equal and does not deserve my respect. At one time, that title may have earned him respect from an Alpha, though that is an old and forgotten tradition in this day and age.

I am Alpha. He will bow to me. I lick my lips, and the sweet remnants of mint and honey sweeten my taste buds.

Sabrina leads him into my office and winks at me before closing the door.

"Garcia," I say as I tilt my head to acknowledge his presence.

"Caiden." Garcia squints as he studies my relaxed posture.

I motion toward the chair in front of me. "Please have a seat."

Garcia glides across the room, surveying the surroundings. Before taking his seat, Garcia performs a slight bow, acknowledging my Alpha status.

Good.

"Caiden, I am here to renew our prior conversations."

My nostrils flare. He came to my parents' funeral as the O'leander pack's official representative. It was an honorable gesture from his Alpha, and the words he spoke about my father were kind and full of compassion. Though, that was where it ended.

After the funeral service, his choice of words and accusatory tone hit a nerve, and my beast reacted. Blood was spilled and threats were exchanged. I was impressed with his fighting skills, but I do not fear him. He is no threat to me.

"There is nothing to be said on that topic," I say.

"Are you that blind?"

A growl slips out. "If that is what you came to discuss, then this meeting is over."

"We've been patient since your father's death, giving you time and space to heal the pack. But now it's time. You must make a choice! Are the Blood Moones siding with the witches or the vampires?"

I grit my teeth and force a swallow. "We want no part of the fairytale. Leave us alone."

"Not making a choice is the same as siding with our foe. If you don't join us, then you're against us." Garcia stands and pounds his fist on my desk.

I lean forward and snarl. "Who is the *us* you refer to?"

"The Wolf Council is divided. That's why we no longer have our annual retreat. Half of the packs side with the witches and the other half with the vampires. This is a centuries-old war—"

"Then why have I never heard of it before?"

"The wolves always stayed neutral in the past, but now it's time. We need to take a stand or die trying." Garcia sits back down and stares at me with black eyes.

I clear my throat. "Who's left to even choose sides?"

"Not many, not many at all. But not only are we fighting the witches, we're also fighting each other."

"Wolves attack wolves? Why?"

"Because they are weak. Your friend Felix kills other wolves for the witches."

"Felix is no friend of mine," I say through a tight jaw. "He sides with the witches?"

"Felix has been lied to and led astray," Garcia whispers. "The Crescent Noir pack sided with the witches, and now they are destroyed. Your father—"

"Don't talk about my father." I curl my fingers and my nails cut into my palms.

"It'll only be a matter of time before your lovely mate tries to persuade you to join our side and fight with the vampires."

"The damn bloodsuckers kidnapped Lucinda's friend. They're the enemy."

"Aren't the witches trying to kill her? So why aren't they the enemy? Have you found out why they want her dead?"

My heart pounds. *No, I haven't. That was their mission—to find the witch and discover why. But then Cody was kidnapped...*

"No? Tsk tsk. It's the same reason the vampires want your precious mate alive. They want her blood." Garcia's eyes sparkle. He's enjoying this too much. Knowing more about the people I love, taunting me with information.

I growl. "Her blood?"

"Yes. Her mixed blood." Garcia's eyes widen and his face pales. "Oh, didn't you know?"

A snarl hisses through my teeth as I fight the urges within me. My wolf yearns for his mate, and the beast rages with a fiery passion.

Garcia stands and walks backward toward the door, his hands in front of his chest, palms facing me. "Caiden, I—"

The door swings open, and Gavin steps into the room. My pulse races, and I take several deep breaths to regain control.

I search the empty hall behind Gavin and study the grim look on his face. "Where's Lucinda?"

"She didn't come home."

CHAPTER 17

LUCINDA

DYLAN INSISTED on sleeping on the floor of my room to keep an eye on me overnight. The only problem with that idea was leaving Felix unattended.

Do I think Felix would leave us? No.

But, would he? If it was in his best interest, he wouldn't hesitate.

I tiptoe around Dylan and enter the common room. It's still dark, but the early morning light peaks through the curtains.

Felix is nowhere to be seen.

Damn him! I crack my knuckles and scurry over to Dylan.

"Dylan, wake up." I nudge him with my foot.

He swats at my leg. "Leave me alone."

"Get up, damn it. This is important." I kick him, this time in his kidney.

"Ouch!" Dylan rolls over, presses up on his elbow, and glares at me.

"What's so important that you had to wake me up at this godforsaken hour?"

I point to the common rom. "Felix is gone."

"Good. I didn't like him traveling with us anyway." Dylan lies back down.

"What are you doing? Come on, get up!" My stomach tightens at the thought of Felix loose in the world, and unsupervised. *I should never have trusted him. I will not be making that mistake, again.*

Dylan yawns as he stands up and stretches his arms out wide. "You are a pain in the ass in the morning, do you know that?"

I smirk. "Get used to it."

"I need a shower—"

A growl vibrates up my throat.

"I'll be quick, I promise," Dylan says as he walks into the bathroom.

I sit on the couch, pull out my phone, and stare at the screen. *What do I say? Anything I say will just set him off again.*

Me: *Hey. How is he?*

Mia: *I don't know.*

Me: *What do you mean?*

Mia: *I'm not home.*

Me: *Where are you?*

Mia: *Will you be home soon.*

Me: *Have you heard from him?*

Mia: *No. You?*

Me: *No.*

Mia: *What happened?*

Me: *He didn't like what I said.*

Mia: *Lol. He'll feel better when you're home. When are you headed back?*

Me: *I'm not.*

Mia: *Shit. Gotta go. TTYL.*

I stare at the wallpaper on my phone. I have it set to a picture of Caiden—his silhouette against the evening sky, with part of him in the shadows so he looks like a dark angel.

A tear falls on the screen, and I blink away the remaining drops before they fall.

Why would an angelic beast like Caiden ever want a dirty half-breed like me? Sighing, I close the phone and tuck it into my pocket.

As soon as we check out of our room and exit the motel office, my nose twitches. The familiar scent of cloves and bayberry swirls in the air. Felix stands leaning against the brick wall just outside the exit. He jiggles a set of keys in his hand and motions for us to follow him across the parking lot.

I restrain a growl as my lips curl. *Jackass.*

But when I follow Felix and turn the corner, I stop in my tracks. A striking Aston Martin Rapide is parallel parked next to the curb.

"Nice ride." Dylan stuffs his hands into his pockets and smirks.

Felix flicks his wrist and waves off the compliment. "This old thing? Not really, but it'll do."

My fingertips glide across the flawless exterior. "This is a beautiful teal—"

"Teal?" Felix clenches his jaw and squints in my direction. "Kitten, it just isn't an ordinary teal. It's ocellus teal."

Dylan opens the passenger side door and folds down the seat for me to climb into the back and says through the mindlink, "Yeah, Lux, don't you know your different teals?"

I study his stern face for a moment, and his cheeks redden.

"It's hard not to laugh, right?" I send back through the mindlink and muffle a laugh under my breath.

I study my reflection in the metallic paint. My hair is tousled and beginning to frizz, so, I pull it back and tie it into a low bun before crawling into the backseat. Dylan takes the front passenger seat. I slide my hand across the smooth leather and admire the soft curves of the interior.

Yeah, nice.

"Chicago is neutral territory," Dylan says. "But we need to cross through the Gibbous territory to get there."

"Do you think we can get in and out without anyone noticing?" I ask.

Felix turns around and raises an eyebrow at me. "In your particular position, I don't think not announcing your presence would be wise."

"What position is that?" I snap.

"For starters, you're half-wolf, half-vampire—"

A growl slips up my throat. "Assumed, not proven!"

I'm not going to believe it just because Felix and a witch, who's trying to kill me, say it's true. Or maybe I don't want to believe it because I'm worried about what Caiden will think.

"Okay, then we'll go with reason number two. You're being tracked and hunted by a witch assassin—"

"We've seen no proof that we're being tracked since we first left. For all we know, Caiden found and killed the witch in the woods."

"They would only send another if that were the case," Felix says. "But the situation I was referring to was your new position. You are Caiden's mate and the Luna of the Blood Moone pack, and Dylan is the Beta. How would it look if we were caught sneaking through a neighboring territory?"

My head falls forward, and I rest my elbows on my knees. *He's right. Why didn't I think of that? I'm no longer a rogue, so I can't act foolishly anymore, not without consequences.*

I look up at them. "By chance, do either of you know their Alpha?"

Felix drums his fingertips on the steering wheel. "We know of each other."

"Is that a good thing?"

Felix looks at me through the rearview mirror. The pointed tips of his teeth shimmer in the rays of sunlight reflecting off the mirror with his grin. A shiver courses up my spine.

"I've met him before," Dylan says.

"What type of Alpha is he?" I ask.

"Haven't you met him?" Felix asks.

"No, why would I?"

"Your friend in Chicago—"

"Oh, right. No, I was, uh, rogue."

"I see," Felix says, and his scowl causes my cheeks to redden.

Did he really just try to reprimand me?

Dylan scoffs. "Alpha Jackson isn't someone you want to play games with, that's for sure."

"I disagree. Games are always fun to play with Jackson." Felix strokes his goatee. "But Dylan is right. For the purpose of this trip—" Felix releases a sigh. "No games. Although..."

My eyebrows raise, and I bite my bottom lip.

"Jackson doesn't need to know everything either. Let's keep the purpose of our trip on a need-to-know basis."

I nod, but Dylan growls.

"Do you disagree?" I ask.

"I don't think it is wise for the Luna and Beta of a fellow pack to be caught lying. Alpha Jackson isn't known to be the most understanding or forgiving Alpha."

"Whoever said anything about lying?" Felix says.

I place my hand on Dylan's shoulder. "Dylan, I understand what you're saying, but I agree with Felix. The fewer people that know what we're doing, the better."

Dylan's nostrils flare and his jaw tightens.

"We won't lie to him," I say. "We'll tell the truth, just in vague terms."

Dylan's eyes narrow. "Just to be sure we're all on the same page, what is our story?"

"We are visiting a friend in Chicago," I say.

"That could work. It would make sense for me, the Beta, to be escorting you, the Luna, to visit a friend." Dylan nods, then motions toward Felix. "But what about him? Why is he with us?"

"That won't matter. Jackson won't ask about me." Felix waves his hand through the air to dismiss the idea.

"Why not?"

"It doesn't matter." Felix returns his attention to the road and grips the steering wheel tight. "But if he mentions witches or vampires, keep your mouths shut. Do you understand me?"

Dylan turns to me, and the vein across his left temple pulses. Through the mindlink, he sends, "I don't trust him."

"Me either. But what other choice do we have?" I send back.

"Stop it with that damn mindlink!" Felix says.

"Why? Do you feel left out?" Dylan crosses his arms over his chest.

Felix snarls in his direction.

"Stop it you two." I shake my head and put my hand on each of their shoulders, then turn to Felix. "We understand and agree. Now, is it too much to ask for you two to be pleasant to each other the rest of the trip? Because it's going to be a long trip."

Dylan laughs. Felix growls and pulls the car over.

"What now?" I ask.

Felix gets out of the car and storms around to Dylan's side and opens the door.

"Out!" he orders.

"You want to fight? Here, now?" Dylan steps out of the car.

Felix sighs. "No, you fool. You're driving."

"Really?" Dylan's eyes widen. He wastes no time jogging around to the driver side and climbing behind the wheel.

"It would be best for the Beta to be seen driving the Luna. Don't you agree?" Felix asks, and Dylan nods.

Smart.

I crawl into the front passenger seat, and Felix grudgingly climbs into the backseat.

"I don't think he likes sitting in the backseat of his own car," I send Dylan through the mindlink, and we both laugh.

Dylan pulls back out onto the empty road and continues driving in silence until we see signs for the interstate.

"Am I continuing on back roads or getting on the interstate?" Dylan asks Felix.

"May as well get on the interstate. It'll be easier to meet one of their patrol members," Felix says.

My stomach swirls just thinking of the meeting with Alpha Jackson, so I slouch in my seat and pull out my phone. Staring at the screen, there's a tightness in my chests.

No messages or missed calls.

I tuck my phone back in my pocket and close my eyes.

Caiden. Where are you?

The next couple of hours blur together. Felix and Dylan engage in never-ending arguments. When they started debating which came first the witch, vampire, or wolf shifter, I climbed in the backseat and covered my head with any loose clothing I could find. I must have fallen asleep because when I open my eyes, we are stopped at the rest area near the state line.

I stretch my arms and ask, "What are we doing?"

"Waiting for a patrol wolf," Dylan says.

Déjà vu.

A husky man with short dark hair and tattoos covering

his forearms steps out from the woods and approaches our car.

"Let's get out and meet him halfway," Felix whispers.

"You don't think that will be seen as threatening?" I ask.

Felix cracks his knuckles. "We don't want to appear too weak to this pack."

"I agree. Let's go." Dylan opens the car door and steps out, with Felix right behind him. I close my eyes, take a deep breath, then catch up to them.

"And this is Lucinda Raven." Dylan's voice carries on the wind, and he motions to me. "Fated Mate to Alpha Caiden Moone, and Luna of the Blood Moone pack."

The man's eyes roam over my body and then linger on my mate's mark. His nose twitches. After piercing me with his unnerving stare, he bows and says, "It is an honor to meet the Fated Mate of Alpha Caiden."

I glance to Dylan and send through the mindlink, "What do I say?"

Dylan shrugs.

"Thank you," I say to the man. "And what do we call you?"

"You may call me Cru," he says. "And to what do we owe this honor?"

"We would like permission to cross through the Gibbous territory."

"You'll need Alpha Jackson's permission for that," Cru says.

Felix nods. "Meeting with Alpha Jackson is most welcomed. Come, ride with us and I'll drive."

Dylan and I climb into the rear seats, while Cru glides into the passenger seat.

A wide grin smears across Cru's face, accentuating the bronze glow of his skin. The late afternoon shadows put him in half light, giving an otherworldly aura surrounding him.

Shivers run down my spine, and I shake off the alarm bells of my wolf.

"Nice car. Is this borrowed?" he asks.

Felix snorts. He slams the door shut, a little harder than normal. "No. It's mine."

"Alpha J would love a car like this," Cru says in a nonchalant manner and shrugs. The unsaid words linger in the air.

"Do you think Felix will trade the car for safe passage?" I ask Dylan through the mindlink.

"Let's hope we don't have to find out," Dylan sends back.

"Agree." I flash a small smile, and Dylan nods with his eyes.

"None of that!" Cru turns around and faces us. "No talking through the mindlink. Not only is it disrespectful, it's also—"

"Oh, calm yourself. They mean no harm. Don't get your panties in a bunch." Felix's dismissive tone makes me giggle.

Cru turns back around and adjusts himself in the leather seat. "Just don't do it in front of Alpha J. He won't like it much."

"Good to know," I say. "Any other dos and don'ts we should know before meeting Alpha J?"

Cru growls. "It is Alpha Jackson to you."

I nod and Dylan jabs me in the rib with his elbow.

Cru turns around to face us. "But since you asked, yes."

I lean forward to hear him better, and Dylan does as well. Our knees touch, and a warmth pulses through my body. I ignore the closeness and focus on Cru.

"Don't speak unless spoken to. Don't look him directly in the eye. Don't tell him what he has to do or can't do. Do answer his questions when asked. Do answer truthfully—he's very good at detecting a lie. Do be grateful—"

"Seriously?" I ask. "Is he a king or some other royalty?"

Cru glares at me.

I clench my fists into tight balls until my knuckles turn white.

"He's not worth it," Dylan says through the mindlink and squeezes my thigh.

"I will not submit to him," I send back to Dylan.

In the corner of my eye, Dylan throws his hands in the air and lean back into his seat.

Refusing to break eye contact with Cru, a growl vibrates up my throat and my upper lip curls, exposing my deadly incisors.

Cru rolls his shoulder forward, and his pupils fully dilate. Leaning toward me, his lips pull back, and a line of drool drops on the armrest.

The tiny hairs on the back of my neck stand tall. My wolf whines, wanting to be released. I lean in close to Cru, only inches from his face. My nose crinkles as a vicious snarl escapes, and I push out a force of power so strong that the car swerves and we all shift in our seats.

Felix growls. "Lucinda, dear, next time you plan to do that —don't."

I nod to Felix through the rearview mirror, then I find Cru's dark brown eyes staring at me with an intensity that gives me the creeps. My eyes narrow, and I lick my lips.

"Enough!" Felix yells.

"Thank you," Dylan mutters to Felix.

"Put a muzzle on her," Cru says through a clenched jaw.

Dylan squeezes my shoulder.

"You may want to watch your mouth." Felix glances at Cru.

"Why? I don't care who she is, and we don't have a pack alliance with the Blood Moones."

"It's not the pack you should fear."

I glare at the back of Felix's head.

"What game is he playing?" I ask Dylan through the mindlink.

Dylan shrugs.

Cru shifts his stare between Felix and me.

"I don't fear Caiden," Cru says.

"And that's your first mistake. Care to guess your second?" Felix drums his fingers on the steering wheel.

I lean back in my seat. *Felix is enjoying this too much. I'm over it.*

Felix turns to Cru. "No? Let's play twenty questions."

"I don't like games."

"Fine, fine. Dylan, be a dear and tell him his second mistake," Felix says over his shoulder.

My head snaps to Dylan. *How does he know?*

Dylan adjusts in his seat and removes his hand from my shoulder.

"Underestimating her strength," Dylan says.

Cru tightens his jaw, but his eyes capture my interest. His pupils are fully dilated, yet instead of being the usual black, they are lined with streaks of red.

Caiden's beast flashes through my thoughts. *Could Cru also be cursed?*

"Just keep her on a short leash when you meet with Alpha J." Cru faces forward.

"If this is how a regular pack member acts, I'm not looking forward to meeting this Alpha J," I send Dylan through the mindlink.

Dylan squeezes my hand. "You'll do fine. Just remember to stay calm."

"Stay calm? How am I supposed to stay calm when we're about to lie to an Alpha, who apparently has a major little man complex?"

"I wouldn't call Alpha J a little man."

"You know what I mean!"

Felix's eyes drift to the rearview mirror, and his expression tells me to calm down.

I close my eyes, take a deep breath, hold it for a second, and release it slowly. After a few more deep breaths, I feel rejuvenated.

With a clear head, I pull out my phone. Two missed calls from Caiden and one from Mia. No voice messages. Six text messages.

Caiden: *Where are you?*

Caiden: *Lucinda?*

Caiden: *Answer me, dammit!*

Mia: *Cinda, what are you doing?*

Mia: *Call Caiden, please.*

Mia: *Call me!*

Dylan sends through the mindlink, "Everything okay?"

"Have you checked your phone recently?" I ask.

Dylan reaches into his back pocket and pulls out his phone. His eyes widen as he looks at the screen.

"Fourteen missed calls. No messages."

"Caiden?" I ask.

He nods.

I bite my lower lip and bang my head back against the seat rest. *Shit.*

My stomach churns as I fight back tears that threaten to escape. I miss Caiden so much; I miss the warmth of my mate. The sound of his voice would be enough to coax me back home.

But no. I can't go back, not yet. Not without Cody.

My fingers fumble over the keypad as I text.

Me: *Caiden, you around?*

There's no instant response, so I send Mia a quick message.

Me: *Hey! Can't call now. Everything ok?*

My hands begin to tremble when I get no response from Mia.

Dylan catches my phone as I drop it before it crashes to the floor.

I send Dylan through the mindlink, "Mia always has her phone with her."

He glances to the unlocked screen and shrugs. "Maybe she's in the shower or something."

"Maybe. But you don't get it. I mean, she always has her phone. Always."

Dylan rubs my shoulder. "Everything's fine. You need to focus on Alpha J."

"Alpha Jackson," I correct, but I can't stop the feeling in the pit of my stomach that all isn't fine. I send Caiden another message.

Me: *Hey. I can't talk now, but call later? Love you.*

Just as I'm about to slip my phone back into my pocket, it vibrates.

Caiden: *Hi.*

Me: *Hey! How are you? Is everything ok?*

Caiden: *Fine. Where are you?*

I bite my lower lip and glance to Dylan. He reads my screen.

Shaking his head, he says through the mindlink, "Don't tell him we're going to see Alpha J. He'll freak."

I raise my eyebrows. "What do you mean, freak?"

"They're rivals. And from what I understand, they don't have the best childhood history."

I rub my temples. "That would've been nice to know yesterday."

Dylan's face smooshes into a weird awkward grin.

I stare at the screen. *What do I say?*

Caiden: *Lucinda?*

Me: *I'm here. Sorry, D had a question.*

Caiden: *K. Where are you?*

Me: *Why? So you can come get me?*

Caiden: *Maybe.*

Me: *I love you. <3*

Caiden: *You're not going to tell me, are you?*

Me: *No.*

Caiden: *Please?*

Me: *I'm sorry, I can't.*

Caiden: *Be careful. Trust no one.*

Me: *I'll always trust you. <3*

Caiden: *Trust only yourself.*

Caiden: *Have to go, call later.*

Caiden: *Love you, stay safe.*

Me: *TTYL. <3*

Caiden's words repeat over and over in my head. *Trust no one. Trust only yourself.* What does he mean? Is he talking about Alpha J? What does he know?

Can I still trust Caiden?

CHAPTER 18

CAIDEN

I STRIDE OVER to my speed bag hanging in the corner of my office and give it a punch. I knew she wasn't coming home; she told me that much last night over text.

Her damn stubbornness. I'd hoped Dylan or Gavin would talk some sense into her. As a last resort, I'd wished she would listen to her wolf and return home, *I was wrong.*

My wolf perks up at the slightest shuffle on the hardwood floor.

"Leave me!" I growl.

A fist connects with my kidney. *Garcia.*

The low blow momentarily cripples me, and I kneel on the floor to catch my breath. I'll never admit weakness, but I can still feel the effects of the poison coursing through my body.

When I raise my head, Gavin has Garcia in a headlock from behind. Mia and Leah walk into the room.

"Gavin!" Mia runs to him with wide eyes and drapes her arms around him.

I stand and nod to him. He lets go of Garcia.

Leah smirks. "You boys having fun without us?"

Garcia's eyes linger on Leah a bit longer than normal, and her eyes flutter. He spins around to face Gavin. "Have we met before?"

I make quick introductions. "This is Garcia, an official representative and first warrior of the O'leander pack."

Gavin dismisses Garcia's uncanny stare. "No, I don't believe we have had the pleasure."

I step forward and face Garcia. "What was the point in attacking me?"

Sabrina walks into the room, followed by Elder Charles and his friends of The Brotherhood.

Garcia doesn't seem to notice or care because he smirks and then shrugs. "To kill you, of course."

Mia's knees wobble and she stumbles back into Gaven's chest.

Sabrina's stare hardens, she crosses her arms over her chest, and drums her fingers on her skin.

One of The Brotherhood steps into the hallway and returns with an older woman.

I dismiss everything but Garcia. "What good would killing me do for your cause?"

"When your mate or Beta return, they will join our cause." Garcia's forehead furrows.

"How can you be so sure?"

"They're both Dark Ravens—"

"Not anymore!" I pound my fist on the table and knock over a glass of water.

"Are you sure about that?"

Gavin smacks Garcia on the head, and Garcia slumps forward, then falls to the floor. *Unconscious.*

"Oops. Must've been harder than I thought." Gavin smirks.

"Garcia has a point, you know," Sabrina says.

"What do you mean?"

"Dylan randomly coming here right after the attack on us. And then Lucinda suddenly showing up years later—"

I grimace and a vein throbs at my temple. "Get to the point."

"They planned it all along."

"No!" Mia protests. "Cinda would never do that!"

"Planned what?" I ask.

The old woman snickers. "And just how well do you know your friend, Cinda? Or is it Lux? Oh wait, it's Lucinda, that's right."

"And you are?" I glower at the woman. The absence of her scent is more noticeable than if she had a vile smell. But her sharp tongue disgusts me more.

"This is Nyla, the witch," Gavin says.

Mia stares into the witch's eyes.

"Did you know she had a mate that rejected her?" The witch continues to speak. "Did you know she was kicked out of her pack? Did you know she was the daughter of an Alpha?"

Mia rolls her eyes.

"It's a pity you didn't know her better. Maybe all of this could've been avoided."

"All of what?" Mia asks.

The witch motions toward Garcia, who is dangling limp in Gavin's arms. "Now we're going to have to kill him."

"No," Mia says.

Elder Charles's voice rings in the silence. "He attacked the Alpha. You must—"

"We must do nothing at this moment." I roll my shoulders back and my fingers get caught in my hair as they comb through the messy bedhead.

"Don't you see?" Sabrina asks. "It makes perfect sense now."

"What does?" I ask.

Sabrina steps closer to me and reaches for my arm. "Dylan and Lucinda."

My right eye twitches.

Nyla clears her throat. "Dylan was cursed and knew how to break it. So he led Lucinda here, to find her mate, for you to break it. They are both Dark Ravens, therefore most likely will side with the Vampire Nation. They've deceived you."

Sabrina's eyes widen and her ruby-stained lips form an O. "OH! Yes, that's it. They used you in order to break the curse. And now, they are in a position to overthrow you and take the Blood Moone pack for themselves."

"I'm afraid they played you the fool." Nyla shakes her head.

Sabrina whispers under her breath, "And now they're both out searching for the Vampire Nation at this very moment—"

"Stop it!" I growl. "You don't know any of that."

"But I do," Nyla says.

"And just a short while ago, weren't you trying to kill her?"

"Yes. And now you know why. She's the enemy."

"Get out!" I push a rippling force of power through the air so that everyone, witch included, couldn't deny the command.

"But what about Garcia?" Mia asks, her eyes wet with tears.

"He should be killed," Sabrina says.

I grit my teeth. "Put him in a cell."

"Alpha, sir, if I may interject," Elder Charles says. "If you don't want to kill him, then he needs to stand trial. We cannot show weakness during these uncertain times. Other packs may get word—"

"Fine. When he wakes up, we'll hold a hearing with the council members. Now, leave me."

I turn around and watch the peacefulness of my sanctuary—the forest—when a text message dings on my phone. *Lucinda.*

The door latches closed, but the presence of someone still lingers. I quickly respond to Lucinda, then turn around and face Elder Charles.

"What do you want?"

His twisted smile mixed with the shadows cast upon his face, gives him a devilish vibe. "To provide my Alpha with advice during times of need."

"And what advice is that?"

"These are dark times. Witches and vampires are resurfacing, so who knows what is in store for us. And with the Wolf Council disbanded, we're on our own to fight against these entities."

"And what would you have me do?" I ask.

"You need to be careful and cautious of whom you let close to you."

I cock an eyebrow and fold my arms across my chest.

"That girl, Leah. How much do you know about her?" Elder Charles asks.

"She's Elizabeth's little sister."

"Of course, of course. But aside from that?"

"What more do you need?"

"Don't you find it uncanny how she showed up right when the witch assassination attempts began?"

"Enough!"

Elder Charles nods and clasps his hands in front of him. "As you wish. Just, please, be careful. There could be spies or more assassins in our midst."

"Thank you for your advice, if that is all..."

"Just one more thing."

I shoot him a death stare. "Fine."

"As much as I dislike saying this, it must be said. If the things Garcia and Nyla said about Lucinda are true—"

A snarl slips free. "They're not!"

"Just think about it from another perspective. No mate, fated or otherwise, would ever leave their mate behind, especially in the company of other men."

My veins bulge as my arm muscles tense.

"I know you love Lucinda, and I have no doubt your fated bond is real. But she is a master of seduction and trickery. I fear she's playing you for your power and position."

I curl my fingers into my palm, and my sharp nails pierce through the calloused skin.

"She will wear you down and poison you in your sleep. You need to stop acting like a broken-hearted little boy and be the man I know you are. Be the man your father raised. The man that this pack needs as our fearless leader."

Numbness spreads over me. Shock. Pain. *Can it be true?*

"We need an Alpha that can make the tough decisions. You can't always follow your heart."

"You know nothing of what you speak. You don't know Lucinda like I do," I growl, forcing myself to believe my own words.

"Fair enough. But the Blood Moone pack needs an Alpha and Luna who are fully committed to this pack and to each other. We need strong and committed leadership, now more than ever. What type of message does it send when the future Luna runs off on little adventures every time something arises?"

"You know it isn't that simple."

"True. But that isn't how other pack members see it. I warned you before not to interfere in others' affairs. You brought this upon us when you chose Lucinda over your pack."

The beast inside me fights for control. I roll my neck and clench my fists, trying to calm the urge to shift.

Elder Charles draws in a deep breath as his eyes widen. His scent is drenched in fear. "I will leave you to reflect on all that has been said."

He steps backward toward the door.

A howl slips from the depths of my soul as my clothes shred to pieces and fall to the floor.

CHAPTER 19

LUCINDA

THE MEETING with Alpha Jackson was ridiculous.

Upon entering his office, he cut off Cru during introductions and ignored Dylan, me, and Felix completely. Instead, he talked to Cru about us, as if we weren't there. The entire situation was obnoxious, and I was glad when he waved us along like he dismissed the wait staff.

What an arrogant, power-tripping Alpha.

And now, Felix and Dylan are back to their petty arguing.

"No," Dylan growls. "The interstate will be quicker."

"Too bad you're not driving," Felix says.

"Enough!" I say. "Can we please have some quiet time? I need to rest."

More like think, but I won't tell them that.

The message from Caiden to trust no one still pulls at my heart.

I understand his hesitation in trusting Felix. I question my trust in him every damn day. And Dylan; though I've had reason not to trust him in the past, is he not redeemable? Does Caiden not trust his own Beta?

Trust only yourself.

Can I no longer trust Caiden, my mate?

My wolf senses a change in the bond. I thought it was the distance put between us, or even the lack of communication.

I should call him. But what do I say? Nothing.

Felix decides to drive through the night, so I take advantage of the silence and try to sleep. Every time I wake up, Dylan sits, scowling in the front passenger seat.

I continue to doze throughout the morning in an attempt to tune out the snide remarks Felix and Dylan continue to exchange.

In the state between sleep and alertness, my wolf whines as she thinks of Caiden.

I fall asleep missing him.

The black wings of a bat soar in the sky, and a raven swoops down to land on Caiden's left shoulder. The bat circles overhead, then lands on his right shoulder.

Caiden's red eyes shimmer in the moonlight, and his lips turn up to expose razor-sharp teeth. Fresh blood drips from them, and Caiden smirks and stares—as if he were looking directly at me.

I gasp for air and claw at my throat.

Dylan's voice slams against my mental barrier. "Lux!"

My eyes flash open, but I don't see anything except images from the awful dream.

Someone slaps me across the face.

Felix's voice fills the air between my snarls. "Calm her down. She's going to cause a damn accident!"

The person I assume is Dylan grabs my wrists and holds them tight to calm my violent spasms.

"Hey, calm down," Dylan coos and presses his forehead against mine.

His touch pulls me from the dark thoughts that threatened to consume me. I stop fighting against his hold and collapse into the backseat.

"Do you want to talk about it?" Dylan sends through the mindlink, his eyes wide with worry.

I curl up and hug my knees. "No."

I don't ever want to think of that dream, though I know I'll never stop thinking of it.

A shiver runs through my body, and I squeeze my legs tighter against my chest.

It wasn't real. It was only a dream. That wasn't Caiden.

But when I close my eyes, his haunting smile and his red eyes are all I see, staring back at me, laughing.

I lie awake for the rest of the drive. Dylan watches me for a while, but then finally falls asleep. Felix glances at me through the rearview mirror every now and again, but thankfully doesn't say anything.

When we enter Chicago's city limits, I pull out my phone to get directions to Katie's new place.

Renelle on the River is so posh! Her text says.

My thumb brushes across Caiden's picture, and my bottom lip quivers.

He's okay. It was just a dream. I'll call him later.

Felix circles the block before parking, and I admire the beautiful eighteen-story condominium complex. The eeriness of the dream has passed, and I want nothing more than to forget about it. No one has spoken since that incident except to give the address.

Dylan breaks the unnerving silence. "So how do you know this person?"

I tilt my head. "Katie?"

He glares at me and nods.

I look up into the late afternoon sky and smile as the warm breeze blows across my cheeks.

"Let's see... After you and I were kicked out of our pack, you pawned me off on that group of rogues—which, luckily, was Cody. I then met and got mixed up with Felix."

I cast dagger eyes at Felix.

Felix winks.

Clearing my throat, I continue, "After leaving Felix, the first time, I came to Chicago."

"That didn't answer the question." Dylan grimaces.

"Katie posted a 'roommate wanted' ad in the paper." I shrug.

Dylan's expression goes blank and he rubs the back of his neck. "You were roommates?"

"Yup." I breeze past him and enter the apartment building.

"Why didn't you just say that in the first place?" he mumbles under his breath as we wait for the elevator.

When we arrive at her door, I turn to Dylan and Felix, "Don't say anything, okay? Let me do the talking."

They roll their eyes but nod in agreement.

Katie opens the door on the third knock, and her eyes land on Dylan.

"Well, hello handsome." She leans against the doorframe, extending her right arm up the wall.

Dylan's cheeks flush.

"Hi, Katie," I say, pulling her attention from Dylan.

"Oh hey, Cinda! You didn't tell me you were traveling with Mr. Yummy."

"Katie, this is Dylan." I motion with my hands. "Dylan, this is Katie."

"Dylan? Like, the Dylan?" Katie's eyes widen.

"Yes," I mumble. Of course, I told her about the boy that broke my heart one night when we had a bonding moment.

"Oh, so you're back together?" she asks.

"No!" Dylan and I say in unison.

"So, you're single?" Katie says in her come-hither voice as she strolls toward Dylan. She offers her hand. "Hi."

Dylan smirks and kisses her hand like a perfect gentleman.

"We don't have time for this nonsense." Felix walks up behind us.

Katie's eyes fix on Felix and then glances at me. "So, is this one yours?"

I roll my eyes and shake my head. "No."

Felix's laugh is deep and rich. It warms my wolf and makes her yearn for our mate.

"Mmm. This will be a fun night." Katie squeals and winks at them both. "Spenser will be so jealous!"

"Wait, what?" My heart skips a beat at the mention of Spenser.

Katie blows a kiss in the air as she turns into her apartment.

I tug her arm and whisper in her ear, "Katie, he doesn't have to know."

"Who's Spenser?" Dylan asks.

Katie spins around to face me and asks, "How's he not going to know? He's—"

"I'm what?" A man's voice echoes from inside the apartment.

Shit. My heart pounds against my chest.

"Guess who's here," Katie says, swinging the door wide to reveal a tall man standing next to the kitchen table. *Spenser.*

He's holding a pot of spaghetti, which slips in his grasp when our eyes meet. A hot flush spreads through my body, and his cheeks burn crimson.

"Hey, Spens, you remember my old roomie, right?" Katie says.

She damn well knows he remembers me.

I bite back a growl that threatens to escape. *If I wasn't in mixed company right now...*

Dylan places a hand on my shoulder.

"Lux, you okay?" he asks through the mindlink.

"Yeah," I send back.

"Fooled me," he says and squeezes my shoulder. "Is he a problem?"

"No." He's not a threat to anyone. *Except my heart.*

After I met Katie, Spenser and I quickly became inseparable. I was falling in love with him, and the situation freaked me out because he's human and I'm not. I didn't know how to handle everything, so it didn't end well.

Spenser's gaze moves from mine to behind me. I follow his stare to Dylan, specifically his hand resting on my shoulder.

I roll my shoulder, unsuccessfully trying to shake off Dylan's unwanted touch.

"Dylan, you can let go now," I send through the mindlink and motion toward his hand.

A woman walks out of the kitchen, holding a stack of plates, and she smiles at Spenser. "Katie, has your friend arrived?"

Katie motions for us to come into the apartment. "We were just getting ready to eat, come and join us. This is my brother, Spenser. Spenser, these are Cinda's friends, Dylan and Felix."

Spenser asks, "Friends?"

"Well, no not really," Dylan says. "Lux and I are old friends, but we don't claim to be friends with him." He motions over his shoulder toward Felix, and I laugh. Surprisingly, so does Felix.

Katie pulls out a chair at the table and slides into it. "If you're not friends, what are you doing together?"

"Traveling alone is such a lonely road," Felix says in a poetic rhythm. "Don't you agree?"

"Whatever." I roll my eyes and pick a seat next to Katie.

I've learned to embrace the solitude.

I extend my hand out to the woman sitting next to Spenser. "Hi, I'm Lucinda."

Spenser drops his napkin. "Since when do you go by Lucinda?"

"She goes by many names," Felix whispers across the table. "It changes with her mood."

I glare at him, but Dylan and Katie laugh.

"See, that's why we're not friends," I say.

"Hi, Lucinda, it's nice to meet you. I'm Thea."

Spenser holds her hand under the table, and I smile. It warms my heart to know he found someone that makes him happy.

My wolf yearns for the tender touch of my bergamot-scented mate. *Soon,* I tell her. *Soon.*

Spenser asks between mouthfuls of pasta, "How long are you staying?"

"Not long." I take a bite of a big meatball.

"A day, two max," Dylan says.

"Do you need somewhere to stay?" Katie flutters her eyelashes at Dylan. "You can stay here."

"Thanks, but we have a place downtown," Dylan says.

My head snaps up, and my eyebrows knit together. Through the mindlink, I say, "We haven't made reservations."

"Not yet. But I'm not staying here," he says and gives me a look from across the table.

I smirk, knowing why he doesn't want to stay here.

After our bond broke, he was ashamed of how he acted toward me and women in general. He made a few resolutions, and so far, he has kept to them.

"I'm proud of you," I say through the mindlink and then focus on finishing my spaghetti.

When I'm done eating, I look up from my plate, and my eyes meet Spenser's questioning look. From time to time, I often wondered if I could have lived a normal life with him.

Will I ever live a normal life?

Spenser wouldn't let me leave, so I told him why I had to

go—I told him my secret. I showed him my wolf. His reaction wasn't what I was expecting. I hoped he would be frightened or at the very least disgusted. Instead, he accepted me. He loved me that much.

But I couldn't do that to him. I cared too much for him to bring him into my world.

After a few run-ins with the surrounding pack members venturing into neutral territory, I worried for his life.

Spenser is a tough guy, but he'd never survive a fight against a wolf.

When he asked me if I would leave my world behind and join his, I explained that we have a certain code about us that we can't ignore—it's built in. And then he asked if I could try to be normal. I acted insulted, but I wasn't, not really. I explained to him it didn't work like that. He was understanding of everything, which made leaving that much harder.

He deserved better than me.

I would never be able to leave my world behind. My children will be shifters, and so would their children... and so on down the line.

Oh shit! Will they be shifters, or will I have little bloodsuckers? Is one dominant over the other? Or will they be a mixed breed of shifting bloodsuckers?

My pulse quickens, and I play with my napkin to steady my shaking hands.

"What?! You're getting married?" Katie's voice fills the room, startling me from my dark thoughts.

My gaze darts to her and then to Dylan.

"Congratulations!" Thea says.

"Yeah, thank you," I say.

My cheeks flush as I look around the table. Dylan is smirking, Katie's eyes are wide with excitement, Felix yawns while he taps his fingernails on the table, Thea is smiling, and Spenser stares at his plate of half-eaten spaghetti in front of him.

Wiggling her eyebrows Katie says, "Start talking, sister."

"His name is Caiden." As his name rolls off my tongue, a pain shoots through my heart. *I miss him.*

"Where did you meet?" Katie asks.

"He's the brother of a good friend," I say. After the words leave my mouth, my eyes lock with Katie, and we both look to Spenser. He's stabbing a meatball with his fork, over and over again.

"This calls for a toast," Thea says as she stands from the table and heads into the kitchen.

She reminds me of Mia. I miss her too. I'll call her and Caiden later, I need to hear their voices.

"When did you meet?" Spenser's deep voice makes my pulse jump. When he lifts his head, his eyes narrow and penetrate my soul.

"A few months ago." My voice quivers under his dark scowl.

"Wow. That's fast." Katie whistles.

"Well, we're not actually getting married until summer," I say.

Thankfully, Thea walks back into the room with a bottle of champagne and a handful of glass flutes.

After the celebratory toast, I excuse myself for a minute and step out onto the balcony. The cool night air blows across my face and calms my wolf.

I pull out my phone and text Caiden.

Me: *Wish you were here. Missing you like crazy!*

Caiden: *Wish you were home.*

Caiden: *Where are you?*

Me: *I'll call later.*

Caiden: *Good. Need to hear your voice.*

I send Mia a quick text too.

Me: *Miss you!*

Mia: *Miss my BFF too! Hurry home.*

"Is he like you?" Spenser's voice causes me to jump. *Wow. Did I really just let him sneak up on me? What the hell?*

Turning around to face Spenser, I say, "Yes, he's my mate."

Spenser nods, then his eyes narrow. "I thought you said your mate rejected you?"

I bite my lip. "Yeah, about that—"

"You lied to me? Why? Was any of it true?" He runs his hands through his short dark hair.

"No, I didn't lie. At the time, it is what I thought was the truth. And yes, all of it was true." I take a step closer to him. "I thought Dylan was my mate and that he rejected me."

I follow Spenser's gaze through the glass window. Our eyes land on Dylan who's clearing the table.

"Yeah, him," I say. "But it turns out he wasn't my real mate. Caiden is."

"How can you be sure?" Spenser asks. "If you were wrong about Dylan, how do you know this Caiden guy is the real deal?"

My heart twists like someone is ringing it out like a wet towel. My wolf whimpers at the thought of Caiden not being my mate.

"It's hard to explain, but I just know. He's the real deal." I look over the balcony at the evening sky.

Spenser closes the distance between us and moves my hair off my neck. His fingertips trace my mark and he asks, "Did he do this to you?"

I push his hand away and cover the mark with my hair. "Yes, and I gave him one."

"What is it?" he asks.

"It's the mark of mates."

"Hey, Cinda." Katie's voice echoes through the open door. "Time to get ready."

"Ready for what?" I ask.

"The club. You're not wearing that," she says and closes the door as she walks away.

Spenser cocks an eyebrow. "Club?"

"Yeah, it's a long story."

He looks over his shoulder again at Dylan and Felix lounging on the sofa.

"I bet it has something to do with them," he says.

"Kinda."

His smirk brings out the dimple on his right cheek. "Probably something I don't want to know about?"

"Exactly." My lips curve into a smile, but I can feel it doesn't reach my eyes. My stomach tightens into knots. This is dangerous ground. I'm walking a tightrope between friends and flirting.

Or am I just imagining it? Nope. That mischievous look in his eyes—

I need to put a stop to this before it goes any further.

I stick out my hand. "Friends?"

"Friends." He swats away my hand and pulls me in for a hug.

His strong arms and warm embrace remind me of why I fell in love with him in the first place. But he doesn't have the same bergamot scent I've come to adore. Human scents are bland and not all that appealing.

The scent of cumin and freshly cut grass drifts through the air, and Dylan clears his throat. "I don't mean to break up whatever this is, but Lux we really need to get going."

"I know." I turn my head toward Dylan, then back to Spencer. "It was good seeing you, Spens. I wish you all the best life has to offer."

I step out of Spenser's embrace.

Dylan says through the mindlink, "We won't tell Caiden about this."

My heart sinks. *What's another lie? I'm the one Caiden shouldn't trust. Does he know that?*

CHAPTER 20

CAIDEN

I DIG my sharp claws into the pillow and feathers littering the bed. The light scent of mint and honey drifts through the air.

The only remaining item with Lucinda's scent is now destroyed. I grab a handful of the feathers and inhale her luscious scent. My head swirls, and my wolf whines for our mate to return.

A light knock on my bedroom door pulls me from my daydream, and I quickly shove all the feathers under the covers.

"Caiden, are you okay?" Mia's soft voice drifts into the room as she cracks open the door.

"I'm fine. Come on in," I send through the mindlink, too exhausted to talk. After the encounter with Garcia, the witch, and Elder Charles, I headed for the woods to let off steam. The run through the forest as my wolf was successful in keeping the beast at bay.

When Mia enters, I turn my head in her direction but remain lounging on the bed.

"Are you sure you're okay?" she asks.

"Yes."

"When you left and didn't come home, I thought..."

"I'm home now."

"When I couldn't reach you through the mindlink yesterday—"

"I'm sorry, I didn't mean to worry you. I just needed time to myself."

"Fair enough. But we need to talk."

"There's nothing to talk about." I close my eyes and place my hands over my chest. The bed dips slightly when she sits next to me.

"Caiden, I know what you're thinking."

"I doubt you do."

"You can't believe."

"Honestly, I don't know what to believe anymore." I let out a deep sigh and open my eyes, staring into Mia's face. Dark circles sag under her eyes and worry lines cover her forehead. "All I know is Lucinda is my Fated Mate, and by choice, she's not by my side."

"You don't know that."

"You're right. I don't know anything. I don't know where she is or what she's doing because she won't tell me." The last words stick in my throat. "She won't even answer her damn phone!"

"Caiden."

"Stop!" I prop myself up, resting on my left elbow, and lean closer to Mia. "With or without Lucinda, I have to think about the safety of this pack. I am their Alpha, and their safety is my number one priority right now."

I fall back into a resting position on the bed. I pushed myself too hard last night, but I'll never admit that to Mia. All night I struggled to retain control over my wolf, but I did. *I think.*

"Okay, and what about their safety? At the current

moment, what do you have to protect them from?"

"If half of what Garcia said is true, then—"

"About Garcia—you can't kill him."

I scowl and pinch the bridge of my nose.

"Caiden, you can't!"

"What would you have me do? I'll be a laughing stock."

"Since when do you care what other people think? You didn't care what the pack said when you announced Dylan was your Beta."

"That was different," I mutter. "You don't understand."

"Understand what?"

"Garcia attacked me!"

"So, what of it? Sabrina's cousin lunged for you last year, and Lucinda took him down. You barely punished him."

"That was a pack member, not a rival pack warrior. And Elder Charles is right, these are dangerous times. I need to think about the safety of this pack. If word gets around that he attempted to kill the Blood Moone Alpha and lived…"

"You're not that type of Alpha."

"Maybe I should be!" I growl.

Mia's eyes widen, and she backs away, sliding off the bed.

"Calm down, okay. I didn't—"

"You didn't what?" I kneel and stalk across the bed, my eyes never leaving Mia's.

Calm down. Breathe.

Mia's shadowy form wavers a few feet from me. Red outlines her silhouette. The beast is vying for control.

NO!

I'm exhausted, but I won't let the beast hurt my sister. Mia must sense my inner struggle for control because she slowly backs toward the door.

"Leave," I call out between snarls. Through the mindlink, I add, "And lock the door behind you."

Her eyes glisten with wetness, and a tear runs down her

cheek. She scurries out of the room and whispers, "Oh, Caiden."

Now she understands the extent of control the beast has over me.

My claws pierce through the mattress. A throaty croak causes me to flip around and face the open window. The quick movement knocks a stray feather into the air, and the scent of mint and honey calms my rapid heartbeat. Another croak and the flapping of wings snap me out of my current daze.

A raven is perched on my windowsill, his beady eyes watching me with an uncanny stare. I shake my head to clear the fogginess of the beast.

That was too close.

With another croak, the raven takes flight and disappears into the midmorning sky.

Rubbing the back of my neck, I climb off the bed and head downstairs. I want more of that herbal tea from either Leah or Sabrina. I need to relax.

When I round the corner into the kitchen, two people stand silhouetted together in the mudroom. My nose twitches as the familiar scents register—leather and tobacco, and apple, rose, and vanilla. Their forms startle as I cross through the kitchen and the back door slams closed.

Gavin enters the kitchen. "Hey, Caiden, we should talk."

My eyes roam his body from head to toe. *What was he doing with Leah? What were they talking about in secret?*

"Later," I say. I'm in no mood to talk right now. Brushing past him, I reach for the canister of tea Sabrina left.

"What's that?" Gavin steps closer to me, eyeing the loose leaf blend with curiosity.

"An herbal tea mix. It helps me relax." I turn my back to reach for a mug and switch on a pot of water to boil.

"Cool. What's in it?"

I shrug and hand him the open pouch. He sniffs the contents.

"Where did you get this?" he asks.

"Sabrina."

Gavin takes another whiff of the contents and puts the lid back on just as Sabrina and Nyla enter the kitchen.

"I'll catch ya later," Gavin says, and I nod.

Sabrina's gaze follows Gavin as he leaves the room.

Nyla pulls out a chair, scraping the legs across the floor, and sits down.

"Pour an extra mug, please," she says.

Sabrina's silky voice drifts through the air. "Caiden, do you have a moment?"

I nod and pour the steaming water into two mugs. Sabrina takes one of the mugs and places it in front of Nyla. I take the other and lean against the counter.

"What's on your mind?" I ask.

"The safety of this pack." Sabrina sits next to Nyla.

"And?" I sip the hot liquid. The tea burns as it coats my throat, but I like the sensation.

"Mia and Leah have returned, so can we talk about The Brotherhood returning to finish the protective wards?"

Another sip sets my throat on fire as it slides down. I take my time, drinking the entire mug. When I'm done, I set it down and return my attention to Sabrina and Nyla.

"Tell me more about these protective wards they want to put up. Who do they protect, and what do they protect us from?"

"The wards will protect anyone within the enclosed space," Nyla says.

I arch an eyebrow. "So why the Pack House? Why not put them up to enclose the entire territory?"

Nyla dismisses me with the wave of her hand and takes a sip of her tea.

"That would be too time-consuming," Sabrina says. "At least, that's my understanding."

"You still haven't answered my questions."

"Come sit down and I will," Nyla says, and Sabrina kicks out a chair from under the table.

Once I'm seated, Nyla speaks. "Protective wards are stronger in close proximity. Your territory is much too large to protect with wards."

I nod. "So, why the Pack House?"

"To protect you, our Alpha, of course," Sabrina says.

"And exactly what are they protecting me from?"

Nyla and Sabrina exchange a look, and my biceps flex. *What do they know that they're not sharing?*

Sabrina clears her throat. "They will protect you from anyone—"

"Anything," Nyla says.

Sabrina nods. "Anything that means you harm."

"So, The Brotherhood will put up these protective wards around the Pack House. And then I will be magically protected from anything that wants to hurt me?"

"Yes. But only when you're within the walls of the Pack House," Sabrina says.

"Which isn't often."

"That's why I also made you this." Nyla lays a chain with a circular gold pendant hanging from it on the table.

"What's that?" I ask.

"The Elders are concerned about assassins trying to kill you. They heard of Garcia's attack—"

My body tenses and I crack my knuckles. *Of course they have. I told Mia this would happen.*

"Elder Charles asked if I could protect you in some way," Nyla says. "And if you won't stay within the walls of the Pack House that will be protected by the wards, then all I can do is give you a charmed talisman to wear."

"This is going to protect me?" I pick up the flat piece of gold and run my fingertips over the strange markings.

Sabrina rests her hand on top of my fingers. "What could it hurt? Even if you're skeptical, it will make the Elders happy."

"And this will do the same thing as the wards, protect me from anything that wants to harm me?"

Nyla's head bows with a slight nod.

"Then why do I need the wards around the Pack House?" As soon as I say it, I bite my lip. *Stupid question. The wards will protect Mia and Gavin, Leah, and Lucinda and Dylan—if they ever return.* "Never mind."

I pick up the protective talisman and slip the chain over my head, then slide the flat pendant under my shirt, where it sits flat against my chest.

"Thanks," I say to Nyla.

Mia pops her head into the kitchen. "Hey, Caiden, can I see you for a minute?"

"Sure, be right there." I stand.

"Real quick," Sabrina says. "Getting back to the question of the wards—"

"Yes, they can finish, that's fine. Just make sure they stay out of my way."

Sabrina's lips curve into a wide grin. "I'll make sure of it. Thanks, Caiden."

I nod and leave to find Mia.

Her scent leads me into the family room, where she sits sprawled out on the couch.

"What's up?" I ask.

"Oh, nothing. I thought I'd save you from those two." Mia's warm eyes glow in the afternoon sun.

"I see. Thanks." I look around the empty family room. "Have you seen Leah?"

"No, why?"

"I haven't had a chance to catch up with her since you two returned from your errand. How did it go?"

Mia smiles, grabs my hand, and pulls me out the front door.

"Our trip was successful," Mia says through the mindlink as we walk down the front porch. "And that book is amaze—"

We turn the corner of the house and the gazebo comes into full view. Two shadows sit side by side, whispering to each other. Lucinda and Dylan flash into my memory. Not too long ago, I saw them in a similar situation.

This time it's Gavin and Leah. *Again?*

I glance at Mia, and she's white as a marshmallow. I fold her arm under mine and walk with purpose toward the gazebo.

My power radiates over the distance, and I know the instant that Gavin and Leah become aware of my presence. They jump apart, and their heads spin around until they meet my scrutinizing stare.

Mia stumbles, and I steady her balance. She tilts her head and stutters. "Actually, I'm tired. I'm going to go lay down."

I divert our direction and head to the back of the house, guiding Mia to my room, where she curls up on my bed.

"Caiden," she reaches for my hand. "What do you think Gavin and Leah were discussing?"

The mattress dips under my weight as I sit next to Mia. "I'm not sure."

"They looked close, almost intimate." She blinks back tears and pulls a blanket closer to her chest.

"Gavin adores you, you have nothing to worry about. He's probably just finding out what's transpired since he left."

"I hope you're right."

I better be right. I'll deal with Gavin and Leah later. And hopefully, the beast won't come out. That won't be good for anyone.

CHAPTER 21

LUCINDA

FELIX DRIVES us to Chateau de Paris and pulls up to the VIP valet parking. Katie rolls down the backseat window and waves to the attendant, who quickly opens our car doors and takes the keys from Felix.

Dylan's forehead furrows. "How do you know this place?"

Felix says, "Some things are best left unknown."

Katie winks at Felix and smirks.

I tell Dylan through the mindlink, "She writes a column for a local magazine about the Who's Who of the Chicago Night Scene. All of the local bars and nightclubs invite her and give her their VIP status in hopes of swaying her opinion."

"Finally, something that makes sense tonight," he mutters under his breath. He gives me a sideways glance, and his gaze roams up and down, causing a slight heat to rise up my neck.

Did he just check me out?

I look down at the black dress Katie gave me to wear. It has a deep plunge V-neck with a snug fit body and it hits me mid-thigh. My mother's necklace sits perfectly between my breasts against my bare chest.

Oh god! He was checking out my cleavage!

He nods and motions for me to exit the car and follow Felix and Katie down the red carpet.

As we near the entrance, I slow my pace to let Dylan step in front of me. He flashes his ID to the bouncer and steps through the doorway.

Maybe it was my imagination.

After I hand my ID to the bouncer, I tug at the hem of my dress. *I hate dresses.*

When the bouncer's gaze drift to my cleavage too, I hold back a snarl from my wolf—she will tolerate it from Dylan, but not from this stranger.

Dylan snatches my ID from the bouncer's hand and pulls me through the entryway.

"You need to calm down, Lux," he says. I can barely hear him over the thumping of the music.

"What?" I say through the mindlink.

"Felix went to find his contact," Dylan says through the mindlink.

"So, what are we supposed to do?"

He shrugs. "Have fun?"

Katie returns from somewhere with her hands full of colorful drinks.

"I'm not drinking that," I say.

"What? I can't hear you, the music's too loud." She hands me and Dylan each a highball glass full of a blue liquid. "Follow me."

She waves her hand and walks toward the rear of the club.

I sniff the electric-blue liquid; it smells like a sweet combination of strawberry, lemon, and lime.

"What is this?" Dylan asks when we stop at an empty high-top bar table.

"It's the Smurf." Katie sips on her drink before tossing her head back.

My phone vibrates in my purse, and I pull it out to see a missed call. *Caiden.* I place my drink on the table and slide it over to Dylan. He seems to be enjoying his Smurf.

I text Caiden.

Me: *Hey. We're playing phone tag tonight. Can't talk now. I'll call later.*

Caiden: *What are you doing?*

Me: *Following a lead.*

Caiden: *Where are you?*

Me: *Chicago.*

Caiden: *I know.*

Me: *How?*

Caiden: *Jackson called.*

Me: *If U knew, why did U ask?*

Caiden: *Where are you right NOW?*

I glance to Dylan. He's enjoying yet another blue whatever drink. I kick him under the table.

His head jerks in my direction. "What the hell?"

I lean in and send through the mindlink, "Caiden wants to know where we are."

"Oh. Tell him Chicago." Dylan throws back another drink.

"He knows that. Jackson called," I say.

Dylan slams his glass down on the table and yells. "Shit."

"I know."

"What's the matter?" Katie asks.

"Nothing." I throw her a small smile.

"Her fiancé wants to know where she is," Dylan says with a slight slur.

Asshole.

"And you don't want him to know?" Katie asks. My eyes meet hers; she doesn't miss anything. "Why not tell him you're at the CDP?"

"What's that?" I ask.

"It sounds like an airport code," Dylan says.

"The abbreviation for this place, Chateau de Paris." Her lips turn up into a wickedly beautiful grin.

My phone vibrates again.

Caiden: ???

Me: *CDP. Gotta power down. Love you.*

I slide my phone back in my purse, but I can't help the burning sensation rising from the pit of my stomach. I reach for a blue drink sitting on the table, and I down the sweet liquid in one motion.

Katie claps her hands together and squeals, "Now it's a party!"

She places another glass on the table in front of me, and I reach for it. *One more won't hurt, right?*

The next thing I know, the three of us are ordering another round with more than a dozen empty glasses on the table.

I glance around and spot Felix walking across the upper tier, following a few steps behind a burly man.

"He must've found his contact," I say to Dylan and motion up with my head.

"Good. I think it's almost time to leave this place," he says.

"Why? Aren't you having fun?"

"It's not that," he says.

"Then what is it?" I glare at him as his eyes roam my body.

"He totally wants you," Katie says.

"What? No!" Dylan says in a defensive tone.

I lean back in my chair and cross my arms over my chest.

He leans across the table and pulls me toward him to speak directly in my ear. "There are too many guys in here that are checking you out."

I start laughing. "Seriously?"

He nods.

"Whatever." *Maybe he wasn't checking me out earlier.*

"Let's dance!" Katie pulls me out of my chair and leads me to the dance floor.

I look over my shoulder, and Dylan is reluctantly following with his hands stuffed in his pant pockets.

Katie starts to grind on Dylan as soon as he catches up to us. She tries to put him between us, but I refuse to grind on him. *That would be crossing some type of line, right?*

But Katie comes and goes. As soon as the music changes beat, she turns to dance with someone else.

Dylan turns to me just as the tempo slows down. He holds out his hand, and I take it.

What am I doing?

He closes the distance between us, puts his right hand around my waist, and holds my hand in his left near our shoulders. Our hips sway together to the slow beat. My heart pounds, drowning out the lyrics.

Dylan asks, "So, who's Spencer?"

I roll my eyes. "I told you, he's Katie's brother."

"Right. I mean who is he to you?"

"A friend."

"I'm calling bullshit on that one."

My head snaps to meet Dylan's stare, and I squint. "Are you jealous?"

"No. I have nothing to be jealous of."

"Then why does it matter to you?"

"I'm just looking out for my Alpha's property," Dylan says with a heated look.

"Your Alpha's property?" My nostrils flare and my hands clench. "I am no one's property."

Turning on my heels, I storm off the dance floor.

"Lux, wait," he calls behind me, but I keep walking.

I stop as I reach the edge of the dance floor. A strong presence in the crowd ruffles and agitates my wolf. I glance over my shoulder, and Dylan's face is pale—he senses it too.

"I think it's time to leave," Dylan sends through the mindlink.

I nod. But when I turn back around, a man stands in my path. I don't know who he is, but he's emitting the strongest wave of power I've ever felt. It ripples through the air and temporarily immobilizes me.

As he walks toward me, my wolf fights against his demand for submission. His deep, dark brooding eyes claim my attention.

He extends a hand to me. "Would you care to dance?"

"Actually, we were just leaving," I say.

He cocks an eyebrow and looks to my side. "We?"

"Yes. I'm here with someone."

"Yes, of course you are."

I follow his stare over my shoulder.

Dylan stands frozen, his forehead pulled taut and his lips fixed in a tight grimace. Power radiates from him, circling around him in a whirlwind.

"What are you doing to him?" I ask.

"I'm not doing anything, but he refuses to play nice," the guy says in a thick Norwegian accent.

"Well, if you'll excuse me—"

"I wasn't done speaking with you," he says, and his hands curve around my waist.

Before I'm able to step away, he pulls me close to his body.

A growl slips out. "I'm sorry but I'm already taken."

"I know you are, my dear. You reek of it." He brushes my hair off my shoulder and exposes the mark on my neck. "Impressive. And to think he could make such a distinctive mark."

I glance over my shoulder to Dylan. "Oh, he's not my mate."

Goose bumps prickle my exposed skin, and my arm

muscles twitch. I try to shrug off the strange man's chilling touch, but a flash of playfulness crosses his eyes.

He looks up to the balcony where we last saw Felix. "Is your mate here?"

"No, but you'd be wise not to provoke him," I say.

"Provoke who? Your mate or the other ones you travel with?" His lips curve into a deeply seductive grin. When his eyes meet mine, his once blue eyes are nothing more than large pieces of black coal.

"Take your pick. Both are strong and powerful and won't take nicely to—"

"I can be very persuasive." His eyes narrow and he scowls. "Let's dance."

He grabs my hand and pulls me onto the dance floor. Two other men step out of the shadows and form a protective barrier around us. They block Dylan from my view and close off any hope of an escape path.

Gritting my teeth, I give him the deadliest stare I can conjure.

He smirks.

Shit.

He wraps his arm around my waist and pulls me close. My breasts are snug against his hard chest, and he nuzzles into my neck. My mark burns on my neck and pulses under my skin.

"You smell wonderful." His warm breath tickles my skin, and my heartbeat quickens. "Is that a Moone I smell?"

I flinch and pull away, but he keeps a firm grip on my waist.

"Miss Raven, you travel with an interesting mix of company. I can only imagine you are the queen among the wolves. But why do you travel so far from your mate?"

"That doesn't concern you."

How you know my name, concerns me.

"Many things concern me." He clears his throat. "How is the Blood Moone pack fairing these days? I worried they would dwindle away after that harsh attack a few years ago."

"They are stronger than ever."

"If they have you, I don't doubt that."

I pull my hand from his clammy palm. "You don't even know me."

White tips of his fangs peek through his lips, and flames dance behind his darkening blue eyes. "You're mistaken. I know more about you than you probably do yourself. The question is, do you know who I am?"

"Who are you?" I ask.

He smiles, followed by a deep and throaty laugh. "It doesn't matter who I am. What matters is who you are and what you will do when the time comes."

"How do you know who I am?" I try to pull away from him, but his iron grip keeps me close. "And what do you mean when the time comes?"

"I know many things."

"Like what?"

"Miss Raven, you travel down a dangerous road, and at the end, you'll come to a narrow path and must make a choice. Which road will you choose to follow?"

"What are you talking about?"

I know our journey is dangerous, but a path and a choice, what?

"Do you trust your companions?"

I bite my lips. *Do I trust Dylan and Felix? Both of them have hurt me in the past, and both have lied and betrayed me on several occasions. Do I trust them now?*

"Yes, I do."

"Noble, but foolish."

"Whatever." I struggle against his tight grip. "I think we're done here."

"I'll say when we're done," he says in a deep, commanding tone and pulls me closer so our noses touch.

I clear my throat. "This is a free zone, you have no—"

His laugh erupts from deep in his chest and startles me. It transforms his face, highlighting laugh lines near his eyes and mouth, which accentuate his glossy red lips.

My heart flutters and blood races through my body.

"I have authority over all," he says in a sensual tone, and his tongue glides over his lips.

"Who are you?" I whisper to myself, a rhetorical question.

He leans in and his front teeth nibble on my earlobe. Between breaths, he asks, "Do you trust your mate?"

I shake my head to fight the building sensation...he is a master at seduction. I fight to free my ear from his mouth. "Of course."

I do trust Caiden with my life. But lately, when I talk to him, he seems distant, and I've been lying to him. I tell myself it's for his own protection, but if I fully trust him, why do I lie?

Felix's smooth English accent sings in my ears as it carries over the music from behind me. "Lucifer, it's nice of you to keep Lucinda company, but we must be on our way now."

The two goons standing protectively around us, step forward and block Felix's approach.

"Lucifer?" I ask.

Chills race through my body as I stare into the dark eyes of the man in front of me. *Should that name ring a bell?*

"It was a pleasure to finally make your acquaintance, Miss Raven." He gives a slight nod to the goons, and they let Felix through, then he releases me and takes a step away, dipping his chest with a bow. Lifting his head, he turns his attention to Felix, who stands behind me. "Felix Noir, always a pleasure."

Felix steps in front of me in a protective stance. A small growl slips through his clenched jaw.

Lucifer asks, "How is your father?"

Felix wrings his hands together behind his back. "Dead. But I'm sure you already knew that."

"Now that you mention it, I do believe I heard that heart-breaking story. I was saddened by the news, my condolences to you and your family."

"I'm sure you were just heartbroken over it," Felix mutters.

"I was ill with sadness, as I always am when a good friend dies."

Felix says something under his breath in another language that I don't recognize. Lucifer's eyes widen and his lips turn into a devilish smirk. He flashes his canines, and I glance at Dylan who stands on the outskirts of this little party, still unable to penetrate the barrier Lucifer somehow put up around him.

"We should go." I touch Felix's shoulder.

He nods and reaches up to take my hand.

Lucifer steps aside to allow us to pass. As I cross by him, he whispers, "Until we next meet."

Dylan files in behind me as we near him, and Felix leads us straight to the exit. Before leaving, I give a cursory look around the place for Katie, but she's nowhere to be seen.

I pull out my phone and send her a quick text.

Me: *Where are you?*

Katie: *I met someone.*

Me: *K. We gotta go.*

Katie: *Don't wait for me.*

Me: *Be safe.*

Katie: *Always!*

Katie: *Don't be a stranger.*

I move close to Felix. "Who was that guy?"

"Lucifer Vârcolac," Felix says.

"You say that like it should mean something," Dylan says.

Felix twists to look over his shoulder. "At one point in time, it did mean something,"

Dylan and I follow his gaze to the roof. Lucifer and his men stand on the ledge, watching us. The way the moonlight casts its shadow, they remind me of gargoyle statues sitting atop buildings for protection.

"Come on, we'll talk more in the car," Felix says.

I don't argue. I'll feel better when we're safely back in the car too, though I know the little metal box won't protect us from the likes of Lucifer or his men if they wanted to harm us.

"Is he a threat?" Dylan asks once all car doors close.

"He's an annoyance more than anything these days," Felix says. He turns the key, and the engine rumbles, then settles into a steady purr.

"He was once someone of importance?" I ask.

Felix sits up straighter and adjusts his seat. "Yes."

"He's powerful," Dylan says.

"You have no idea." Felix grips the steering wheel so hard his knuckles turn white.

"So, who is he?" I ask. "And don't tell me his name again because it doesn't mean anything to me."

Felix relaxes his grip on the steering wheel and melts into his leather seat. "He's the Prince of Wolves."

I glance at Dylan in the backseat—his eyes are as wide as mine—and then I return my gaze back to Felix.

Dylan and I say in unison, "Who?"

CHAPTER 22

CAIDEN

M ia's cinnamon and honey scent drifts through the air, swirling around me. She slept peacefully in my bed while I battled with my inner beast for control. I stand at my window, gazing out at the forest.

Mia stands from the bed and crosses the room toward me. "What's wrong?"

My chest tightens and my right eye twitches. I send through the mindlink, "Please leave me alone."

"No." Her hand touches my shoulder, and I let loose a growl.

Mia steps between me and my sanctuary, the only thing currently keeping the raging beast in check. I keep my gaze fixed on the forest just outside my window. Only a thin piece of glass separates me from it. I could jump through the window of my bedroom...

"What happened while I was sleeping?" Mia asks.

My fists clench, and I divert my gaze to her. "Nothing."

"Bullshit!"

I startle and raise my eyebrows. *Did my little sister just curse?*

She crosses her arms over her chest and pops a hip. "Something happened, and I want to know what. Stop trying to protect me. If it's about Gavin—"

"It's not about Gavin."

She relaxes her tense posture and exhales a long sigh. I return my gaze to just beyond Mia.

The haunting stillness of the forest calls my name. I was waiting until Mia woke to make sure she was okay, but an evening storm threatens and dark thunderheads roll across the black sky. My wolf grows restless.

"Caiden." Mia grabs my hand, and my attention focuses on her. "What's going on?"

My phone dings, signaling a message. I squeeze Mia's hand and flash a smile. "I'm fine."

I step over to the nightstand and pick up my phone. A message from Lucinda pops up on the screen, and my heart pounds. *Finally.*

Mia sits on the bed next to me as I respond.

My jaw muscles tighten, and my stomach turns sour as I read her response.

"Why does she have to be so stubborn?" I mumble under my breath.

Mia rubs my back until her phone dings with a message. She glances at me before quickly replying. I don't need to ask; I know who it's from.

A knock on the door pulls my attention away from dwelling on Lucinda's stubbornness and secrecy. Plenty of time for that later. All night, every night, dark dreams haunt my sleep...

I open the door and peer at Gavin. He ignores my snarl and says, "Garcia's awake."

As I palm the phone in my hand, a growing tightness pinches at my stomach. I can't think of her now. I need to focus on the task at hand. *Garcia.*

Tossing the phone across the room, it lands on the bed next to Mia. Her eyebrows raise and her chin lifts, but I sidestep Gavin and leave the room before she has a chance to speak. I know what she'll say, and I don't want to argue.

The pack's safety comes first. If Garcia must die to protect the pack, so be it. *I think.*

Mia and Gavin's whispers travel down the hall behind me. I pause at the top of the steps and glance over my shoulder. My heart eases when I see Mia and Gavin tangled in a lovers embrace.

But then a sharp pain rolls through my gut, and I wince. My wolf longs for his mate. *She'll return soon, I hope.* I understand Lucinda's decision to leave, sorta, but not returning—it's not right! She should be here, with me.

I want to be able to rely on my Luna's advice and guidance at a time like this. But I can't. A growl rumbles from deep in my chest, and my nails pierce the tough skin of my palms.

Grayness starts to encroach on my vision, but then my nose twitches. Mint drifts through the air, and something else. *Honey?*

I take a deep breath and inhale the relaxing scents. When I reach the bottom of the steps, my heart pounds, and I turn into the family room.

"Caiden." Leah's soft voice is barely audible.

I freeze and my heartbeat quickens. *How did she catch me by surprise?*

"Leah?" I scan the room. *Where's that damn mint and honey smell coming from? Is Lucinda home?*

Leah lounges on the couch with her feet resting against the coffee table. Her apple, rose, and vanilla scent floods my senses and overpowers my ability to pinpoint the mint.

"Was anyone else here?" I ask.

"When?"

"Just a few minutes ago?"

"No. I mean, Gavin passed through a while ago, but then he went to find you." She raises a large mug up to her lips. The steam from the warm liquid fogs up her rose-colored glasses on her head.

"What are you drinking?" I ask.

"It's a new herbal tea mix I made. It's a mixture of several different types of mint, calendula, catnip, and rose. And of course, sweetened with a splash of honey." Her fingers wrap around the mug as she walks across the room. Holding the mug out to me, she says, "Here, try a sip."

"Caiden!" Sabrina blurts from behind me.

I glance over my shoulder, and Sabrina stands in the entryway with her hands crossed and a hip popped.

"What do you think you're doing?" she asks.

"Excuse me?"

"The council members have assembled."

"Good." I grit my teeth and stare into Sabrina's lavender eyes. My flesh burns, and my temples throb. The beast wants out.

"Are you coming? Let's not keep the council waiting." She reaches out her hand.

I snarl. "They can wait all damn night."

"You may be the Alpha, but the council will still hold the hearing without you. They're used to you not showing up."

My canines protrude over my lips, and a deep, full-bodied growl erupts from my chest. My prey is ensnared as I stalk across the room, closing the gap between us.

"You should run," I warn through the mindlink.

But Sabrina remains still, a deer caught in headlights, unsure what to do or where to go. Her bottom lip quivers.

"Caiden!" Mia's voice penetrates through the haze, and the veil of fog lifts. I close my eyes and give a slight shake of my head. *What's happening to me?*

Warm skin touches mine. *Cinnamon.*

"You're ice cold!" Mia gasps and begins to rub my hand frantically.

I swat her hands away and say, "I'm fine."

"Caiden, you're not. What's going on?" Mia asks through the mindlink.

"Nothing."

Mia looks over her shoulder and narrows her eyes at Sabrina.

"What did you do?" she asks.

Sabrina's forehead wrinkles. "Me? I didn't do anything."

My eyes meet Sabrina's, and her pale blue irises stand out against her unusually pale skin tone. *Should I apologize?*

Sabrina adjusts her weight and says, "We really should go."

Leah calls from the family room, "I don't think Caiden should go anywhere with you."

Sabrina moves quicker than I expect and lunges for Leah with a battle cry. Leah dodges and steps into the center of the family room, squaring off with Sabrina.

"Stop this nonsense." Mia's high-pitched scream echoes in my ears.

Leah's eyes melt into a deep amethyst, and she holds her hands out in front of her chest, shielding her body.

I divert my attention away from the family room when Gavin comes clambering down the stairs.

"What?" he asks with raised eyebrows.

Mia shakes my shoulder. "Caiden, stop them!"

I shake my head. "Fine."

As I turn around, a loud cracking noise sends Mia, Gavin, and me all kneeling to the floor for cover. When I raise my head, Leah is on the floor under one of the faux support beams from the ceiling.

"Leah!" Gavin and Mia run to her side.

I survey the room for Sabrina. Her dark hair is sprawled on the floor under another part of the beam.

"Sabrina."

When I reach her, her eyes flutter open.

"Mia, Gavin, I'm going to lift the beam. When it's clear, you pull both Leah and Sabrina away."

The faux beam is hollow inside, so it's not as heavy as I thought. And once the girls are pulled to safety, I gently lay the beam back on the ground.

"Are you two okay?" I ask.

"Yes," Leah says.

"I'm fine," Sabrina says.

"What happened?" Mia asks.

Leah and Sabrina look at each other, then they both shrug.

They know more than they're saying. I'll have to speak to them later. I don't like secrets.

"Caiden." Sabrina coughs. "You really should go to the hearing."

I nod, and ask through the mindlink, "Mia, can you look after them?"

"No," she says.

My head snaps to her. "Why not?"

"Because I'm going with you. Gavin will watch over these two."

I grit my teeth and clench my jaw. "Fine."

Mia hands me my cell phone. "In case you want it."

I slip it into my pocket, and my pulse quickens. I'm torn. I want it in case Lucinda calls. But at the same time, it's a burden. The silent dead weight burns a hole in my pocket.

When we reach the steps to the old school house where the council meets to discuss business, Elder Charles glides out from the shadows to greet us.

"Caiden, so good of you to join us."

"Charles." I acknowledge him with a slide dip of my head.

"Mia, I didn't expect to see you here."

"Why not?" Mia's upper lip curls.

"Don't you have cakes to order and flowers to arrange?" Elder Charles scoffs.

I roll my eyes. *Is this what he thinks of my sister?*

"I have more pressing issues at hand—"

"What's more pressing than planning parties?"

"Looking out for my brother's well-being."

"I see. That's very thoughtful of you, but don't worry, your brother is in good hands." Elder Charles glances over his shoulder to the shadows from which he came. Several figures stand huddled in the darkness. *The Brotherhood.*

My wolf stirs within me. He's eager to be released. I hold my breath to control the tearing of my soul.

I am calm and in control, I tell the beast raging inside me.

Mia jerks her head, motioning me inside. She walks by Elder Charles and knocks him in the shoulder.

I smirk. *When did my little sister become so protective?*

She turns over her shoulder and raises her eyebrows. Through the mindlink, she asks, "Are you coming?"

My smirk widens. *My little sister is growing up.*

Just then, my phone dings, and a small bubble of hope soothes my mood. *It's my mate—her voice will calm the beast.*

But when I look at the screen, I snarl.

Jackson.

I wave Mia on and turn back outside, steering clear of Elder Charles and The Brotherhood.

"Hello?" I say.

"Caiden Moone," Jackson's rough voice says through the phone.

"Jackson."

"I'm sorry I wasn't able to stick around at your parents' funeral—"

"What do you want?"

"You don't call, you don't write."

"There's a reason for that."

"You're an Alpha now, so we should keep in touch," Jackson says.

My fists clench. "I'll take your suggestion into consideration."

"Good. And, I'll admit, I was taken by surprise when your lovely mate showed up unannounced in my territory."

My pulse quickens and a bead of sweat drips down my temple. *What is she doing there?*

"I know we've had our issues in the past, but we were boys. We're men now."

"What is it you want?" I snarl.

"Moone, I don't like surprises. Your Beta escorting your Luna makes sense, but the damn Noir? Really? Sending him into the depths of Lucifer's lair, what were you thinking? Do you know what happened the last time Felix went there?"

No, I don't. But I'll never tell him that.

"Oh, never mind. But you surprise me yet again. Last I heard, you were holding Felix Noir prisoner. And now I hear you have Garcia."

"That is none of your business."

"You're right. An Alpha has to do what an Alpha has to do. If he attacked me, I would've killed him on the spot."

"I think we're done."

"Yes, yes. I have other business to attend to anyway. But a little piece of advice before I go."

"I'm listening."

"Your pretty little mate is walking on a tightrope. If she's not careful, she's going to fall. And there's no safety net."

My vision blurs and I clench my fists into tight balls.

"If she were my Luna, I never would've let her go near Lucifer's lair—Lucinda is a goldmine for someone of Lucifer's pedigree. I'd keep her on a tight leash before Lucifer digs his claws in her. But I'm sure you know what you're doing."

My throat swells and I struggle to speak. "Thanks for the tip."

"It's what we do, we look out for each other. We're practically family. Now, don't be shy and keep in touch."

I take deep breaths to calm my racing heart once Jackson hangs up.

Chicago?

I dial Lucinda.

No answer.

I text.

The three dots appear, she's actively responding.

Finally, a response—vague and distant, but she responded. But "has to power down"?! I growl and my claws extend, almost puncturing the phone.

Mia steps out of the building and walks toward me. I motion her away.

"Don't come near me," I send through the mindlink.

I squeeze the phone until my knuckles turn white, then I raise my arm.

Mia pries the phone from my hand before I'm able to throw it against the brick wall. My claw catches Mia's palm and slices through her delicate skin.

"Caiden." Mia's sweet voice quivers as she grabs my face, forcing me to focus on her. "Breathe. Deep breaths just like Dad taught you. Just breathe."

My right eye twitches. With every inhale, Mia's cinnamon and honey scent flood my senses.

Her hand moves to my chest, and she whispers, "Everything is going to be okay. Just breathe."

Finally, the tension in my shoulders relaxes and my vision clears. My head falls forward near Mia's ear, and I whisper, "She's keeping secrets from me."

CHAPTER 23

LUCINDA

FELIX LOUNGES back in the driver seat, shakes his head and twists his lips with disgust. "Lucifer Vàrcolac, Prince of the Wolves, our prince, the last remaining royalty... Did your Alpha and Elders teach you nothing?"

"There's wolf royalty?" Dylan asks.

Felix mutters under his breath. "Figures. Just like all the others. Rewriting history one generation at a time. But not this wolf. Oh no, I'll never forget. The Noirs will never forget—"

"I don't mean to interrupt your little self-reflective moment or change the subject, but where are we going?"

"My house."

"You have a house in Chicago?" I ask.

"No."

"Then where is it?"

"Seattle."

My head snaps to Dylan, and my eyes widen as I mouth, "Seattle?"

"How long of a drive is that?" he asks.

"We're not driving you fool." Felix rolls his eyes.

"Then..."

"Private jet," he says. "Now, enough questions. Get some sleep—it may be your last chance to rest for a while."

"One more question," I say.

Felix tightens his grip on the steering wheel.

"What did you find out from your contact?" I ask. "Do you know where Cody is, and why do we need to go to your house?"

"Those are three separate questions, my dear. But the answers are you don't need to know, yes, and to prepare."

"Wh—"

"No more!" The gentle roll of power that emits off Felix forces me to sit back.

Fine, for now. A low growl gurgles in my throat, and I wrinkle my nose.

Felix pulls into the parking lot of a small airstrip.

"Wait here," he says.

I glance at the phone in my hand. The little silver rectangular device weighs heavy on my heart. I brush my fingers across Caiden's picture, and tears threaten to wet my eyes.

There's a rustling from the backseat, then Dylan exits the car. My pulse quickens, and before I realize what I'm doing, I dial Caiden's number.

But he doesn't answer.

"It's Caiden. Leave a message."

I bite my lip and wait for the beep.

What do I say?

"Hey Caiden, it's me, Lucinda. I'm sorry I haven't called too often... it's just that I miss you so much. The sound of your voice causes my wolf to whine. She misses you too. And, I'm sorry I didn't tell you about Chicago and Alpha Jackson. There's no excuse. I'm sorry. We have another lead, but Felix hasn't shared it with us yet. We're headed to his family's house in Seattle. I hope you're doing okay. Call when you have time. Love you."

Felix whistles for me and motions to a small jet. Tucking my phone into my back pocket, I nod and head toward the plane.

Once I'm seated, I pull out my phone again and send a quick text to Mia.

Me: *Call when you have time.*

My phone vibrates within a minute.

I slouch down in my chair and cross my legs. "Hello?"

"Cinda, where are you?" Mia asks in a shaky voice.

I sit up a little straighter. "Mia, what's wrong?"

"You have to come home."

"I can't, not yet—"

"It's Caiden. He needs you."

"Is he okay?"

"No."

"What do you mean? What's going on? I just tried to call him."

"Cinda, I don't know what's going on with him. But something isn't right."

"What do you mean, not right?"

"He's agreed to kill Garcia."

I lean forward and scoot to the edge of my seat. "What? Who's Garcia?"

"He's the first warrior of the O'leander pack."

"What is a first warrior, and why is Caiden going to kill someone from the O'leander pack?"

Felix crosses his legs and grunts at the sound of *O'leander.*

I bite my lip and listen as Mia talks. Rocking back and forth in my seat, I attempt to calm my nerves and settle my wolf.

"Hey, Cinda, I have to go. But please hurry home, for Caiden." Mia hangs up.

Felix clears his throat. "Trouble back home?"

"Do you know Garcia, the first warrior of the O'leander pack?" I ask.

"Our paths have crossed once or twice," Felix says with fleeting eye contact.

Dylan leans forward in his chair. "Why are you asking about him?"

"Apparently, he tried to kill Caiden—"

"WHAT?" Dylan jumps out of his seat.

"Caiden's fine," I assure.

Felix plays with a glass of whisky. "And Garcia?"

"Still alive, for now."

Dylan paces in the narrow aisle of the jet. "What would provoke him to do that?"

"Mia said it was something about picking sides, joining forces with the O'leander—"

"No!" Felix's lips pull taut into a vicious snarl. "Caiden must not join with the likes of them."

"He's not. That's why Garcia attacked."

Felix nods, but his body remains tense.

Dylan sits down in one of the oversized black leather seats and stretches his hands high above his head. "I don't understand. The O'leanders have always kept to themselves."

Felix swirls the liquid in his glass. "Not always."

My eyebrows raise. "Go on."

Felix rolls his eyes. "Not now."

Whatever.

"Then tell us what your contact said about Cody," I say through a clenched jaw.

Felix waves his hand in the air. "Fine, the O'leanders it is."

Dylan sends me through the mindlink, "I guess he really doesn't want to talk about where Cody is."

I nod in agreement.

"The Alpha of the O'leander pack took a mate," Felix says.

"Not his Fated Mate, nor someone he loved. It was an arranged mating by their fathers. Though I've heard that despite the fact it was arranged, they did learn to love each other. However, the Alpha joined sides with the dirty blood-suckers. And much like the Dark Ravens, he entered into a blood pact with the damn vampires to give up his firstborn son. When his mate found out she was pregnant, she fled."

"Where did she go?" I ask.

"No one knows. She's never been seen or heard from again."

"She has a set of balls on her!" Dylan roars with laughter.

"I take it the Alpha wasn't overzealous about this?" I ask.

Felix's lips rise into a lopsided smirk that accentuates his cheekbones. "Would you be?"

"So, what did he do?"

"He sent his warriors to every pack with instructions to tear the place apart until she was found."

"That is a sure way to make enemies," Dylan says.

"And enemies he made. More than one of his warriors didn't return."

"Did they ever find her?" I ask.

"No—"

The jet hits turbulence, and I tumble from my seat to the floor.

"Sorry about that, sir," the captain calls from the cockpit. "A little pocket of turbulence, but we'll be through it soon."

We take another dip and dive. I climb back into my seat and buckle the seat belt.

"You okay?" Dylan asks.

I nod and then close my eyes. I try to focus on anything other than Caiden or Cody, the vampires, or even the assassin the witches hired to kill me.

Is he even still tracking me?

I wake as we land. When the jet door opens, a chill races up my spine and the hair on the back of my neck prickles with goose bumps. The night air is cool and damp, but something else is causing my wolf to stand on alert.

Dylan catches up to me as I cross the vacant lot of the small landing strip.

"You okay?" he asks.

"Do you feel it?"

"Feel what?"

I glance over my shoulder and peer into the darkness just beyond the jet. "I'm not sure, but I don't like it."

Dylan's hand brushes against my lower back. At first, it startles me, but the warmth of his touch calms my nerves and puts my wolf at ease.

"Come on." He leads me toward the lights in the hangar.

Felix catches up to us and motions us toward a single black town car that's waiting in the parking lot.

"Why the rush?" Dylan asks.

Felix shrugs as he unlocks the doors, climbs in, and turns on the high beams of the car.

"What's out there?" I ask.

He relocks the doors behind us. "Kitten, you don't want to know about the things that linger in the darkness."

"Is it the vampires?" Dylan asks.

Felix turns on the car and drives away without answering.

"Is Cody dead?" I ask.

Felix's head snaps to me. "No."

My heart pounds in my chest. "Will they kill him?"

"No."

"Why not?" Dylan asks.

Felix studies me; his expression tells me everything.

"Because of me."

Felix returns his attention to the road and tightens his grip on the steering wheel.

"So, they're using him as bait, and we're walking right into the trap?" Dylan leans back in his seat and rests his hands behind his head. "Great plan."

The rest of the car ride goes by in a welcomed silence. But I sit up straighter in my seat as we turn off the main road. A twelve-foot wrought iron gate stands in front of us. Felix drives through it and continues to follow the tree-lined driveway.

"Where are we?" I whisper.

"Welcome to the Noir Family Manor," Felix says as he parks the car in front of a stone mansion that screams Gothic Revival.

The gargoyles that perch on top of the peaked roof give off a spooky vibe, but as I exit the car and climb the stairs, the entryway and entire structure is enchanting.

"Does anyone live here?" I ask.

"Hurry up and don't linger." Felix leads us down a grand hallway. When we reach the end, Felix points to the ground. "Stay here."

As Felix slips through the door to our right, Dylan bumps my shoulder with his elbow and motions to a statue a few feet in front of us.

I tiptoe over and admire the beautiful artwork. And then, a few feet farther into the darkness, something shimmery catches my eye. *Armor.*

Dylan follows me to the next set of display pieces.

"Wow! Check this out." I squeeze my head through the enormous base of an old helmet.

Dylan stifles a laugh and takes it from me. Rolling it over in his hands several times, he examines every inch of it with a keen eye.

"What?" I ask.

"I think it's made to be worn by a wolf." He frowns.

"Why would a wolf need to wear a helmet?"

"Check out these markings." He points to etchings made above the eyes.

When I brush my fingertips over the intricate design, the etchings appear to come to life and swirl under my touch. I brush the cold metal again. My eyes widen as they meet Dylan's. "Did you see that?"

"Are we having fun?" Felix's voice echoes down the marble-lined hall.

Dylan hands me the helmet as we turn around to face Felix.

Holding up the helmet, I ask, "What is this?"

The design now resembles that of an elegant dragon, with his wings spread wide, ready to take flight. Pointed scales adorn his back, all the way down to his tail, and his sharp claws are drawn in defense. Shivers race through my body as I take in the full image.

Felix closes the distance between us, his footsteps so light, they make no sound on the hard marble floor.

"I see you've made yourself at home," he mutters under his breath and takes the helmet from my grasp. "This, my dear, is my great-great-great grandfather's battle helmet. He was a famous general in the Great Pack Wars."

"The what?" Dylan asks before I can process what Felix said.

"The Pack Wars," Felix repeats in his annoyed tone. He gently buffs out the fingerprints we left on the helmet and replaces it on the bookshelf.

Looking around the room, an eerie feeling begins to take hold. Everything in this room is old, historic, and powerful; I get a sense of importance as well. Though I've never heard of the Pack Wars, I know they must have been tragic.

"What are the Pack Wars?" I ask when my mouth catches up with my brain.

Felix looks from me to Dylan and back again. Dylan and I turn to look at each other and back at Felix.

"Interesting how history is changed through the generations," Felix muses to himself. Stroking his well-groomed goatee, he spins on his heels and starts down the hallway.

Turning to Dylan, I shrug, and he rolls his eyes.

We've been traveling with Felix long enough to know his expectations. He expects us to know what he wants, and right now he wants us to follow him.

"Well, are you coming?" he says without turning to face us.

"After you," Dylan says through the mindlink and gestures with his extended right hand.

I nod and give him a wry grin as I quickly follow in Felix's wake.

Hurrying down the hall, we catch up as he turns and opens a hidden door concealed within the wall.

"Watch your step," he says, holding the door open for us.

Dylan enters first and I follow. Felix hurries past us to lead the way.

The tiny corridor is dark, but a dim light shines up ahead, which opens into a circular room full of books. The walls are floor to ceiling bookcases with sliding ladders, and row after row of bookshelves fill the middle of the room. Even though these don't extend floor to ceiling, they're close.

The ceiling is a large, round colorful mosaic stained glass window. *Stunning.*

Continuing my search around the room, I spot a catwalk across the top tier on the left side of the door. It looks like a loft area, with a couch and telescope. *I bet the stars look amazing through that at night.*

"What is this place?" I ask, my tone full of wonder as I take in the antiquities this room holds with wide eyes.

"My dearest Lucinda," Felix says over my shoulder, "this is our history."

Dylan whistles. "The Crescent Noir pack must be old for all of this to be their pack history."

Felix's deep, rich laugh stirs my emotions, making my heart yearn for Caiden's soothing touch.

"What's so funny?" Dylan asks.

"Yes, the Crescent Noir is an ancient pack. However, the books in this room contain the history of our kind. The wolves."

"The entire history of our kind?" I ask.

"Yes, kitten. For all time, the council members elected a representative from the Crescent Noir pack to serve on the board as the historian, documenting everything in history."

"What happened? Why did you stop?" I have every reason in the world not to believe him, however, for some reason, I do believe him.

"Times have changed. The people in charge wanted to erase the past and rewrite history," he says with his characteristic shrug. "Haven't you ever wondered what happened to those missing pages in the Dark Raven pack journal? And I'm sure the Blood Moone pack journal has missing pages as well."

Dylan's mouth twitches, but he doesn't show any other signs of agreement.

"Through the years, different packs wanted their deepest and darkest secrets to be erased from history and forgotten in time. The easiest way to do that, of course, is to remove the journal entries. If you look at enough pack records, you'll notice a pattern. The same pages for a certain time frame are torn, lost, or misplaced. Some packs have even gone as far as rewriting the lost pages."

"How—"

"Agreements were written, handshakes made. Aren't you curious about your birth? Here is a little bedtime reading for the two of you." Felix crosses the room and hands me an old leather-bound book, titled *The Dark Raven Pack Chronicles*. "There is plenty of time for more questions later. You two need your rest, and I need my beauty sleep."

Pulling the book close to my chest, I take a deep breath and steal one last look behind me before following Felix back through the narrow passageway.

The book burns my skin, but it must be my imagination, right? Do I really want to read what's in here and find out everything I've always known is possibly a lie? Or do I want to continue blindly believing as I always have? *Sigh.*

At times like this, I wish Caiden was here to comfort me and settle my raging wolf within. I hope he knows how much I miss him.

After Felix escorts us to the guest quarters and leaves, I turn to Dylan. "What do you think about what Felix said?"

"Honestly, I'm not entirely sure. I never saw the Dark Raven pack records, but the Blood Moones journal was missing several pages."

"What do you mean missing?"

"It looked like they had been torn out," he whispers.

"Do you think Felix could—"

"No, I noticed this last year when you first arrived." Dylan holds out his hands for the book. "Come on, let's take a look."

I tighten my grip around the edges of the leather journal as I hug it against my chest.

After a minute of the burning sensation against my skin, I hold the journal out to Dylan. "Okay, here, you read it first. I'm not sure I want to know what it says."

I toss the journal on the floor at his feet, and Dylan steps closer to me. He opens his arms. "Come here."

I clumsily crash into his firm chest. My head finds the crook between his arm and chest, and I nuzzle myself into his warm embrace.

His arms tighten, and a rush of relief washes over my stressed body. My shoulders relax, then my back, neck, and legs.

I haven't felt safe since I left Caiden. But in this moment, Dylan's wolf makes me feel safe, and next thing I know, my eyes are drooping.

I'm faintly aware of him scooping me up with both hands and carrying me bridal style to the bed. My head rests comfortably on his shoulder, tucked under his chin, and my wolf gives a little whimper when he places me in bed and the warmth of his body is replaced with the cool night air. My security blanket has been taken away from me, and I'm left to fend for myself once again.

My wolf protests, and he must sense my uneasiness because he crawls into bed next to me in an upright sitting position.

Peeking one eye open, I see him reading the journal. My wolf yearns for her mate, but she doesn't protest against Dylan's proximity. So, I roll over and lie on his chest, wrapped up in the security of Dylan's arms.

Maybe I can sneak a peek at the journal—a few words here and there without reading the entire thing.

CHAPTER 24

CAIDEN

As I stand in an embrace with Mia, I peer over her shoulder. The council members are exiting the building. *Shit.*

Elder Charles's voice drifts on the light breeze. "Isn't this a heartwarming picture."

I step away from Mia and my pulse quickens. "Is it over?" I ask.

"Yes, my boy. We didn't need long. It's a shame you came all this way and didn't make it inside. I trust whatever kept you was more important."

Mia steps in front of me. "What kept him is none of your business."

Elder Charles bows his head. "Of course."

I clear my throat. "What was decided?"

"The only course of action that we can afford. Garcia must die—"

"No!" Mia spins around, and her hair whips across my face. "Caiden, please don't."

"I'll think about it," I say.

"It's what the council has decided." Elder Charles's

uncanny stare ruffles my wolf, and I let loose a warning growl.

His lips twitch, and he glances over his shoulder toward the shadows. *The Brotherhood.*

"Mia, please tell the other council members that I'll take their decision under consideration. But I'll decide Garcia's fate and if he must die, then I'll be the one to do it."

Mia responds through the mindlink. "Why don't you tell them yourself?"

My biceps flex and I respond through the mindlink. "If I want to take back control of this pack, I cannot allow them to view themselves as an equal to me."

Mia reaches up on her tippytoes and places a kiss on my cheek. "That's my brother, the true and rightful leader of the Blood Moone pack."

A smirk plays at my lips. "I'll see you back at the Pack House."

I give a nod to Elder Charles and take leave.

On my walk home, I stroll through town for a distraction. An unfamiliar voice calls from behind, "Caiden."

When I turn around, Nyla is beckoning her hand in the air and attempting to flag me down.

"A moment of your time?" she asks.

As I wait for her to approach, I kick the gravel under my boot. "What can I do for you?"

"I noticed you were missing at the hearing, and when I stepped out to find you, I couldn't help but overhear your conversation with the conniving Alpha Jackson."

My forehead creases. "You were eavesdropping?"

"It was not my intent." She makes a dismissive gesture with her hand. "But you know, these ears of mine."

Whatever.

"Do you have something to say?" The muscles in my forearms ripple under my skin as I rein in my anger. I force a smile and nod to an innocent mother and daughter walking past us down the street. *Stupid humans.*

"That is an endearing scene, isn't it?"

I return my attention back to the vile creature standing next to me. "What is?"

"Mother and daughter, smiling and laughing as they walk hand in hand down the street. Oblivious of imminent danger."

My nails pierce into my palm, and I take a deep breath to clear my mind. My interactions with Nyla have been limited, but she has given me no reason to love witches.

"Imminent danger? Do you know something I don't?"

"It's only a matter of time."

"What is?"

"You believe in your heart that Lucinda will return—and I believe you. However..."

"Get to your point."

"Caiden, you need to stop pining over Lucinda and entertain the idea she may not return the same person she was when she left."

"Stop talking in riddles, witch! If anyone touches her—"

"It's not a matter of what someone will do to her, but what she does to herself. She's on a self-destructive course. I can feel it in her energy."

"Once she returns, I will help her find her way."

"It won't be that easy. If Lucinda chooses to side with the vampires, she may return as an assassin or a spy. Will you be able to interrogate her, if needed?"

Shit.

"If she gives me reason to suspect her, yes."

"And are you prepared to do what needs to be done in order to protect your pack?"

My lips curl, and a snarl slips through my teeth.

"Caiden, no one holds you responsible for falling in love with your enemy."

"Lucinda is my mate. Not my enemy."

Nyla nods. "At least, not yet."

My patience is fading, and my wolf is begging to be released. "Tell me, friend, are you still trying to kill her?"

"I will not lie. Yes, my assassin is still tracking her. When they return, if Felix can vouch for her—"

"Felix?"

"Yes. He is a dear friend and has been loyal to me for many years. I trust him."

I squint and wrinkle my nose. "You do understand that Felix is still my prisoner upon his return."

"I'm sure that mess will work itself out. You have more important things to worry about than him."

My canines pierce my lip as they extend from my mouth. "Thank you for your words of wisdom during these difficult times. I will take your guidance under consideration."

"It's not your fault. You two were doomed before you were born. Fate played an evil trick on you, but only you control your destiny. Choose the right path. You need to listen to reason, even if your heart tells you otherwise." Nyla speaks with an air of authority.

Who is this woman that waltzed into my territory and has the audacity to make these accusations?

"The question hanging heavy on everyone's heart is, what are you going to do now?"

I step forward, closing the distance between us. My heavy breath stirs the loose hair around Nyla's face.

"I am the Alpha. The safety of my pack will always come first—no matter the threat."

Her lips curve into a crooked smirk. "Good, my boy. There is hope yet."

"Caiden!" Mia's voice cuts through the air.

I turn to gaze at Mia's soft hand as it touches my fore-arms. My vision darkens and everything tints red.

NO! Not now.

I toss my cell phone to Mia.

"I'll be back later," I tell her through the mindlink, and I run toward the tree line just beyond the edge of town.

My muscles bulge from my shoulders as I fight against the beast. *Almost there.*

I focus on the forest, but my vision blurs and the objects in front of me become dark and foggy around the edges.

As soon as I step into the protection of the forest, I shift into my wolf, remaining in control—for now.

My paws hit the ground, and I take off running at full speed, dodging bushes in my path, jumping over boulders, and diving under fallen trees. The cool breeze ruffles my fur, and the farther I get from town, the clearer my mind becomes. A heaviness lifts, and the beast subsides his push for control.

When I arrive at a small clearing in the middle of the forest, I slow my pace and come to a stop. The sun filters through the canopy of leaves and shines upon a woman sitting on the limb of an old, gnarly black walnut tree.

I've never liked this tree.

Nothing grows around it because of the toxin released by its roots. It's always given me an eerie feeling, much like it does now. The fur on my neck bristles, and a low growl emits from deep inside my chest.

The woman closes the book in her hands and leaps to the ground, gracefully landing on two feet. *Did she float down?* My nose twitches, and I spot a gray fox baring his teeth at me in the tree.

"Leah?" I send through the mindlink.

"Hi, Caiden." She walks toward me.

I crouch back on my hind legs and my lips curl, exposing my incisors.

She extends her hand. "I wasn't expecting to see you, but I'm glad you're here."

My ears pull back and lie flat against my head. I snarl.

"You don't need to fear me." Her soft voice echoes in my ears as she steps closer.

"You should leave," I send through the mindlink. *The beast isn't fond of her presence.*

"I'm not going anywhere." She reaches out and rubs my ear.

My chest rips with a seething pain as the beast threatens to take control.

"LEAVE!" I push a dominating message through the mindlink, and a force powerful enough to bring the strongest pack members to their knees flows through the air.

"Caiden." Leah speaks in a sing-song voice. She kneels before me and stares into my eyes.

How can she fight my dominant wolf? I'm her Alpha! I growl. *Insubordinate.*

"Shhh..." A low hum vibrates from her lips, and she strokes my wolf from my ear down to my neck.

A coolness floods my senses and calms my burning veins. I shift into human form.

The moist dirt against my bare skin brings a clarity I haven't experienced in a long time. I glance at Leah and gaze into her amethyst eyes.

"How did you—"

"It doesn't matter," she says.

"The beast—"

"The burden of the beast is suppressed, but only for now."

"How long?"

"Not long, so we need to talk fast."

"Talk about what?"

"Garcia."

I roll my neck to loosen the tight muscles and release an audible sigh.

"Caiden, please! You can't let them kill him."

"It won't be them killing him."

"What do you mean?"

"I'm the Alpha. He attacked me. If he must die, I'll kill him myself."

Leah inhales a sharp breath and covers her mouth. Her eyes water, and a tear threatens to drip down her crimson cheek.

"Please," she whispers. "Caiden, I beg you. Please don't kill him."

I run my hand through my hair and close my eyes. Pain stabs my heart. I reach for her chin and tilt her face to meet mine. "Leah, he attacked me. If I don't, we'll look weak."

"You're not that type of Alpha." She sniffles.

I lower my hand to my side and punch the dirt at my knees. "No, I'm not, and look where we are now."

"We have strong pack members, just lead us. Lead us with your heart."

"With my heart?" I laugh. "Don't you mean with my head?"

My fingers dig into the soft earth, and I grit my teeth. *The beast returns.*

"No decision has been made, yet. But you need to leave —now."

She nods and stands. Her fox scurries to her side, and they both disappear into the darkened forest.

CHAPTER 25

LUCINDA

A LOUD CRASH startles me awake. I rub my eyes and peer around. The room is dark, and I'm alone.

"Dylan, where are you?" I send through the mindlink.

"Stay in your room," he responds.

I grab my cell phone and check the time, five a.m.

No missed calls or text messages from Caiden.

The pit of my stomach tightens into a ball of anxious nerves, and another loud shattering sound from somewhere in the hall sends my pulse racing. *What is going on?*

My nose twitches and my wolf pleas for control. I race to the door and swing it open. The early morning light filters through the glass ceiling and illuminates the grand library below. I peer across the balcony and catch a glimpse of something moving in the shadows.

Dylan yells, "Get down!"

I duck just in time for an arrow to fly above my head.

Felix grunts and rushes toward me from the staircase. "You fool."

Another arrow hisses through the air and misses my head by less than an inch. I study the arrow that's lodged in the doorframe, and a growl slips from deep within. The broadhead cut off a few strands of my hair. *That was close.*

I shift instinctively.

My wolf spots the intruder on the other side of the stairwell. I swerve around Felix and race toward the stranger who has a pungent scent that triggers thoughts of Caiden being weak and paralyzed.

The man sends arrow after arrow in my direction, but with the adrenaline racing through me, I dodge them all.

Why isn't he retreating? I snarl and let loose a howl as I charge toward him. *Only a few more feet.*

He notches another arrow and pulls back on his bow. I leap into the air, and he adjusts his aim to my exposed chest. The arrow whistles as it flies through the air.

A heavy mass jumps on my back and twists my wolf just in time to avoid the arrow. I shift back into human form upon impact with the hard ground, but I don't miss a beat. I spin around, ready to fight my assailant. *Felix.*

A smile spreads across his face. "Expecting someone else, kitten?"

I roll my eyes and turn toward the arrow-firing intruder, but he's gone. *Damn it!*

"Who was that?" I ask.

Dylan runs toward us from the other side of the hallway. "Are you okay?"

Felix brushes off his pants. "I'm fine."

"Lux?"

My nostrils flare. "Felix, if you didn't—"

"Didn't what? Save you from the arrow that was aimed at your heart?"

"I would've had him."

"No, kitten. You would be dead."

I snarl. I hate that Felix is right.

Dylan hands me a robe to slip on. "How did the assassin find us?"

Felix cups his chin. "I'd like to know that as well. But we need to leave. This location has been compromised."

"Where will we go?" I ask.

Felix rests his head back and pinches the bridge of his nose. "We'll talk about it in the car. Go get dressed and meet me downstairs."

I hurry back to the guest room, slip on fresh clothes from my bag, and head downstairs. When I arrive, Felix ushers Dylan and me outside toward the town car.

Once we're on the road, I ask, "So, who was that back there?"

"The assassin," Dylan says.

"I thought—"

"That they would just give up?" Felix shakes his head and flashes a twisted smile. "No, my dear. They will never give up until you're dead."

My chest tightens. *How can I return to Caiden with an assassin still tracking me?*

"Where are we going now?" Dylan asks.

"Not too far," Felix says.

I glare at him. "Does this destination have a name?"

"Not one you'd recognize. Walla Walla is the closest city."

"And why are we going there? Another secret family home?"

Felix grips the steering wheel. "I took you to the private Noir Family Manor with the intention to train and educate you two before we went after Cody. But things changed. So, you two will just have to follow my lead."

My heart pounds. "We're going after Cody now?"

"Yes."

"And facing off against the vampires." Dylan's dry tone

makes me wince. He's risking his life for Cody, but who is Cody to him?

I turn to face Dylan. "You should go back."

His eyes widen and his pupils constrict. "Nope. I'm here to protect you. I go where you go."

I nod and turn back around in my seat. My fingers find a loose string hanging from the hem of my shirt, and we sit in silence. When my thoughts drift to Caiden, I soon fall asleep.

―――――

Red eyes pierce through the shadows, and a shiver races up my back. A man steps from the cover of darkness, his flaming eyes turning to a solid onyx. Caiden.

The intensity of his haunting stare causes my heart to flutter, but his stern expression stirs something else—fear. I gasp and stumble backward, tripping over my sluggish feet that won't move. I lie on the moist dirt and peer at the man-beast that looms over me.

Wake up, Lucinda! It's just a dream. Wake up!

My head slams against the dashboard of the car. *Ouch.*

"Bad dream?" Felix asks.

I glare at him without moving, and he smirks.

If only he knew.

"Lux, you okay?" Dylan asks.

"Fine." I pat my forehead and wipe away the beads of sweat that have gathered on my brow line.

"Good, because we're here," Felix says.

I steal a glance out the window. Archaic headstones cast gloomy shadows in the afternoon sun as we drive past an old cemetery. When we round the corner, I gasp. St. Lucian's Cathedral comes into full view with its stone architecture giving it a gothic beauty.

"Drop me off at the corner," I say.

"Why?" Dylan asks.

"It'll be easier to search the perimeter on foot."

"Which is precisely why I'm parking," Felix says. He pulls into a nearby alley, then pulls into a parking spot along the street. His long, cold fingers wrap around my forearm. "Lucinda, be careful."

"Aren't I always?" I flash a smile.

"Damn it, Lucinda. I mean it! This isn't a game." Felix tightens his grip on my arm.

"I know." I stare him down. *He is not in control here. And he does not control me.*

His hand locks in an iron grip on my arm. Glaring at him, I yank out of his hold and climb out of the car.

Dylan steps next to me. "Don't do anything spontaneous or stupid."

"Who me? Never." My voice raises to an unusually high pitch.

"Yes, you." He tucks a piece of hair behind my ear and my cheeks light on fire at his touch. His soft lips pull to a lopsided grin.

"Hey, lovebirds." Felix's voice carries from a few feet away, and I jump away from Dylan. "Are we going to stand here all night?"

"Let's go." I turn my back to Dylan and start walking down the street.

"Where are you going?" Dylan asks.

"Haven't a clue," I say.

"I think we should go this way." He points in the other direction.

My eyes narrow and I peer down the dark alley. "Down there, why?"

"That is an interesting choice." Felix strokes his goatee.

Dylan's gaze shifts between me and Felix and then to the

dark alley again. Closing his eyes, he takes a long inhale through his nose.

"Don't you smell it?" he asks.

All I smell is rotting trash and the salty stench of death—probably a rat.

"Humor me," Dylan says.

I lift my nose into the air and take a deep sniff. Felix does the same.

My eyes open wide in alarm. "Wolf blood."

"But it's not Cody's," Felix says with a tone of certainty.

Dylan twitches his nose. "Being this close to the bloodsucker lair—"

"St. Lucian's," Felix corrects.

"Yeah, whatever. It can't be a coincidence. I bet that wolf was either *going to* or *coming from* St. Lucian's," Dylan says with extra emphasis.

"Maybe," I say.

"Or it could be a trap," Felix says.

"True." I hate agreeing with Felix, but he does have a valid point.

We huddle together and stroll down the sidewalk, talking in hushed tones. The possibility of spies looming about, watching our movements and listening to our conversations, is unnerving. But I won't dismiss the possibility.

Dylan nudges me in the shoulder and his pupils dilate. I know this look from our closeness in childhood. *He's pissed.*

I bite my lower lip and fiddle with my pockets.

"Fine. You two go that way." Dylan points to the street. "But I'm going this way."

I blurt, "We're not splitting up."

Felix nods. "She's right."

Dylan asks, "Did hell freeze over?"

My eyes drift to Felix and back to Dylan. "What?"

Dylan gives a lopsided grin. "Felix said you were right."

"Enjoy it all you want, I'm sure it will be the only time," Felix says.

I lift my eyebrows to him; he flashes a fake smile before he turns and walks toward the street.

Dylan looks to Felix and then to his watch. "I'll meet you two back here in an hour."

"What? No," I say. "Dylan, just hear me out. If that is a wolf going in or out of St. Lucian's, then before we follow it, we want to check things out, right? That way we know exactly what we're up against?"

"Listen to her, Dylan. Don't be stupid," Felix says. "Stupid gets you killed, or worse."

I turn to face Felix. "Or worse?"

He nods and takes long strides to close the distance between us. "Yes. The damn bloodsuckers like to experiment. You could end up as one of their guinea pigs."

Chills race up my back. *Poor Cody!*

"Guinea pig? Don't you mean lab rat?" Dylan says in a dry, sarcastic tone.

"Same thing." Felix dismisses the conversation with a brief wave of his hand.

"Come on." I reach for Dylan's hand and tug him behind me. He shuffles his feet and reluctantly follows.

When we reach the street, Dylan asks, "So what's the plan?"

Felix rolls his eyes. "Do we need a plan?"

Dylan looks at me and shrugs.

"How about we just act normal?" I say.

"Normal?" Dylan gives me a skeptical look.

"Yes, like normal tourists. I'm sure this cathedral must be well-known, possibly even some type of town historic site."

Dylan nods, but he's staring off into space. "Okay, that's actually pretty smart."

I smack him upside the back of his head. "Duh."

"Where do we start?" he asks.

"If we're going to do this, then we should go to the local library or visiting center and ask for tourist information," Felix says.

"Will a bookstore work? Because there's one over there on the corner." I point to a big rectangular sign that hangs above a narrow doorway.

We scurry across the pothole-ridden street, and as Felix opens the door, a bell rings from above.

"Cozy," Felix mutters under his breath.

"Hello," a man calls.

Taking in the surroundings, my eyes land on a short, round man with red hair who's standing behind a counter several feet away.

"Hi," I say.

"Never seen you folk around these parts before."

"Nope. Just passing through," Dylan says.

I walk toward the counter. "Maybe you can help us."

"Well, seeing how I'm the shopkeeper, then if anyone can, hopefully, I can." His face beams with cheerfulness.

"Do you have any books about that church down the street?"

"St. Lucian's Cathedral?" The man's Adam's apple bobs up and down.

"Yes, I think that is the name. It's beautiful," I say. "I bet it has a rich history."

"We're touring the lesser-known historic sites in America," Dylan says and winks at me.

"You should cross that place off your list," the shopkeeper drums his fingers on the counter.

"Why?" I ask.

"It does have a rich history, only it's a dark and devilish tale."

"Dark?" Dylan moves to stand next to me.

The shopkeeper grabs a stack of papers and attempts to straighten them as he gulps. "I shouldn't be telling you this, but, yes, it's dark—as in evil. Things live there that shouldn't exist."

"What kind of things?" Dylan asks.

The shopkeeper leans across the counter and motions for us to do the same. "Dead things."

"Can you tell us how many?" Felix asks from across the room. He snaps closed the book in his hand and places it back on the shelf.

The shopkeeper's face scrunches, and his nose wrinkles.

"Or can you tell us how to get in?" Dylan asks.

The shopkeeper looks between the three of us, then releases a high-pitch whistle.

Felix rushes across the room. Reaching the counter, he grabs the shopkeeper by his collar. "That was stupid."

Dylan growls.

I yell, "What are you doing?"

Felix tosses the shopkeeper on the ground and spits. "Get ready for company."

I turn to Dylan and both our eyes widen.

Shit.

CHAPTER 26

CAIDEN

A BEAD of sweat rolls down my face and lands in the dirt next to my hands. I jump to my feet and thrash wildly in the open space between me and the walnut tree.

Storm clouds cover the setting sun and cast spine-tingling shadows on the forest floor. Unfortunately, the images have no effect since the raging beast within me is relentless in his fight for control.

I spit and snarl, but then a gentle breeze cools my moist skin. As I clench my fists, I lift my head to the gloomy sky and let loose a deep and throaty howl.

Birds spook from the treetops, but not the one I hope for. The raven.

My head falls forward and rests against the rough bark of the tree trunk. I sigh.

Have you deserted me too? Maybe you aren't my forest friend, after all.

I grab the trunk and my nails extend into the hardwood. A warm sensation ignites in my skin, building through my hands and up my arms. I step away from the tree, but my palms continue to burn where they made contact.

What the...?

A loud crack of thunder rumbles overhead, and a chain of lightning follows. I pause to gaze at the mysterious tree before shifting into my wolf.

The storm continues through the night, but it exhilarates my wolf-beast, and I relish in the freedom it offers. In the morning, I head home. Large drops of rain puddle on the ground as I near the Pack House.

When I open the back door, another crack of thunder causes my shoulders to flinch, and a flash of lightning illuminates the mudroom. A shadow crosses the room.

I call out, "Lucinda?"

Sabrina steps closer and hands me a robe. "No, it's me."

"Thanks. How are you feeling?"

"I'm fine, but—"

"No!" An irate voice carries through the wall from the other room. "I'm not going anywhere until I speak with MY Alpha!"

Sabrina rolls her eyes. "It's Mr. Willow. He won't leave until he speaks with you."

Eva's father. My chest tightens. *I hope she hasn't run away.*

I stroll to the kitchen; I'm in no rush to talk about pack business.

"Hi, Tom," I say and extend my hand.

"Alpha." His handshake is strong with a firm grip.

"Is everything okay?"

"I'm not sure. I would like to speak with you in private, if that's okay?"

I smile at Mia who's standing next to Tom and nod. "Mia, will you please show him to my office. I'll be there in a moment."

"Thank you," Tom says and follows Mia out of the kitchen.

Sabrina steps next to me. "I have a feeling he's bringing trouble."

In slow motion, I turn to gaze at her and cock an eyebrow. A smile spreads across her face, and I shake my head. As I cross the room, I ask, "Will you brew two mugs of coffee, please?"

"I think we're all out of coffee, but how about some tea?"

"Fine." I head upstairs to find clean clothes.

After dressing, I glance at my phone lying on the nightstand. Heat rushes to my head and my heart drops.

Nothing. No missed calls, voice messages, or texts.

I take a deep breath, leave the phone on the nightstand, and head downstairs.

"Thank you for your patience," I say to Tom as I walk into my office.

He stands as I cross the room to sit at my desk.

My hands wrap around the mug of hot tea Sabrina left. "Now, what do you need to talk about?"

"It's Eva." Tom sits back in the chair across from my desk.

"Is she okay?" The steam from the tea tickles my nose as I take a sip of the hot liquid.

"Yes, at least for the moment." Tom sighs and rubs his temples.

"Then what's the problem?"

"Eva is desperate to find her Fated Mate, but honestly, she'd be happy with any mate that was honorable and treated her well. The boys in this pack that are her age are all too stupid and immature." Tom punches the arm of the chair. He takes a deep breath and exhales. "She's of good stock."

I lean back in my chair.

"You don't know me well. I've kept my distance over the

years. But your father and I were once best friends, much like you and that Sammy kid."

"What happened?"

Tom shrugs as his gaze finds the ground. "Everyone knew he'd name me his Beta when the time came—"

"But he didn't."

"No, he didn't. Much like you and Sammy. But Sammy is a better man than I was. He stood by you and supported your decision." Tom looks me in the eye. "I regret how my friendship ended with your father. Our last words were full of bitterness and hate."

"How does this relate to Eva, and what's your point in telling me this now?"

"My point is that Eva comes from a good family. She has pedigree. She would make a great Luna—"

"This pack already has a Luna!" My eyes burn as I stare him down. *So, this is what he wants to talk about.*

"Where is she?"

"She has an important task to deal with."

"More important than the safety and well-being of her pack?"

My lips draw back in a snarl.

Tom motions with his hand to calm me down. "I like Lucinda, I really do. I made it a point to get to know her during those social events."

"Why?" I ask through a clenched jaw.

"To make sure she was deserving of you, our Alpha. I owed it to your father. Lucinda is strong and powerful, yes, but—"

"Why is there always a but?" I roll my eyes.

"May I speak freely?"

I nod.

"She would be a great leader, but it's hard to lead when you're not here. It doesn't seem like she's thinking as a Luna should. I can't blame her. It'll take time to readjust to pack life after living as a rogue. But time is of the essence. An Alpha and Luna should think of the pack first, and then their own."

"What are you trying to say? Spit it out."

"She's being selfish. Leaving the pack—and you—when we need strong leadership the most, makes us vulnerable."

I rest my head back and close my eyes. "She'll return as soon as she can."

"Until the next time, right?" Tom adds.

I growl.

"My apologies, that was out of line. But we need your combined strength and leadership right now. Strange men with bald heads and robes wander through our streets. Witches are openly living in our communities. I can't even run through the forest without my nose twitching and fur bristling because the forest is full of spies now. And word of an attack on you, our Alpha, has spread like wildfire. People are scared. There's talk of leaving and heading west."

"What?" *Why am I just hearing of this?*

"This is my home. I don't plan to leave. I will die here, protecting my family if it comes to that." Tom runs his hand through his hair and sighs. "What I'm saying is, my daughter has the pedigree to mate with an Alpha. She is strong but also has a soft heart and gentle nature. Her mom raised her to be the epitome of a Luna. She would do this pack a wonder of good if you'll have her."

I lean forward over my desk and meet Tom's wide eyes. "I have a mate."

"Yes, I know. And I'm not asking you to necessarily mark Eva as a mate. Just as the Luna."

"You're suggesting I mark two women?" I weave my fingers together around the mug, and I sip the hot liquid so it coats my throat.

Tom nods and stands, extending a hand across the desk. I shake his hand with a firmer handshake than before.

He says, "I realize this is a lot for you to think about..."

My chest tightens at the thought of taking two mates. I'm not sure I can control the beast raging within me.

How could I do that to Lucinda? But if I don't, could I lose the pack's approval?

CHAPTER 27

LUCINDA

FELIX PULLS the shopkeeper off the floor and snarls in his face. "Who did you signal?"

A deep voice echoes from the shadows near the rear of the bookstore. "The Night Watch."

"There goes our recon mission," Dylan mutters.

Felix slides across the counter and pulls the shopkeeper in front of him. His claws extend, and he applies pressure to the man's throat.

I don't care who these people are, Felix should not show his claws! I breathe deeply then snap in my dominant tone, "Felix!"

He glares at me but retracts his claws before anyone notices. *I hope.*

Half a dozen men step out from the shadows of the bookstore, all carrying shotguns, which are aimed at us. They stalk slowly and form a circle around us. In a matter of seconds, we're outnumbered and surrounded.

Shit.

A redhead with a shaggy beard shakes his fist to Felix and says, "Let him go."

Felix smiles his frightful grin. I know what he's thinking; I've seen that look many times before. Death is a game to him. No. I will not let him kill these men.

I step forward to face the redheaded man. "I think there's been a misunderstanding."

"Is that right?"

I nod and flash my most innocent smile.

"Then why is that goon holding Neil?" another man asks.

My head snaps to the tall, thin man. He reminds me of a beanpole. Under my gaze, he pushes his round glasses up on his nose.

I turn to Felix. "Let him go."

Felix stares at me with dark eyes. He will escalate this situation further if he can, and I will not let that happen. I call upon my wolf, and my dominant Alpha pushes a force of power through the air.

Felix's eyes widen as it hits him. His jaw tenses, but he lowers his arms. Neil, scoots away from Felix's reach and hides behind one of the men with a gun.

I turn my attention back to the man with the glasses. "See, we mean you no harm. That was pure instinct. We didn't know who he signaled. Felix was just trying to protect us. As I'm sure that's what you are doing."

A few of the men nod at my explanation.

"Neil, why did you sound the alarm?" An older man with graying hair and a face covered in day-old stubble asks.

"They were asking a lot of questions about the cathedral," Neil says.

"What kind of questions?" the older man asks.

"How to get inside and how many dead ones there are."

The older man turns to me. His eyes roam over my body and then study Dylan and Felix.

"Are you one of them?" he asks in a hostile tone.

Felix makes a sound of disgust. "No."

"Do you want to be one?"

"Ew. No." Dylan says.

"Then why the interest?"

"They have one of our friends, and we plan to get him back," I say.

"And there goes our cover story," Dylan says under his breath.

"How long have they had your friend?" the redheaded man asks.

"About a week, give or take a few days or more," I say. *How long has it been? So much has happened, I've lost track of time.*

"Then save yourself and forget about it. He's probably already one of them, or if he's lucky, he's dead," the man with the glasses says.

"How do you know he's here?" the old man asks.

"We have contacts," Felix says.

"Contacts?" The old man eyes Felix with a skeptical gaze.

Felix dismisses it with a wave of his hand.

A flash of movement sends me crouching on the ground and pulling Dylan down with me. Just in time for the man behind us to shoulder his gun, take aim, and shoot into the rafters of the bookstore.

"What the hell, Bob?" the old man says.

I turn, and a scruffy man wearing a flannel shirt removes his smoking shell.

"A damn bat," he says.

Everyone looks up, and I follow their gaze. I spot it high up in the rafters, covered in the darkness of the far corner. But I don't tell the men. I recognize the bat by the small white V on his chest.

This is the same bat that's followed me around for as long as I can remember. He annoys me most of the time, but I've also found a calmness in his presence. *I won't let these men kill him.*

I stand up and brush off my thighs. "Are you going to help us or not?"

"We don't need their help," Felix says.

"Lux, I agree with Felix on this one. No need to involve them."

The somber stillness that was in the room, explodes with laughter.

"Did you hear that," the redheaded man says between laughs. "They don't need us."

"Young kids these days," the man with the glasses says. "They keep getting stupider."

Dylan's fists curl into tight balls and his pupils dilate. "Who are you anyway?"

"Calm down," I send through the mindlink. I grab his hand and rub his arm to soothe his rising anger.

"We are the Night Watch," the old man says. "We serve and protect this town from the evils that live within the cathedral walls."

"If you go poking around the cathedral, you'll make trouble for us," Neil says.

"And as I said earlier," I say, "We aren't here to make trouble or harm you or the people of this town. We just want our friend back."

The old man studies us for several awkward moments. "You've dealt with this kind before?"

"Unfortunately," Felix says drily.

"So, you know what you're up against?" the man with glasses asks.

"Yes." Dylan releases a sigh.

"Okay, then your lives are not our concern, and your deaths will not be on our conscience."

"Fair enough," Dylan says, and Felix rolls his eyes.

"Follow me." The old man heads toward the rear of the bookshop. He removes a book from a dusty shelf and reaches behind the remaining books. With a loud click, a door opens in the side wall, revealing a secret passageway.

My heart pounds.

The foul stench that blows in from the darkness causes my wolf to whimper. She doesn't want to go down there. I don't blame her.

"If this leads directly to the bloodsuckers, I think it's safe to say we got played," Dylan says through the mindlink. He grabs my hand and squeezes.

The warmth of his touch calms my wolf. *Why am I so nervous?*

"If it does lead to them, great! It'll make quick work of what we came here to do," I send back through the mindlink.

The old man pulls out a flashlight and shines it in Felix's face, which causes him to snarl.

"Who are you?" the old man whispers and steps closer to Felix.

I rush between them. No need to agitate the situation when our wolves are already on edge.

"Where does this lead?" I ask, diverting the old man's attention away from Felix.

"To the outskirts of town."

Felix growls. "We don't want to leave."

"I know. And you aren't, just trust me," he says and turns down the dark passageway.

I glance at Dylan and Felix and then follow the old man into the darkness.

We exit next to a large boulder and several other grated passages.

"These are the sewage systems that run under the town.

From here, you can gain access to the old catacombs under the cathedral."

"The cathedral has a catacomb?" I ask.

"Oh yeah, long forgotten. And we hope to keep it that way," the man says.

"Why?" Dylan asks.

"We don't need the media poking around or tourists coming here." His voice is stern and gravely.

"You protect the bloodsuckers." Felix's face contorts and his nose scrunches.

"The who?"

"The dead ones," I say.

"You know more than you're letting on," the old man says, staring into my unfaltering gaze. Finally, he gives up and continues, "No. We protect our own. But when things get bad for the dead ones, they take it out on our town."

"Do you have a map?" Dylan asks.

The man shakes his head.

Felix steps forward and growls at the man. "Is this a game to you?"

"Follow this straight until it opens into a large circular room. You'll see three other tunnels. Take the one to your right, and follow that until you come to a fork. Stay to the left, then you'll come to another smaller room with three more tunnels. Take the one on the right. Follow that until you see a stairwell on the left-hand side. Those stairs will lead you up to the catacombs."

I repeat, "Right, left, right, stairs on the left. Got it."

Dylan asks, "And once we get to the catacombs?"

The old man shrugs. "Anyone that's ever ventured up there has never returned."

I nod and give Dylan a sideways glance.

"I don't like it," he says through the mindlink.

"I know, but it's our only chance to save Cody. We've come this far..."

"We could find another way."

"No. Let's just do it. The assassin is still out there, so we can't waste any more time." I turn to the old man. "Thank you for all your help."

"Good luck." He steps back into the secret passage from which we came. "Oh, if you happen to see a boy around the age of twelve with dark hair and brown eyes, will you tell him his papa loves him?" The old man's eyes glimmer with tears.

"Yes." My heart aches for him. *I wonder who the boy is?*

I snap my head to the wooded area just beyond the large boulders providing our cover. A rancid scent drifts in the air, and my nose twitches.

"We're not alone," I whisper.

Felix and Dylan are already scanning the area.

I turn back to the old man. "Go! Get out of here."

"Watch out!" Dylan jumps on me, and we both collapse on the dirt ground as an arrow flies over us.

Damn assassin!

"That was a close one," Dylan says, helping me off the ground.

I stick my finger through a tear in my shirt near the shoulder. "Yeah, too close."

WHOOSH. I duck as another arrow zips past my shoulder.

"We need to move," Felix says.

I spare one last look over my shoulder; the old man is gone. *Good.*

We dart into the dark sewage tunnels, and I'm thankful for my heightened vision, which makes it easier to see in the shadows of the setting sun. But the assassin pursuing isn't so lucky. His dull flashlight illuminates the tunnels several yards behind us.

I wish we could transform. Our wolves would be much faster and quieter, but that would be awkward when we transform back. All our spare clothes are in the car in town.

The room opens out ahead, and I remember the directions and call out, "Right."

I hope our pursuer isn't a good tracker. With any luck, he'll get lost down here.

Unfortunately, it sounds like he's still behind us. Taking a quick look, his light bobs along the wall.

"Left," I tell Dylan through the mindlink as I see the fork ahead.

Another arrow whizzes by my head. *Damn it!*

"Quick, the stairs!" Dylan calls. We hurry up the stairs but stop, wide-eyed. We've stumbled into a long corridor that extends in two directions.

"Which way?" Dylan asks.

Felix tugs on his goatee and kicks the ground. "We don't have time for this."

I raise my eyes to the ceiling and a shadow moves in one direction. It's a bat, my bat.

"Wait, I think we should go to the left," I say.

"How do you know?" Felix asks.

"I have a feeling." I start walking in the direction of the bat.

"Oh, you have a feeling," Felix mimics my words in a whiny voice.

"Just trust me, okay?"

Felix and Dylan follow me into the dark and down the corridor of the catacombs.

A stench of sewage and hot garbage drifts through the air and causes my head to throb. It's mixed with stale air, and my lungs protest with each breath.

Finally, we step into a more spacious room with torches to light the way, and the air clears.

"Now where?" Dylan asks.

I look around, but the bat is gone.

I shrug. "Your guess is as good as mine."

CHAPTER 28

LUCINDA

A WOMAN'S voice echoes through the room. "Well, well look who it is."

I whip my head around, and I startle. A stunning woman appears from the darkness. Her long red hair and soft waves stand out against her pale skin, and my heart flutters. *Is this a vampire?*

Her movements are graceful as she glides across the floor. Her off-the-shoulder black dress has long sleeves, a deep V-neck, a side slit up to her mid-thigh, and a mermaid style skirt. I'm drawn to her bright green eyes. *Who is she?*

"Hello, Morticia." Felix licks his lips in disgust. "I would say it is good to see you. However, it's not."

"I see you're still a jokester," Morticia says. Her voice is bewitching. Something I would expect a siren to sound like if they were real.

"It wasn't a joke," Felix says.

"You really know how to win over a girl's heart." Morticia comes to stand only inches from him. "Let's put all theater tricks aside. It's nice to see you, Felix."

Felix huffs out a large sigh and turns his head away from her.

Morticia clasps her hands together in front of her face. "Good. Now we can move on to bigger and brighter things."

"And what would that be?" Felix asks in a dry tone.

"Aren't you going to introduce me to your friends?" Her eyes widen as they rake over Dylan's body.

"No."

"That's no way to treat your lover."

"Lover?" I ask. *Has Felix been playing us the entire time?*

Felix glares at me. "Ex. It was a long time ago."

"You always have to be negative, don't you?" Morticia says. "Well, let's not waste time with introductions. I already know who everyone is."

Felix snarls. "How?"

"It's of no concern to you."

"But we're at a disadvantage," I say.

The woman turns her attention to me. "How is that, love?"

I swallow before answering. "Because we don't know who you are."

She raises her hand to cover her heart, seemingly in pain, as she whines, "That hurts. Felix, you haven't told them anything about me? That crushes my heart."

"That's impossible, because you don't have a heart." Felix's lips curl and his incisors peek through his lips.

The woman straightens her posture, and her face turns dark and serious. "Very well, if that's how you want it. All business."

Felix nods.

She turns her attention to Dylan and me. "Hello, I'm Morticia, Queen of the Vampires, and welcome to my house. Now let's get down to business. I have something you want, and you have something I want."

I glance at Felix. His eyes blaze with fire, boring a hole into Morticia's otherworldly stare.

So, this is the Queen of the Bloodsuckers. The leader of those trying to kidnap me.

I force a swallow, and send Dylan a message through the mindlink. "Hey, if they try to experiment on me or turn me into a vicious bloodsucking monster, you'll take care of it, right?"

He grimaces. "What do you mean take care of it?"

"You'll kill me if needed, right? Promise me."

His chest raises with an inhale as he nods. And then he adds, "Ditto."

I nod and then step forward, focused on Morticia. "Here I am. Where is he?"

Morticia laughs. "My dear, as much as I would love to have you, you're not what I want."

I turn and look at Dylan with an alarmed expression. *Does she want Dylan? No, that's not how it's supposed to be.* And then I glance at Felix. His tense posture and set jaw say it all. *He knows what she wants.*

"You are impossible, woman." Felix's voice echoes down the catacombs.

With a seductive wink, Morticia says, "I like to think of myself as a perfectly aged bottle of wine. You need an acquired taste to fully appreciate—"

"No one will ever fully appreciate everything you have to offer."

An alluring smile spreads across her face. "I think you meant that as an insult, but I'll take it as a compliment."

"Where's Cody?" I ask.

"He's fine," she says, not moving her gaze from Felix.

"I didn't ask how he was, I asked where."

"Upstairs." She waves her hand in the air above her head.

"If you've done anything to him..."

Her head snaps to me, and her eyes light with fire. She grabs her heart again and fakes an insult. "First you break into my house. And then you threaten me?"

"If you didn't kidnap him in the first place, we wouldn't be here."

She stares into my eyes and then turns on her heels. "Very well, come along. We've wasted enough time down here anyway."

"Agreed," Felix says.

Morticia's eyebrows raise as a new scent fills the room.

With a brisk motion, Felix steps next to Morticia and whispers, "We're not alone down here."

Stupid humans. They always underestimate our sense of smell.

Dylan steps up next to me and places his hand on my lower back to give me a gentle push. "Come on, let's go."

My feet reluctantly stumble forward, and Dylan and I follow in step behind Felix and Morticia.

"You were followed, I assume?" Morticia asks.

"Yeah. There's an assassin trying to kill Lux," Dylan says. His bitter tone upsets my wolf, so I bite my lip and slap his arm.

"What was that for?" He rubs his arm.

I shrug. "I don't know. The way you said it makes it sound like it's my fault."

"Now, now, children. No need to bicker," Morticia says with a rueful grin.

Felix clears his throat. "But of course, it's not just any assassin that's after you, my dear."

Morticia's eyebrows raise. "Is it...?"

"I'm afraid so." Felix nods.

I quicken my pace and step between Felix and Morticia. "What? Who is it?"

"He belongs to a group called the Brotherhood of Assassins," Felix says.

"What is the Brotherhood?" Dylan asks.

"Not what, but who is the correct question." Felix stares at the ground as he paces a couple steps in each direction, then he stops and looks up at Dylan and me. "They are a fanatic group of warlocks that became a league of assassins trained by the witches."

"No, you mean trained by the dark Lord himself," Morticia says.

"The who and the what?" I ask.

"Don't concern yourself with the finer details right now," Morticia says.

"All along, you knew the assassin that's been following us?" I ask.

Felix's eye twitches.

Stepping in front of him to block his path, I raise my hands to my hips and glare at him. "Why didn't you tell us before?"

"I wasn't entirely sure, not until now," he says.

"Why are you sure now?" I ask.

"Because of this." Felix holds up an arrow that was aimed at us earlier.

"What's so special about that?" Dylan reaches for the tip.

"Don't touch that." Felix pulls the arrow out of reach.

"Why, is it poisoned or something?"

"Or something," Morticia says. "Why is she a target?"

"The witches put out a contract," Felix says.

"Interesting." Morticia runs her fingers through her long hair. "Let's waste no more time getting upstairs. At dusk, I'll send out a search and kill party."

Dylan looks over his shoulder. "Agreed, let's keep moving."

I cross my arms over my chest and let Felix walk past me as I wait for Dylan to step up next to me.

I grind my teeth and send him a message through the

mindlink. "Felix is keeping secrets from us. He knows more than he lets on. When we get out of here, he's going to tell us everything."

"Let's focus on getting out of here—alive," Dylan says with his signature smirk.

Yes. That will be an achievement in itself. Who's the main threat here, the bloodsuckers or the highly trained assassin?

We follow Morticia through the maze of the underground catacombs sparsely lit with oil lamps. As we pass by each one, they cause my heart to ache for Caiden and the comfort of his embrace.

I pull out my phone and check for a signal. Surprisingly, one bar appears. I send Caiden a quick text.

Me: *Thinking of you.*

Caiden: *Can you talk?*

Me: *Not now.*

Caiden: *When?*

Me: *Not sure.*

I tuck the phone back in my pocket before he responds. I know his next question will be to ask where I am, and it'll lead me to another lie on top of the rest.

What type of relationship can withstand so many lies? I sigh with a heavy heart.

Dylan asks through the mindlink, "You okay?"

I turn and look up at him; his face flushes with worry.

"Yeah, I just miss—" My stomach twists. I feel awkward telling Dylan that I miss Caiden, but why?

His eyes widen with concern and his eyebrows raise, waiting for me to continue.

"I miss home." *Lie. Why am I lying to everyone I care about?*

"I miss home too." He reaches for my hand and gives it a reassuring squeeze, but he doesn't let go.

It's been a long time since I've walked holding hands with someone, much less Dylan. My pulse spikes.

Calm down, Lucinda, it's only Dylan. He's a good friend. My wolf stirs restlessly within me. I think she misses her mate more than I miss Caiden.

We climb a circular stone staircase that leads up to the aging cathedral. The air is cool, but that isn't what's giving me goose bumps. The deeper we walk into the large room, the more things move in the shadows that line the walls.

"We're here. Now where is Cody?" I ask when we come to a halt.

"All in good time, love," Morticia says. *What is it with her and Felix calling everyone love?*

"I don't like the sound of that," Dylan says through the mindlink and pulls me closer to him.

"Felix, lover," Morticia says. "About that trade."

"No." Felix crosses his arms. He stands unfaltering as she licks his neck and kisses his lips. Her hands roam over Felix's body, and she grinds against his lower half.

"Why did you kidnap Cody?" I ask.

Morticia glares at me.

"Did you kidnap him just to lure Felix here?"

"Why not just take Felix in the first place?" Dylan asks.

"Because where would be the fun in that?" Morticia asks in a silky voice.

Did Felix know this all along? And I thought the bloodsuckers wanted to kill me! Why am I still so gullible when it comes to trusting him? Never again. I'm done trusting him. I mean it this time.

An arrow flies through the air, but I hear it too late to react. Felix pushes me out of the way, and I stumble for a few feet before finding my balance.

A bat circles above me and swoops down to knock another arrow out of the air. One that was aimed for my head.

I startle at the bat's closeness, but then I glance to Felix's hunched form. Waves of power radiate through the room. *Something is wrong.*

He rests in a sitting position and then lies down on his back. I gasp at the arrow lodged deep in his chest and his bloodstained shirt.

"Felix?" I run and slide down on my knees, skidding to a stop when I reach him. Another arrow zips through the air and nicks the tip of my ear. The bat darts toward the intruder, distracting him for now.

Through blurred vision, I reach for the arrow in Felix's chest.

"No, don't touch that." Morticia glides across the marble floor to stand over Felix's fallen body.

I retract my hand but examine the arrow from a safe distance. "It's another one of those poisoned—"

"Or something," Dylan says.

"What will it do to him?" I ask.

"Kill him, of course," Morticia says.

"I thought you said it wasn't poisoned?" Dylan asks.

"The Brotherhood uses arrowheads that are laced with dark magic. Only the witch caster, or warlock in this case, can reverse the spell."

"What spell?" Beads of collect on my browline and I frantically wave my hands over his body with no purpose.

"A painful death."

I cover my mouth and gasp. "Isn't there anything we can do?"

Morticia taps her red nails across her ruby lips. "There is one thing I can try. But no promises it will work."

Felix coughs, and blood drips from his lips. "No. Kitten, Lucinda, don't let her—"

A creek in the wooden rafters overhead causes us to jump. I lean over and cover Felix with my body, and Dylan takes a protective stance in front of me. I look over my shoulder as an arrow whizzes by, less than an inch from my head. Dylan takes off running in the direction from where the arrow came.

With a loud clunk, the large merlot velvet curtain covering the giant window falls to the ground. In pours the remaining sunlight, and I instinctively squint and turn away as it cascades over the floor, illuminating Felix's bloody body.

As my eyes adjust, I peer over my shoulder again. Dylan stands in the middle of the room, arms sheltering his face from the light.

High-pitched moans and weeping wails pull my attention to the retreating bloodsuckers, including Morticia, who slither to the rear of the room where they tremble in the shadows.

Another arrow zings through the air, and I roll out of the way, successfully dodging it as it hits the floor and skids into the shadows. A raven soars out of the shadows, then a body tumbles to the ground from the rafters and lands at Dylan's feet.

He kneels beside the crumpled body and places his two fingers against the man's throat. "He's dead."

"Of course, he is, you fool," Morticia calls, her voice trembling from the other side of the room. "He won't let himself be taken alive."

"Kitten," Felix whispers and motions with his fingers for me to come closer.

I crawl across the floor and lean in close.

"Kill me," he says. His eyes roll back, and his body constricts in a violent spasm.

"What?" *Did he just ask me to kill him?*

"Please, kill me," he says after his muscles relax. "You must do it before she gets to me."

My gaze wanders to the shadows. Morticia's kneeling on

the floor, and the pain of watching her lover die is plastered on her face.

"You can't save him, but I can," Morticia says. "I am the only one that can save him now."

"No!" Felix yells. "Kill me, damn it."

A flush spreads through my body. My head spins. "I... I can't."

Felix looks deep into my eyes. "Kill me before she turns me into one of her experiments. I don't want to be an undead bloodsucker. Lucinda, please, kill me and make sure I'm dead."

Dylan's hand rests on my shoulder. "Hey, I'll do it."

"No, it should be me," I whisper.

I follow Dylan's gaze to the window. "Then you better do it quick. The sun is setting."

I place my hand on Felix's chest, careful not to touch the arrow. Taking a deep breath, I close my eyes.

Caiden, please forgive me for what I'm about to do. I hope you understand, and I pray that I'm able to forgive myself one day.

I call upon my wolf for her added strength, and my mouth transforms, exposing my razor-sharp canines.

"Sever my head," Felix says. "It's the only way to make sure I stay dead."

I lean in for the kill. My mouth hovers over his throat, saliva dripping from my heavy panting.

"Lux, it's a mercy killing," Dylan sends through the mindlink. "Everyone will understand."

Not everyone. I promised Caiden I would bring Felix back.

In one swift motion, my jaw clamps down on his throat. My canines pierce through his soft flesh, and with a jerk of my head, his skin tears. One more bite, and his head rolls away from his body.

I hover over the headless body and rock back and forth.

I'm vaguely aware of Dylan kneeling next to me, wiping

the blood off my mouth. He helps me stand and then holds me under his arm. I turn into his chest and tears run down my cheeks.

Why am I crying over Felix? It wasn't too long ago that I wanted him dead.

CHAPTER 29

CAIDEN

A TREMBLE ROLLS through my shoulders and up my neck. I close my eyes and shake my head. *What happened?*

I glance over my shoulder at the clock on the wall. It was midmorning when Tom left.

I clench my fists and growl. I've lost four hours. *I blacked out, again.* This has been happening more often than before. I pat my chest to make sure I'm still in human form, and I let out an audible sigh. Luckily, the beast didn't come out this time. *I hope.*

"Caiden," Sabrina's voice drifts through the air.

"Not now." I say without turning around.

"Caiden."

My heartbeat quickens at the seductive tone in her voice.

"Leave me alone!" I spin around to growl in her face, but no one is there.

The door to my office is closed and the room is empty. I close my eyes and run my hand through my hair. *What is happening to me?*

After a deep cleansing breath to calm my racing nerves, I

turn to take one last look at my sanctuary before getting on with my day. But movement catches my attention.

Two people emerge from the forest, but they're careful to stay to the tree line for protection from the light. *Who is it?* The distance and shadows cast from the afternoon sun make them hard to identify. So, I reach out to them in the mindlink. I only pick up the trace of one person—Sabrina.

I should've known.

And I bet the witch is with her. They've been spending a lot of time together.

They stop walking, and their heads turn toward the Pack House. *Do they see me in the window?*

"Caiden, are you spying on us?" Sabrina asks through the mindlink.

I cross my arms over my chest and grunt as I continue watching them. I am the Alpha; I have no shame in watching them.

Sabrina steps from the shadows. The sunlight puddles around her small frame and illuminates her glossy black hair.

"Caiden, is everything okay?" Her tone is soft and tender, as if she were speaking to a child.

"You tell me," I send back through the mindlink.

"Are you free at the moment? Nyla and I would like to speak with you."

"I'll come out." I'm in need of fresh air anyway.

"No, if it's okay, we'll come to you. We'd rather speak in the privacy of your office."

Tom's words cross my mind—spies lurking in the forest. *Do Sabrina and Nyla sense it too?* I'll check it out later today.

"Fine. Hurry up." I turn from the window. A fresh mug of tea sits on my desk. *When did that get here?*

My nose twitches, but I don't pick up a fresh scent. The mug is still warm, but not hot. I take a sip and release a breath as the liquid rushes down my throat and coats my stomach.

Sabrina and Nyla enter as I swallow the last sip of tea.

"Caiden, are you okay?" Sabrina's eyes widen and her eyebrows raise.

"Fine," I say.

As they cross the room, I sit in my chair behind the desk and motion toward the two chairs across from me. "Ladies."

"Caiden, are you sure you're okay?" Sabrina's voice quivers. She leans over the desk and her hand raises toward my forehead. "You're so pale."

I grab her hand and squeeze it tight before throwing it back at her. "Don't touch me."

She leans back in her chair and exchanges a scowl with Nyla.

"What do you want?" I ask.

"Your pack grows weaker every day that Garcia stays alive," Nyla says.

"Who are you to judge?"

"I can feel it in my bones and deep in my soul," Nyla spits through her dry, cracked lips.

Who is she to take that tone with me?

"Caiden," Sabrina's silky voice diverts my attention. She slides her arms across the desk and reaches for my hand. She blinks away the tears in her eyes before they fall. "It's true. The pack is losing faith in you."

I know what she says is true. Tom told me as much. *How can I be so stupid? I'm the shittiest Alpha ever!*

I jerk my hand from Sabrina's grasp as my arms begin to shake. I stand with such force that my chair tips over and crashes to the floor.

"Sit down and get control of yourself," Nyla demands.

I hunch over the desk and glare at her.

She rolls her eyes and shakes her head. "Your intimidation and power tricks won't work on me. I'm immune to your Alpha control, so it's best you stop trying."

I growl. "Speak, witch, or leave."

"You have a traitor lurking about."

"A traitor?" Power ripples through my veins. My wolf wants out.

Nyla nods.

"You're sure?"

She nods again.

My eyes narrow and my claws extend. "Who?"

"I'm still working on that," she says, and I lean closer. "It's not as easy as you may think."

Sabrina rubs the back of my shoulder blade. "Caiden, while she's working on uncovering the traitor, you should—"

I spin around and grab Sabrina by the neck. My claws slightly pierce the delicate skin near her pulse point. "Are you telling me what to do?"

"No," she manages to mutter, and I release my grip.

"Good. Tread lightly because you are speaking to the Alpha."

Sabrina rubs her neck and exchanges a glance with Nyla. After a slight nod, Sabrina sits in her chair and crosses her legs. I take this chance to straighten my chair and take a few calming breaths before sitting down again.

Sabrina licks her lips and clutches her heart. "The thing is, you're right. You are the Alpha. And as the Alpha, you swore an oath to protect our pack and always put the pack's needs above all else. We need you now, more than ever."

"You don't need me."

"We need you to lead us!"

"Lead you to what? Death?" I pound my fist on the desk, and Sabrina jumps.

"If you keep doing what you're doing, yes, your pack will meet death," Nyla says.

"And exactly what is it that I'm doing?"

"You can't keep waiting for Lucinda to return. You are the Alpha. You must act and make the final decision now! We can't wait any longer or else more bad things will happen. You need to kill Garcia."

My eyebrows raise and the tightness in my chest eases. "So, this is all about Garcia?"

"Yes, you imbecile!" Nyla grunts.

Sabrina swats at Nyla's arm and turns to me with her bright blue eyes and fluttering dark eyelashes. "We fear the traitor will try to set Garcia free."

"And then what's left of your entire pack will see you as the fool you are." Nyla glares at me.

This witch questions my authority and tests not only my patience but also my control. Which is failing.

I stand. My lip curls as I snarl. "Fine."

Sabrina sighs and Nyla nods.

I storm out the door and head toward Garcia's holding cell. *What am I doing?*

This needs to be done. I've known it all along. Everything they've said is true. Any other Alpha would've killed him on the spot. Attacking an Alpha is the highest offense. But what did I do? Threw him in a holding cell and granted him a hearing. *Stupid, Caiden! End this now. He needs to die.*

As I near the holding cell a shiver courses up my neck, and prickles cover my scalp. I race toward the open door and step over the pack member assigned to watch Garcia. He's sprawled on the floor with blood gushing from his head, and Garcia's cell is empty.

Sabrina and Nyla rush in behind me. Nyla mutters ancient words of another language.

"We're too late," Sabrina whispers.

A searing hot pain rips up my spine, tearing the flesh from my bones. This is not another transformation.

I cry out as my shift continues. My vision dances between light and dark.

The horror on Sabrina's face flashes through my sight. Nyla steps in front of her with an outreached arm, protecting her as a mother would a child.

A fire burns in my veins, and the edges of my vision narrow. I turn toward the door and race out, heading toward the forest as the darkness fully encompasses me.

I open my eyes and squint at my room. The bright light flooding the room temporarily blinds me. I groan and cover my face with my hands, rolling onto my side.

Somehow, at some point in time, I made it home. I'm back in the Pack House.

After my eyes adjust to the morning light, I swing my legs over the side of the bed and reach for my phone on the nightstand. I stare at the picture of Lucinda, and my wolf aches for the return of his mate.

No missed calls, nor messages.

Everyone knew but me. They've been right all along. She's not coming home.

I drop the phone, and it crashes on the hardwood floor. The device spins at my feet, and my hands fall idle in my lap. Heat rises up my chest and my pulse quickens.

The mindlink explodes with anxiety and fear; whispers spread, and my head pounds. I reach up to cradle my head, but the faint tint of red stains my hands.

What is that?

I sniff my fingers. *Blood!*

A jumble of messages flood through the mindlink.

"Garcia!"

"A horrific sight."

"Who would do such a thing?"

"...strung to that old gnarly tree in the forest."

"His skin was shredded down to the bone."

"Flayed alive—"

I slide off the bed and kneel on the floor. My shoulders fall as my eyes graze over a trail of bloody footprints leading into my room.

What have I done?

I pick up my phone, and my thumbs circle over Lucinda's picture.

I hope Lucinda never returns. The man she loves doesn't exist anymore.

CHAPTER 30

LUCINDA

"DON'T CRY," Morticia says, "he wouldn't want that."

I blink back tears and wipe my nose on the back of my hand. *I know he wouldn't.*

"Felix and I were once lovers," she says, her voice only a whisper floating in the air. "It was a long time ago before his father died. I made a grave mistake—one that he could never forgive—and it wedged a knife between us forever."

After an awkward moment of silence, she says, "You're lucky."

"Lucky?" I ask, my voice raising a notch.

"Yes. You're lucky to have such good friends. Not everyone has faithful friends." She motions to Felix's dead body, and I twitch my nose to stop more tears that threaten to fall.

Why am I crying over Felix?

Because it's my fault he's dead. He was protecting me. Damn him!

Morticia continues to talk, motioning to Dylan. "And you're fortunate to be so young and have a dedicated lover."

"Oh no, he's not my lover," I say.

"No?" Her face perks up.

The sorrow that was in her eyes has been replaced with something else. *Is she really thinking of seducing Dylan? But if she is, that's none of my business. Why should I care?*

"No. He's like a brother," I say.

"Like a brother." She fixes her eyes to the rear of the room. I follow her gaze. *Cody.*

Tears fill my eyes. He rushes toward me and I collapse in his arms.

"We found you," I whisper. "Are you okay?"

He pulls back and studies my face. "You shouldn't have come."

Morticia clears her throat. "This is touching, let's have a family reunion."

"What?" The amount of wrinkles my face will have when I'm older has doubled in the past few weeks with all the frowning I've done.

"You and your brothers reunite," she says, a little unsure of herself.

"My brother is dead."

"Is he now?" She looks up to a black bat flying down from the rafters. It circles me once and then takes a human form.

I step away from Cody and a young man stands in front of me. His eyes glisten moss-green and his golden chestnut hair falls shaggy with short, gentle waves.

My eyes widen as I stand there, frozen in place, directly across from him. He's taller than me, but we're about the same build.

"Hi, Lucinda," he says in a rich, silky voice. "It's nice to finally meet you."

His lips turn up into a smile, and a flash of sharp white fangs reveals his true identity—if the bat turning into a human didn't already give it away.

He's a vampire. A male vampire version of me.

"Hi," I say, barely audible even for our impeccable hearing.

"I'm sorry, I know this must be awkward. I've known you your entire life, but you just learned about me."

"Lucinda, this is Braeden," Morticia says. "He's your twin brother."

"Right." I glance to Dylan, hoping for moral support.

"Lux, he's the spitting image of you," Dylan says through the mindlink and takes a protective step closer to me. "I don't think they're trying to trick you."

The proximity of my twin brother makes me nervous. *Is it because he's the twin I thought was dead? Or because he's a vampire? Or is it because this only confirms that I am a hybrid after all?* My heartbeat quickens. *What will Caiden think of all this?*

"And let's not forget about your older brother." Morticia steps forward and her lips curve into a seductive grin.

"Who?" I ask.

"Well, he's only a half brother," Braeden says.

"What are you talking about?" Dylan asks.

"Please don't say that you're my half brother," I say to Dylan through the mindlink. "Oh god, I think I'm going to be sick."

Dylan stifles a laugh, but his stomach convulses at the thought as well. My gaze darts over the cold body of Felix on the stone floor. Nausea rolls through me, and I grab my stomach.

Morticia glides over to Cody and says, "You were so young when you were taken. Do you remember me at all?"

Cody's gaze darts from her to me to Dylan to Felix to Braeden and back to Morticia.

"Of course, you don't," she says. "You were only a baby

when Raul gave you to me and those wretched witches kidnapped you."

She pinches the bridge of her nose as she speaks the word *witch* and shakes her head.

Cody's pupils fully dilate, and his focus is on Felix's dead body.

"He knew, didn't he?" Cody asks. His tone is strained, but firm.

"Yes," Morticia says.

Dylan bumps my shoulder and raises his eyebrows. I'm on sensory overload, but I shake it off and stumble over to Cody.

Reaching for his hand, I say, "Hey, big bro."

He looks at our entwined hands and then to my face. His eyes clear and a smile forms. He reaches his arms around me and pulls me into a crushing hug.

My heart pounds. *Cody is my real-life big brother, well half brother, but close enough. My family is still alive.* I always felt a special connection with Cody, and now I know why.

Braeden clears his throat, and Cody and I separate. Cody walks over to Braeden and offers his hand. They do a forearm handshake. *I guess that's a start for long-lost brothers.*

"The holidays will be interesting this year," I say to Dylan through the mindlink.

"I can see it now. Caiden and Braeden—"

My face falls flat, and I try to swallow the lump in my throat. *How will Caiden react to all of this? After all, it was the vampires that were behind the attack that killed his parents. Or was it?*

"Lux, just relax. Caiden loves you more than life itself. He'll accept you no matter who your family is."

Dylan's words provide little comfort. As much as I'd like to believe that, my stomach twists remembering our last conversation.

He may love me, but his duty as Alpha comes first.

I push that to the back of my mind for now.

"Why are you trying to kidnap me?" I blurt out.

"You misunderstand us," Morticia says. "We've never wanted any harm to come to you. That's why Braeden has watched over you."

Dark wings flapping in the sky and a black bat circling overhead.

"The bat—" I say, and he nods. "You've been spying on me?"

"Spying? No." He crosses his arms in front of his chest and lifts his chin. "I was watching over you—to protect you."

He gets defensive easily.

Dylan nudges me with his elbow and says through the mindlink, "Lighten up."

"So why are you at war with the witch coven?" I ask. "Why did you attack the Blood Moone pack?"

"The who?" Morticia asks.

Braeden walks to her and whispers into her ear. I only catch snippets, but it sounds like he's telling her who the Blood Moone pack is.

Heat rises in my veins. *Enough games.*

"The Blood Moone pack. Now my pack. Caiden Moone is the Alpha and my mate," I say, revealing my neck, showing my mark. "And Dylan is his Beta, second-in-command."

"Ah yes. I remember hearing about that tragedy. Just like I heard about the horrific tragedy that befell the Dark Raven pack. Neither of which were at the hands of vampires." She dismisses the thought with the wave of her hand.

Just like Felix would do.

My pulse races. I squeeze my eyes shut and take a deep breath.

"No, but the vampires were behind the attack on the Blood Moones," I say.

"Where did you ever hear such a thing?" she asks.

She is a good actress, or have I really shocked her?

"Are you denying it?" I ask.

"If you're accusing the Vampire Nation of having anything to do with the attack on the Blood Moone pack, then yes. I am denying it."

"Then who—"

"My guess is the witches orchestrated it." Braeden shrugs.

"But why?" Dylan asks.

Braeden tilts his head and puckers his lips. "Maybe to push Caiden into position faster than its natural course."

"Who is Caiden to you? Why is he such a threat?" I ask. *Will he—could he—battle against my brother?*

"The witches wish to annihilate us from existence," Morticia says, bitterness dripping from every word.

"Is that so? And why should we trust you?"

"Have I given you any reason not to trust me?" Morticia asks. "Let me remind you that it is a witch that hired an assassin to kill you. And it is the witch's assassin that killed my dear lover, Felix."

Pain rips through my chest at the sound of Felix's name. My claws pierce into the soft flesh of my palm. *Physical pain will override emotions,* my dad always said.

"If Felix was your lover, why was he working with the witches, against you?"

Morticia floats the close the gap between us. "He was brainwashed, the witches had his head so messed up he couldn't make any decisions himself—"

"But you ordered the Alphas to give up their firstborn sons! Why? What purpose did that serve?" I throw my hands up in the air and shake my head.

"No, that is a lie. I never asked for that, and I never wanted it. What would I do with a child?"

"But—"

"Then what was that story about me?" Cody asks.

"Yes, Alpha Raul gave you, his firstborn son, to me. But not because I told or asked him to do so."

"Then why did he do it?" Cody asks.

"I have often wondered that myself," Morticia muses. "But then I became so tired of all the possibilities that I stopped thinking about it."

"Nice. So tactful," I say to Dylan through the mindlink.

"Easy now, tiger," he says in return and flashes a wink.

"What were you planning to do with me once you had me?" Cody asks.

Morticia crosses the room to stand in front of Cody. "I decided to raise you to be our guard. To watch over us during the day while we were at our most vulnerable."

"To be a watchdog, you mean?"

"No. To be our protector."

"Protector from the witches?" I ask.

"My my, you are a quick study," she says. Her scrutinizing gaze sends chills coursing through my body as she looks me up and down.

I massage my temples and mindlessly walk in circles while I process this new information.

Felix was working with the witches, we were lead to believe the vampires were the threat. Though, stopping to think about Felix and the witch, their alliance does beg question because it was the same witch that cursed him, Dylan, and Caiden.

"And why do the witches want to kill you?" Dylan asks Morticia.

"They lost control over us centuries ago, and they aren't happy about it."

"They used to control you?" Cody asks.

She nods. "The Wolf Council too, only you haven't realized it yet. They still control most of you."

"Wha—"

"They are sneaky and manipulative. You probably have them living in your territory and don't even know it. There are probably also half-breed wolf-witches in your pack that poison the minds of others."

If only she knew how much truth there is to that. We just discovered one living in the pack. I wonder how many more there are. And half-breeds? A shiver courses down my body. I never knew they existed and now I am one.

"Felix knew everything and the damn witches still got to him. They're skillful at slowly poisoning one's mind by twisting facts and events. They start by clouding judgment and clarity of thought and then move into total control by brainwashing. It's only a matter of time until they get to Caiden," Braeden says.

His eyes bore into mine, willing me to understand the urgency. I have noticed Caiden becoming more irritated, but I thought it was due to his mate being away.

I step next to Dylan and send through the mindlink, "I don't know what to believe."

He tilts his head. "If the vampires are the enemy, then I guess we won't be leaving here alive. But, if the vampires aren't the villain, and Felix was a puppet being used by the witches…"

I inhale and exclaim outloud, "Caiden is in grave danger."

Morticia glides over to face me. "Yes, love. The wolves have long been a pawn in someone else's game."

"Gavin and the witch!" My voice cracks. I kneel to combat the dizziness that rolls through me.

Dylan mutters, "We delivered her right where she wanted to be."

"Where is that?" Morticia asks.

"As counsel to Caiden," Cody says. He scurries next to me and reaches out a hand to help me up.

What have we done? I fiddle in my pocket, reaching for my phone.

No signal.

"We need to act fast," Braeden says. "Lucinda, you make haste back to Caiden to warn him and protect him from the witches."

"I'm going with her," Dylan says.

"No, I'll go with her," Braeden says. "You and Cody need to travel to as many wolf packs as you can and plead your case. You need to unite the packs to follow one leader."

"Who will lead them?" Cody asks.

"Dylan, you will need to lead them, if it comes to that," Braeden says.

"Lead them to what?" Dylan asks.

"To march into battle against the witch coven," Morticia says.

I roll my shoulders back and step forward. "If the witches are congregating in the Blood Moone pack territory—"

"You need to choose your side. Where is your allegiance?" Morticia's pearly white fangs glint in contrast to her deep red lips.

"She's with us," Dylan says in a firm tone.

I glare at him and rein in my wolf. "Do I get a say in this plan?"

"No," Dylan, Cody, and Braeden say in unison.

"Lux, he's right," Dylan says.

"Yeah. You need to go back to Caiden, but we can't. Not yet," Cody says.

I search the faces of the men in front of me. Dylan's stare is intense and his glare sends shivers up my spine. And I've never seen Cody's expression so stern. But Braeden's eyes have a spark of mischievousness to them.

My stomach grows uneasy the longer I hold his stare.

Could I ever battle against Caiden, my fated mate? Let's hope I don't ever have to find out.

"It'll be fun. It'll give us time for some much-needed sibling bonding," Braeden says with a wink.

My shoulders slouch and I hang my head in defeat. I am interested in Braeden. He is my twin brother after all. But the thought of being trapped in the car with a bloodsucking dead thing for several days sends chills creeping through my body.

THE END... Continue with Lucinda and Caiden's journey in The Witch's Betrayal, Book 3 in The Raven Chronicles.

ABOUT THE AUTHOR

USA Today Bestselling Author Missy De Graff writes Urban Fantasy, Fantasy, and Paranormal Romance. Drawing inspiration from her vast array of interests, she weaves together worlds of romance and intrigue, mixed with supernatural elements, suspenseful storylines, and addicting characters.

When she isn't writing about sassy heroines, forbidden romances, and enemies to lovers; she enjoys fresh air, sunshine, hiking, and river time. A dedicated lover of sweet treats, a collector of antiques, and fascinated by all things mystical.

Missy resides in Virginia at the foothills of the Appalachian Mountains with her husband and son. She can often be found wandering through their Southern Heirloom Apple Orchard with their mountain cur dog and barns cats close on her heels. She is a bohemian by nature and a Gemini by birth.

Stay up to date on all the latest scoop from book releases to exclusive reader content subscribe to Missy's monthly newsletter today! linktr.ee/authormissydegraff

Fire Glass (Realm of the Fire Fae)

Crimson Legacies

www.ingramcontent.com/pod-product-compliance
Lightning Source LLC
Chambersburg PA
CBHW011034190726
48290CB00011B/2833